LAW
OF
LIMBO

BY TARINA MARCINKOWSKI

LAW OF
LIMBO

ISBN: **E-book-** 978-0-6482955-8-7

ISBN: **Paperback-** 978-0-6482955-3-2

I am in gratitude to God who created the dream that was sent to me one night so clearly.

A dream that stayed with me completely and never faulted.

I dreamt that night like I had never dreamt before and have never done again.

In that perfect dream I watched a movie from start to finish in its entirety and when I woke I felt energised and wonderful.

Law of Limbo was that very dream that was sent to me, it's birth came from the moment I awoke and wrote down the core of its existence.

Since then it has flourished, grown and become a finished product that I am proud to have the honour of calling my own creation.

Thank You my dear maker for gifting me with this treasure, thank you for choosing me with the job to produce this very special masterpiece.

I hope the faith you have in my abilities is warranted, and I pray that I have given your gift that you bestowed upon me that night in my sleep, the justice it deserves.

Thank You!

LIMBO:

An uncertain period of awaiting a decision or resolution.

An intermediate state or condition.

PREFACE

L ife has this ability to do what is best for us, it works for us, not against us, although many times we do not understand its purpose.

The debate of where we go when we die, still to this day becomes the foremost fear in our lives, in our religions and in our minds. The fear that we may not be good enough on this planet, that we may not deserve to go to that beautiful place in the sky called Heaven.

There is that individual fear of, will I go to hell?

We have been taught many things, we have been shown many things, and we have heard many things. But still to this day, there is no more knowledge given to any of us about death and its secrets. We still continue to fear its unexplained vagueness.

But what if death was just a beautiful transition?

What if heaven was already on earth?

What if hell did not exist?

What if we wasted all of our life worrying, to the very point that we *forgot to live*? Isn't that more fearful?

The universe has its own magical way of putting us just were we need to be. So, we can learn the very important lessons of our existence. These lessons push us forward towards our soul's enlightenment, every time we live a life.

Life is about learning its laws and then never turning back. Most people get caught in limbo at some stage in their human lives, that place where we feel stuck. The answer, is whether or not we learn how to move on from it, or if we choose to stay and let it consume us.

CHAPTER 1

What if, heaven was all around us and the only problem we faced was not that we couldn't see it, but because we chose not to.

The night outside was bitterly cold, and lightening filled the darkened sky with its majestic dancing. Jane looked deep into the mirror at her well-tanned body, and soft slender figure that was gracefully being hugged by her black sparkling dinner gown.

She watched intently at her right ear lobe as she slowly poked her dangly crystal earring through it. It was like she was in a zombie state, while getting ready for her husband Oliver's awards night. She had done this so many times before. This time her mind was lost within the repetitious voice in her head that told her that she did not want to go. Not this time.

Gone were the days that getting ready for such an event was fun and exciting. Jane smiled a little. The memory of her and Oliver drinking champagne while dancing around their bedroom, had forced upon her a moment of joy. Together they had pretended to act out Oliver's award presentation and speech the very first time he had received one for the company that he worked for. That was so long ago, over a decade at least.

He was an amazing man, her husband, with his extraordinary mind. His whole life had been dedicated to his photos. The creations that he caught through the lens of his camera were indescribable. Jane fell in love with his ability to capture the pure emotion in everything and everyone he shot.

Although the beginning was so exciting and fulfilling for both of them, Jane now seemed to feel as if her soul had started to become suffocated. They were always a team, her and Oliver. They bounced off each other in a way that was unstoppable, Oliver with his pictures and Jane with her words, but lately this perfect unity was feeling forced.

Jane watched in the mirror at her perfectly crafted blonde hair that didn't move an inch. She took a deep breath in and slowly exhaled as if tired of life, she did not even want to move. Life was too hard.

Jane had given up her career as a journalist when she became pregnant with their son Alex, who was now eight. Her life revolved around him. Not that that was a bad thing for she adored him more than life itself. It wasn't just the school runs or the after-school activities that kept her busy, that was uplifting. Instead it was the continuous task of presenting herself as an immaculately well groomed, faultless mum who was happy with her expensive lifestyle. One who enjoyed and appreciated the benefits from a husband who was very successful.

The green envious eyes that stalked her every movement was from other mothers who also had such a life. They would always send daggers Jane's way, she saw them from beneath her sunglasses. Jane knew they were jealous, wishing to score something more than what they already had. They wanted to have what she had. Jane found herself amongst wives of lawyers, doctors and dentists, none of whom seemed truly happy. Their false exteriors always tried to confirm that they were, but she knew differently. It was like playing a continual game of charades that was tiring and conflicting for her.

Most of the stories these fake friends of hers would tell, would be about how wonderful their husbands were. Then they would secretly confide in a close friend the truth, that their husbands no longer gave them the affection that they needed. Then these honourable close friends would feel the need to tell every other living soul in the neighbourhood the dark secrets they had been entrusted with. They could not bear holding such gossip inside. The burning tongues of the mothers in this neighbourhood were venomous and scarring. Jane had watched families painfully collapse.

Gossip seemed like the most golden reward to them all. Jane wouldn't play in their games, instead she teased them about her amazing life and her loving relationship. She told them nothing. Instead she played the part of fake Jane very well, to perfection even. She did not want these nosy women fishing around in her private life.

Sadly, it was only now as Jane stared deep into the mirror, that she thought how she had slowly become overtaken by this fake Jane. Had she forgotten who she really was, losing her true self in this facade.

Where is the Jane who used to stand up for what was right in the world? Where is the Jane who didn't care what people thought about her? I don't know who I am anymore.

Who was she now except an actress playing a part in a role that she no longer wanted to play. Was it even possible for her to remember who she used to be.

A slight feeling of anxiety swept through her body. She took a moment to shake off the ever-gruesome thought that she may never return to the old Jane. It scared her so very much.

Am I lost? What is wrong with me?

Here she was, looking stunning once again, ready to hang off of the arm of her beloved creative soulmate. The very soulmate who always told her that she was his muse, but this time she felt tired. Jane couldn't even remember the last time she dressed in a tracksuit. Or sitting in front of the screen watching a good TV series, hugging a bowl of potato chips and devouring a block of chocolate. That would be insane. Not to the real Jane, that was her release. That was fun.

After years and years of practice Jane had now perfected making herself look amazing, even if it was just to go to the local shops. She never lost her cool, never in public. She always moved gracefully with a smile on her face. It was exhausting. She remembered there for a moment, as her eyes looked deep into their refection in the mirror, how easy everything seemed to be before all their dreams had come true. Well Oliver's dreams.

3

Looking down and letting out another deep sigh she closed her blue eyes, telling herself that all she had to do was to get through this night.

You can do it, you're tough. Just one moment at a time is all you need to deal with.

When Jane opened her eyes, she forced a big smile onto her reflection, trying to immerse herself into the role that she was ever so good at playing. Maybe she should be the one accepting an award tonight.

And the award for best actress goes to… Fake Jane.

Jane left her bathroom and entered her bedroom, she sat on the bed as she placed her shiny black heels upon her feet. Oliver walked into the bedroom while talking on his phone and lovingly placed a kiss upon her head. Jane graced him with an affectionate smile.

He was a handsome tall man, with short dark hair that flowed perfectly over the top of his head. Big white teeth, not straight but perfect for him. He was strong, independent and kind. These traits seemed to ooze from his aura, making him a delight to be around. People were captivated by him. In his tuxedo he was irresistible.

Jane stood up and headed downstairs, ready to take on the night, against her minds pleading request to stay home.

How am I going to get through tonight's torture?

Grace was Jane's mother. She had been preparing dinner for Alex, Jane and Oliver's eight-year-old son. Alex sat on a stool across the kitchen bench watching over Grace as she cooked.

"GG is making me spaghetti and meatballs mum!" Alex said as Jane came through the kitchen entrance.

"Oh, that sounds delicious sweetheart," Jane ruffled Alex's hair while walking behind him. She fetched herself a glass of water to try and ease the dryness inside her mouth.

"There isn't much food in your fridge darling, did you want me to go and get some shopping for you tomorrow?" Grace asked. "I did bring over Alex's favourite chocolate chip cookies though."

Alex grinned with happiness.

"That's fine thanks mum, I have food getting delivered tomorrow morning, I did an order online today."

"What happened to the good old days when you just went to the store to get whatever you needed. I don't understand how you can even know what you want from a screen!"

Jane smiled, "It's quite easy mum and it saves me time, which is something I don't seem to have much of anymore."

Jane peered out the kitchen window into the darkness watching it light up in the distance. It felt as though her lungs were starving for oxygen. So tight. She did hate going out in storms.

"What's wrong Jane, you seem a little off tonight?" Grace asked her.

Jane turned towards her mother giving her a small grin, "Nothing Mum, it's just another night. I would kill to just stay in and have spaghetti and meatballs with you guys."

"Don't be silly! You look amazing darling. Go out and have fun, enjoy yourself!" Grace urged her.

Jane was humoured by Grace's energy, even a little jealous. She did not know what Jane was really feeling. There was no excitement at all inside of her. She was tired, so very tired of her life. Jane felt like everything she had become was nothing more than a lie. A lie which had grown deep inside, due to her pleasing everyone around her, everyone except herself. Her mind had become consumed by negative thoughts that told her that she was no longer worthy. She had lost who she truly was. But, she would not let Oliver down, he had worked so hard as he always did, and it was her duty to be by his side. She was a good wife and a good mother.

Oliver suddenly danced through the kitchen doorway ending the conversation that he was having on his phone. He danced all the way up to Jane grabbing her around her tiny waist. He began swinging her around, finally dipping her. She giggled at his funny ways and so did Alex and Grace. He was spontaneous like that.

Alex quickly climbed down from his stool and raced over to his parents so that he could be a part of the fun. Jane started to dance with Alex until Oliver lifted him up tickling him under his arms. Grace loved that they were such a beautiful family together, it brought great joy to her heart knowing that her daughter was so happy.

"You had better go otherwise you will be late for your own party!" Grace grabbed Alex from Oliver's arms.

"Your right! Let's go, shall we?" Oliver said looking over towards Jane.

"Yes, let's go!" Jane swallowed one last mouthful of her water, dabbing her lips gently with her fingertips so that she didn't mess up her perfectly drawn lipstick.

Oliver grabbed his keys and Jane her designer black clutch. They both gave Alex a kiss and Jane hugged her mother goodbye.

"We won't be any later than midnight," Jane told Grace.

"No worries!" Grace replied, "go and have fun, we will be just fine."

Grace was a wonderful woman, she was hip and fun. When Jane was growing up she remembered how much she loved her mother playing so many different games with her. It was this very trait that Alex loved about her also. He was not going to be bored tonight, not with Grandma Grace around, or GG as Alex called her.

It really was a terrible night for going out in. The rain belted down hard upon the boot of the car as Oliver slowly backed their black BMW out from behind the electric roller door.

Jane stared out of the car window at the lights that shone from their dream home glowing in the darkness. It gave it a sense of beauty within such a blackened night. The two-storey self-designed masterpiece had distracted her mind for over eighteen months while they built it. They were the envy of the neighbourhood. All the mothers from school were desperate to be the first ones to see the inside of such a magnificent residence. Jane teased them with a morning tea invite, never allowing anyone a look before that party took place a month after they had moved in.

During the drive to the awards ceremony the storm made it hard for Oliver to see clearly in the distance. Large puddles were starting to form on the road. Jane looked upon the gloomy sky with a sense of fear. Every time they hit a puddle it sent water flying onto the windscreen, Jane let out a small muttered noise. It showed Oliver that she was not comfortable about being out in this wild weather. Lightening lit up the sky and Jane awaited the deafening boom that would vibrate throughout her body.

Oliver placed his hand onto her knee to comfort her. Jane squeezed it in appreciation and then kindly asked him to return both of his hands back onto the steering wheel. He laughed at how on edge she was.

"Everything okay?" he questioned her.

"Yes, of course," she replied as she continued to nod her head to confirm her answer.

"I don't believe you."

Oliver smiled at her and then returned his gaze towards the road, he knew her too well. Jane's mind had become entangled within her negative state, and she was finding it hard to let it go.

Why am I feeling this way? Why can't I just enjoy myself, be happy Jane. There is going to be dancing and lots of wine. It will be fun!

She loved Oliver with all her heart and she knew that they were soul mates, but there was something missing. Maybe it was just her over analysing everything, as she normally did. The voices in her head started to eat away at her once tender heart.

No-one would miss you Jane if you were gone. That's why you are feeling this way, because you know that it is true. No-one. Not one person would care.

She had become unhappy, lost in some way. Daily she had begun to toss around the thoughts about the best way she could do away with herself. Hopefully without causing pain or causing any horrible side effects if she failed miserably.

Maybe taking lots of pills would be best way to get the job done right.

Deep down she knew it was just a thought. She also knew that she could never do such a thing to her beloved boys and her mother. The toying of the thought to finalise herself gave her some control over her life, it made her feel like she still had some choice.

Oh shit!

Jane thought as a truck load of adrenaline coursed through her veins. Marianne had organised a catch-up tomorrow, which was Sunday. It was so that the soccer mothers could discuss what they were going to bring to the soccer finals trophy day next weekend. Everything had to be planned perfectly with Marianne, it was annoying.

Here we go again, another waste of my time! Having to talk to Marianne for three hours about how I will be making the homemade sausage rolls. Not using my own recipe of course, instead I will be making them using Marianne's special recipe, passed down through generations. It had to be done properly, the Marianne way. Oh hell, how am I going to get through it? Is this my life now?

Three long hours of listening to Marianne and all the other mothers whinging about their lives, bitching about all the woman that had not turned up. How unbearable. Jane knew that she had survived these meetings hundreds of times before, but having a tooth pulled out in the dentist chair without any drugs seemed more preferable to her at this moment.

Had Jane given too much of herself away, that now she felt like she had nothing left to give. She was empty inside. In the past she just grinned and beared it, but now she had no energy left to hold up the mask that hid her feelings. No more pretending. Oliver could see that Jane was deep in thought, her mind was somewhere else.

"Jane, are you sure you're okay?"

"I'm fine," she lied.

Ooops, I thought I was going to stop pretending!

"I've just remembered that I have to meet Marianne tomorrow to discuss the preparation for the Soccer day. All the mothers will be there, I'm not looking forward to it. You know what they are like!"

Oliver grinned and nodded, while Jane relaxed her elbow onto the car window ledge and began to bite her fingernails. There was a time Oliver remembered, that she loved doing all those PTA things with the other mums. He had noticed that lately it was getting her down. Jane wasn't like the rest of them, she couldn't care less what they ate on the awards night, in fact she would have been happy organising pizzas to be delivered to the event. She loved pizza.

"You know that you don't have to go, they all just go so that they can talk about their husbands behind their backs," Oliver mocked.

Jane lightly giggled, he was right, but if she didn't go then she would be in the line of fire. It will be her that they would all be bitching about.

"If only I had something I could whinge to them about with you my dear husband, it might just get me excited about going! Oh, the gossip I could spread about you."

"Hmm," Oliver started, "tell Marianne that I will meet her later tonight behind the change rooms at school and I will snog her. That should get those gossiping geese going!"

Jane whacked Oliver fiercely on the arm, while Oliver made a grossed-out face pretending to vomit. Marianne was a good looking middle-aged woman, but she could talk a fish to sleep underwater, a trait that Oliver found very agitating.

"Stop it!" Jane begged.

He had managed to do it again, make her smile. Oliver was perfect. Jane knew that he would never cheat on her, he was too gold-hearted for that. Her life was amazing in every way. Her husband was the most genuine man you could ever meet, and she could not remember a time that she was not in awe of him.

The memory of the moment that Oliver had photographed the children in the hospital chemotherapy ward popped into her head. The moments he captured were breath taking. It was the first moment where

Jane felt like she was not participating actively within the world anymore. She knew that Oliver belonged, his images were his gift, but she no longer felt that way about herself. Her gift was no longer being used. Her words not being told.

Oliver's talent was like no other, and no one had ever met a person so dedicated and so good at capturing a human being's emotions as he did. How could she ask him to let go of his work, his dreams so that she could return to hers. She couldn't, and she wouldn't.

She was the mum, that was her job. She could not disturb the career that Oliver had built up over the last two decades. He had invested so much time and energy.

Jane loved to tell stories, to report on what was happening within the world, but how could she do such a job knowing that she would have to travel. It would take her away from Alex, and it would be a burden on Oliver.

Oliver had always told Jane that he would take care of her, so that she would never have to work again, but she loved to work. Jane enjoyed actively helping others and standing up for those in need. When she saw those photos of the children in that chemotherapy ward that Oliver had taken, she knew in her heart that her soul was not fulfilled in doing what it had come here to do. She wanted to do more.

Maybe I should start volunteering somewhere, Jane thought until she realised that she had no time left in her life to give. She was too busy pretending.

"We're here," Oliver said as he pulled up to the valet. Oliver sheltered Jane from the rain with his coat until they both made it inside the venue. In the lobby they met their much-loved friends Sarah and Andrew, they had known them since Oliver started working with Andy over ten years ago. They greeted each other happily and went to the bar to have a drink and a few nibbles before the night officially started.

CHAPTER 2

Perception is a tricky thing, it can make anything become real in the mind of a believer.

The night seemed longer and drawn out this time. Even though Sarah was great company and it was her presence that made these events bearable, it wasn't enough. Jane could not stop the feelings inside of her, it was like she was drowning.

Is this night ever going to end? I don't think I can take much more of this. Bloody Marianne! If she even looks at me sideways tomorrow I am going to smash-up her pretty little face! Oh God please make her cancel, give her gastro or something so that she has to cancel. Please, please, I beg you! It's too loud, the music is just too loud in here. There is so many people, I can't breathe, I can't breathe, I need air!

"Excuse me!" Jane said as she abruptly rose from her chair, "I need to powder my nose."

As she went to collect her bag she felt a hand grab her wrist, it was Sarah.

"Are you feeling okay, you seem quiet tonight."

"I'm fine, I just have a bit of a headache and… well I have this stupid PTA thing tomorrow, it's just, I don't know. Anyway, I have to pee."

Sarah looked up at her knowing that she just wasn't herself, "When you come back we will talk about it."

"Oh, it's not worth talking about! Just a bunch of stale old women thinking they are organising the Queen of England's wedding, instead of a soccer trophy day."

They both giggled, and Jane headed towards the toilets.

A huge surge of adrenaline flooded Jane's body. She quickly entered into the toilets and locked the cubicle door behind her. She closed the lid of the toilet seat down and just sat on it trying to compose herself. Jane was losing her ability to keep it together. There was a time that she was good at hiding her feelings, but the cracks of keeping up such a demanding role were starting to appear.

Why am I feeling this way? Why can't I control it?

She couldn't even describe the loneliness and depression which had suddenly consumed her. Jane just wanted control again.

Breathe, breathe.

Tears began to well within her eyes, covering her face with both of her hands she hoped that she could hold in her emotional break-down and stay quiet. Slowly within her darkened hands she breathed in and out trying to stabilise her attack.

The darkness seemed like a nice friend, a place to hide away from in this overwhelming world that she lived in. It gradually calmed her and brought her breath back to a slow peaceful rhythm. She began to fall into a meditative slumber within her hands gentle cradle. As she sat on that toilet lid, she finally found a moment of peace, her mind lost all of its banter. It was silent.

Jane jumped frantically from the unexpected bang. A cubicle door that had been allowed to slam shut.

Holy shit!

She naturally moved her right hand towards her chest as she comforted her pounding heart. Once again, she breathed deeply to comfort her nerves, the noise had startled her back to reality.

When Jane was ready and composed she adjusted herself making sure everything was where it was meant to be. She headed out towards the mirror to touch up her already perfect face.

Standing next to her was a tall beautiful woman with long dark hair. The woman was re-fixing the bright red lipstick that she was wearing. Jane could feel the exotic woman's intense gaze upon her. She peered into the mirror to casually see why this stranger was looking at her. They were the only two women in the restroom, this privacy appeared to give the woman an opportunity to talk to Jane.

"You're Oliver's wife, aren't you?" she asked seductively into the mirror.

"Yes, I am," Jane answered with curiosity.

"He is such a talented man, you must be so very proud of him!" the stranger blushed.

"Yes, he is very good at what he does," Jane smiled as she fidgeted through her handbag for her powder.

Who is this woman and why is she talking to me?

The brunette put her lipstick away, puckered her lips together, made a few adjustments with the tips of her fingers upon her lips, and then went to leave. Instead she stopped and turned back around. She looked over at Jane as if judging her with her eyes. Up and down. Up and down.

"You know, you're a very lucky woman. Don't you miss Oliver when he is away so much? I miss my husband desperately when he is away. I get lonely, really lonely."

Jane just smiled unsure if she was meant to answer. The beautiful stranger smiled back showing her perfect white teeth and then she left the ladies lounge.

What the hell was that all about?

The look the woman had just given Jane was strange. Was it jealousy or was it more than that. It was like this woman was trying to prove to Jane that she knew Oliver, personally. Jane stood there for a moment unsure of what had just happened. It was the first time in her life that she had ever questioned Oliver's commitment to her.

Has she been with Oliver? No! She is definitely not Oliver's type...is she? She is stunning, her boobs are amazing! Oliver would never cheat on me...would he? No! But...He has been away a lot more lately. More late nights. How does she know how often Oliver is away?

Oh my God! Is he cheating on me?

Jane had dealt with these types of women before, she would watch as the mothers at school would fuss over Oliver, vying for his attention. It didn't bother Jane. She knew Oliver would never have time for such annoying and fake barbie dolls. Their fascination with him is what annoyed him the most. But this brunette was different. It was if she was trying to rub it into Jane that she knew Oliver was a good catch, because she had test driven him. Jane was alone and consumed with her thoughts. Sarah suddenly headed through the ladies' restroom door.

"There you are, are you okay Jane, you've been a while."

"Hey," Jane snapped out of her trance. "Do you know who that brunette was who just left?"

"Yes, that's Damian's wife, Giselle. She is the one who pushed for Oliver to be the photographer on the new project they are doing at the beginning of next year."

"The project that Oliver needs to travel throughout Europe for?"

Sarah nodded noticing that Jane was uneasy, "Why, what's going on Jane?"

Jane stopped what she was doing, looking down at the sponge and powder in her hands, she couldn't stop thinking about Oliver and this Giselle woman.

Fucking asshole! I can't believe it, he is lying to me! Don't be stupid Jane, he would never lie to you. Oliver is the most honest man you have ever met. He loves you! But it all makes sense, why would she talk to me like she had a crush on him. Fuck!

"Jane, seriously what's going on? I'm worried."

"Nothing," Jane answered Sarah.

Jane packed her make-up into her handbag. She went to walk past Sarah and leave the ladies lounge without saying another word.

"Jane!" Sarah tried to stop her, wondering why she seemed so agitated. "What on earth is going on with you, you are not yourself tonight. Talk to me!"

A group of women entered the ladies' restroom all at the same time. Both Jane and Sarah just looked at each other.

"I'm your friend, I want to know what is going on," Sarah said in a softer voice so that the other woman could not overhear what she was saying.

Jane began to doubt herself. She was not thinking clearly, this was just something that was taunting her for absolutely no reason at all. She knew very well that Oliver was the most faithful man ever created. Her mind was just making it bigger than what it was.

Jane took a deep breath in, "You know what, I think I'm just over doing it at the moment. I feel exhausted and I just keep going, I'm so tired. I don't think I should have come tonight, but I didn't want to let Oliver down."

Sarah gave Jane a big hug, "You're always trying to do so much all of the time. You do know that you are allowed to stop and relax for five minutes. Oliver would not have cared it you weren't up to tonight, he loves you!"

"I know," Jane said realising that Sarah was right. "Maybe I'm coming down with something."

"You need to take better care of yourself Jane," Sarah rubbed Jane's arm to comfort her.

The two friends left the restroom and headed back to the table arm in arm where Oliver and Andy were awaiting their return. Both men stood in their honour. As they sat back down Oliver laid a hard kiss onto Jane's lips. Opening her eyes, Jane glanced across the room to see Giselle watching her and Oliver's movements. A sly smile slid across Giselle's face, but she was quickly distracted by someone on her table, turning her attention away from Jane.

This woman had planted a seed of doubt in Jane's mind that no other woman had ever come near to doing. Jane could not get Giselle out of her head. All throughout the night Jane watched Giselle's eyes lock onto Oliver; While he was giving his speech, at the bar buying drinks, shaking hands with his workmates and while he sat at the table with Jane and her friends.

During Oliver's speech Jane noticed Giselle was captivated by him. Small flicks of a smile would illuminate Giselle's face as she watched in awe every word Oliver spoke. He mentioned his new project briefly and thanked Damien and Giselle for the opportunity. Giselle's overreaction taunted Jane even more.

After another hour the awards night was over, and it was time to leave. It was a bit earlier than what they would normally leave but Oliver knew that Jane was not feeling one hundred percent. Of course, all of Oliver's work colleagues were trying to make him stay for a drink, against Jane's wishes. Oliver was a smart man and knew that if he wanted to live another day he would ensure that he said no to them. He remembered the old saying, happy wife, happy life.

Sarah and Andy said their goodbyes to Jane and Oliver as the valet brought up their BMW out the front of the facility first. The night was still full of heavy rain, the air so cold it almost took Jane's breath away.

"Call me!" Sarah yelled through the rain as she opened the door for them to leave.

Jane rushed out towards the car hoping not to get too wet, "I will, I promise!"

The conditions of the night had become worse, and the storm was making Jane feel even more nervous than before. Oliver was a confident driver. Although Jane desperately needed Oliver to concentrate on the wet road she also wanted to ask him about Giselle.

"So, everything seemed to go well tonight, are you happy?" Jane asked Oliver.

"Yeah, it was good," Oliver answered as he gave her a quick glance and smile.

"Tell me about this new project next year that you are thinking about doing?"

"Oh, Damien hasn't told me all the details yet, but I think it's going to be quite a unique experience. You know me, I'm always up for a challenge."

Jane paused for a moment thinking about what she should say next.

Tell him you don't want him to go. Tell him you miss him and that you want him to stop travelling so much. Ask him if he is having an affair with that stupid bimbo with the huge bazookas.

"What if, I didn't want you to go?"

Oliver was quiet at first, he was caught off guard by what Jane had asked.

"Why wouldn't you want me to go?"

Jane didn't know how to answer him. Was she now going to ask him if he was cheating on her, how could she. Jane herself didn't even believe it. What happened in that ladies' room tonight was nothing, absolutely nothing.

Oh my God I'm such an idiot, how could I have ever thought such a horrible thing about Oliver!

"No reason, I just miss you when you are away. It would be nice if you were home a bit more, that's all."

Jane began to just stare out of the window ashamed of her thoughts. Oliver could sense there was something wrong with her. This was not like Jane at all. She never complained or worried about him going away for his work, in fact she encouraged it.

"Jane," Oliver made her look his way, "seriously what's going on with you, are you all right? You can talk to me, you know that."

He placed his free hand onto her hand, but she pulled away not even knowing why. They had stopped at a red light, it was silent and awkward inside the car. As the light turned green Oliver went to say something but retracted. He was scared to keep pushing her. She had become edgy lately.

He began to pick up speed seeing the next set of lights showing another green light in the distance. He was deep in thought. He put his foot down on the accelerator just going slightly over the area limit. He wanted to get through the next set of lights quickly without stopping, he just wanted to get home.

Jane became agitated, she could not hold it in any longer. This woman tonight had started a chain of thoughts in her head that she could not stop. Her accusations made her feel guilty, but her ego would encourage her doubt. Telling her that she had every right to ask.

You know that there is something wrong. You can feel it. You need to know the answer, you need to know if he is betraying you. You have every right to ask him. Ask him! Ask him!

"Are you cheating on me with that Giselle bird?" Jane blurted out while looking at him. Oliver quickly turned his gaze from the road and to her, he was in disbelief. Their eyes met, hers were angry, his were blank.

There was a moment when the world seemed to slow down, almost stopping. Then Jane saw it. Oliver didn't. Oliver was still staring straight into her eyes. Jane saw the light, the light that began to grow bigger and bigger from behind Oliver's head.

"Look out!" she screamed as a huge truck hurled viciously towards Oliver's side door. It had come out of nowhere.

There was no time. Oliver swerved the car abruptly, the BMW's brakes screeched. They were suddenly spinning out of control, but there was no impact felt from the truck. Jane was just screaming holding on for her life. She watched as Oliver tried with all of his might to regain control of the car.

We are going to die, this is it! This is how it ends.

They spun off the edge of the slippery wet road as they hit the grass edge. The car stopped spinning, instead it gripped the grass and continued forward rapidly down the hillside. Jane had one hand pressed on her side window and the other grabbing the bottom of her seat belt trying to hold on.

Oliver moved the wheel side to side swaying in desperation to miss the randomly growing trees, he braked even harder. The car finally came to a stop at the bottom of the hill, where it just cut out. The final halt was hard, but a welcomed relief for the both of them. They were finally still and safe.

"Are you okay!" Oliver frantically undid his seatbelt and leant over to Jane analysing every inch of her body.

"Are you hurt?" he questioned her again.

Jane was shaken up, "I think I'm fine, how about you?"

Oliver had a cut on his forehead, "You're hurt," she said as she started to reach her fingers towards his head.

Oliver felt the wound himself, "It's fine, it's not too big to worry about."

It appeared that they were in a forest like area that was extremely dark and foggy. The head lights remained on even though the car was no longer running. The light showed the outline of many trees, but it was just too hard to see through the thick mist that had swallowed them up. The rain had stopped thankfully.

"Where are we?" Jane was confused about why they were in a forest. They had been driving this busy road for years and had never encounter this type of area before. Strangely her bag was by her feet, it had not moved during the accident. She took her phone out and tried to use it, but there was no signal. Oliver did the same, but once again the phone was useless.

"We could walk up to the top of the hill, back to the main road and flag down a car, it shouldn't be too hard," Oliver suggested.

They both emerged out of the car and Oliver decided that it would be easier if he went alone. Jane's heels probably weren't appropriate for climbing. She stood back watching him as he slowly climbed this medium sized hill in his expensive tux. Ironically, she was watching his amazing toush as he climbed.

I can't believe it, the last thing I did was accuse my husband of having an affair! Now I'm perving on him. What the hell is wrong with me?

Clutching her coat around herself, Jane watched every breath she took freeze up in front of her face. It was so cold, but thankfully the rain had stopped for now. Her heart was still pounding. Jane watched as Oliver slipped a little while he climbed. His right hand grasped into the side of the hill to stop himself from falling.

"Damn it!" he yelled out as his right knee collapsed into the muddy ground.

The rain had softened the dirt to a point where it was making it hard for him to reach the top. With a lot of effort, he finally made it. As he stood up and looked out, he was stunned.

"What the hell?" he muttered under his breath.

There were no roads, no cars, no nothing. Just land for miles. Oliver could not understand what on earth was going on. Where had they ended up. Jane watched Oliver standing at the top of the hill, it was so dark that she could only just see his silhouette. It seemed strange that the cars that were driving past on the main road were not lighting him up every time they passed. It was late, but this road was always busy.

"What's going on?" Jane yelled to him hoping that her voice was strong enough to reach him.

Oliver looked down at her, but he did not know what to say. He rubbed his head with his clean hand. He couldn't understand where they were. He made his way back down the hill and back to the car.

"What's wrong?" Jane questioned him.

"There's no road up there, no cars, there's nothing."

"Nothing, what do you mean nothing? Don't be silly!"

Jane started to get frustrated with Oliver. Being a woman and a mother, she was used to her boys not being good at having a proper look for anything. She desperately wanted to look for herself, but the thought of her heels sinking into the mud held her back.

Oliver looked drained. He tried to flick the excess mud from his hand that had braced his fall. Nothing was adding up.

"We can't be that far away from the road, we have only just skidded off of it," Jane said sensibly.

"I know. That's what I thought."

Oliver was concentrating on the mud on his hand, but in his mind, he was trying to cope with what he was being faced with. He stopped flicking his hand and looked over to Jane.

"Maybe we spun a few more times than we thought we did. Maybe we drove down this edge longer than what it seemed. All I know is that there is nothing but land for miles up there."

Jane pulled out her phone and tried once again to make a call to her mother. It was getting late and she didn't want her to worry, but the phone still would not work. Her thoughts went to Alex and she began to miss him so. She just wanted to be home kissing him on the head. Then she imagined being in her amazing hot shower washing her cares away down the drain.

Oh, how I would kill to have a shower right now!

As Jane looked at the car she noticed its headlights shone on what seemed to be another road further on. She had not noticed the road before, the fog had slightly cleared.

"Look," Jane said as she pointed.

Oliver reached in and carefully restarted the car, which was mechanically fine.

"Maybe someone lives along here somewhere," Oliver said. "We will just have to follow the road and see where it takes us."

Jane happily agreed with him as they both hopped back into the car. Jane handed Oliver a few wet wipes to clean the dirt from his hands before he started driving.

Oliver slowly got the car moving. He prayed that nothing would disrupt this forward motion towards the dirt road, their only exit. Images of parts of the car falling off plagued his mind. The darkness was eerie with the fog surrounding them, making it hard to see the road ahead.

Suddenly something black flew out of nowhere straight into their windscreen. Jane's scream was loud and piercing.

"Holy crap!" Oliver yelled out, braking the car hard.

Stunned, the animal made its way back into the air again, struggling to flap its wings in synchronicity. They both sat there for a moment in silence. They looked at each other, with no words exchanged.

Oliver took a deep breath and started to accelerate the car slowly forward again. They hit the dirt road which was long and windy, the car was travelling along nicely. The trees around them appeared to become thicker, taller and darker the more they continued forward. It was like the surroundings were closing in on them.

"I don't know about this," Oliver said. "Maybe we should turn around and go the other way."

"This is freaking me out," Jane said peering through her side window. She alternated her gaze from the side window to the windscreen, watching on guard to see if anything else was ready to jump out at them.

The rain began to pour down again, and the temperature seemed to drop dramatically. This is definitely not what they needed right now. Oliver noticed the cars head lights were reflecting on something shiny in the distance.

"Look! Maybe that is a sign telling us where we are!"

The car made it all the way to the sign before cutting out and refusing to start again. No matter how hard Oliver tried, the car would not turn over.

Jane looked out the windscreen as the headlights beamed at the sign which read, 'Welcome to LIMBO.'

There were dim flickering lights in the sky's distance which lit up the tops of the trees. This indicated to Jane that there just may be someone living further up the road. Oliver announced that the car was a hopeless cause. There was no other option for them but to walk. If they wanted to explore the road further for signs of life, they were going to have to wrestle the harsh conditions.

"I've never heard of a town called Limbo before," said Jane.

She was right, Oliver had never heard of such a place either and found it weird that they were sitting in front of its welcoming sign. Who would call a town Limbo, that just seemed odd.

"I think we are going to have to walk from here, I'm sorry to say. Unless you want me to go alone and check it out first?"

"No way!" Jane was adamant. "There's no way I'm staying here alone while you go off by yourself into the depths of darkness. Can't we just wait until it's light?"

Oliver sat there for a moment and thought about Jane's offer. They could decide to spend the night in the car and wait for the morning to come. Their bearings would be easier to gauge in the day time.

"What about Alex and Grace," he said, "they will be worried about us."

"You're right," Jane looked down at her phone which still had no signal. "Let's go and see if those lights are a house. They may have a phone we could use."

They both knew they had to do something. If they waited till morning Grace would be beside herself, and Alex would not understand why they were not home.

"Let's do it!" Oliver tried to encourage Jane. He knew that she would be hating the thought of walking in the cold and miserable night.

"Do you want my jacket to cover your head from the rain?" Oliver sincerely asked her.

"No, you will need it, I will be fine."

Why is he so damn nice all of the time? How can I be angry at him when he is always thinking of me? That proves how much he loves me. Maybe he is just trying to cover up. The last thing I asked him was if he was having an affair. Why hasn't he said anything more about it? Why hasn't he answered me? Because it's true!

CHAPTER 3

Walls are built slowly one brick at a time, but walls can be taken down with a sledge hammer in minutes.

The conversation that had ended abruptly before the accident had not been brought up again. Although both Oliver and Jane had it rotting away inside the back of their minds, they did not think the time was appropriate to return to its vulnerable content.

They prepared themselves for the pounding of the rain on their bodies and the chill of the frozen night air. They each stepped out of the car and began walking quickly along the pebbled dirt road. Only tall trees lined both sides. There were puddles of water everywhere. It was hard to see them. At times it took Jane and Oliver by surprise as they lost their balance momentarily as they stepped into one. Jane's heels were causing her so much grief. Eventually the two of them merged together as they walked, hugging arm in arm, becoming each other's strength. Oliver began to laugh, he couldn't help it.

"How the hell did we get here!" he yelled through the rain.

Jane was becoming annoyed.

How could he find this funny? This is not funny at all. We are stuck in the middle of nowhere, in a storm! I'm wet, dirty and cold. NOT FUNNY!

She pushed him away a little. Oliver looked down at Jane as they walked. The rain had washed all her mascara down her face, her hair was wet and stuck across her cheeks and partially covering her eyes.

She was a mess and he loved it. Oliver could not help himself, he forced her to stop in the middle of the road, the rain pouring down over them. Jane's lower lip began to quiver in the conditions as she looked at Oliver waiting for him to say something.

"What! What!" she pushed.

Oliver grabbed both of Jane's upper arms as he fiercely stared at her. While looking deeply into each other's eyes Oliver smiled that smile, the one that would normally melt her legs away. He was captivating.

"It's you my Jane," he spoke with meaning, "it's always been you and it will always be you!"

Moving in he kissed her, Jane closed her eyes for the honourable moment, but she barely kissed him back. Her heart did not jump, it did not melt. Instead it went cold like the night.

You're just trying to cover up your mistakes. I don't trust you! You're lying. I know that you are lying to me.

Oliver knew, he felt it. He was devastated that Jane did not believe him. Jane pulled away from his grasp and began to walk on in the rain alone, she headed towards the lights in the distance. She did not have time for his childish behaviour. Not now.

Oliver just stood there shaking his head, allowing Jane her space. Her stone-hearted attitude was like a kick in his guts. He watched as the love of his life walked further and further into the night without him. He would never betray her, never.

Jane had been acting strangely lately. He had watched his blossoming flower slowly withering. She had become negative to almost everything. Even though Oliver loved her with all of his heart, her coldness had started to take its toll on him. He missed her.

If he were to be honest with himself, Oliver knew that this had been happening for a while. There was a distance that had slowly crept between them. His ignorance to it was his way of hoping that it would fix itself miraculously somehow. They used to be so perfect together. The guilt of his success began to haunt him, maybe he had asked Jane to give up too much for him.

Slowly Oliver began to follow Jane, making sure that he kept his distance, but also ensuring that she did not get too far away. He was over protective of her, even though she had hurt him deeply. They walked separately for a little while. The horrible weather giving no relief, only adding to their torment.

Jane arrived at a bend in the road. She continued on knowing very well that it would agitate Oliver not being able to see her. There was a small feeling of guilt for teasing him.

Don't be silly, why would he care if something happened to you, he is finding his needs somewhere else. Keep going. You're a strong woman and you can take care of yourself.

As Jane continued walking the enormous trees started to thin out and the lights grew brighter. A long bitumen road opened up in the near distance. It joined onto the end of the dirt road they had been walking along. It was lit up and it looked like a beautiful normal looking street. There was many houses and street lamps running down the left side of it, the thick forest on the right. Butterflies filled Jane's stomach.

"There's people living here!" Jane called back to Oliver.

Oliver ran quickly towards her voice, his eyes lighting up with relief as he came around the bend, "Thank God!"

It looked as though the street went on forever, the fog deceiving their vision. Jane looked at her watch, rubbing the droplets off its face to reveal that it was 11.30pm. She was hopeful that someone in this street would be awake, if not she would drag someone out of bed if she had to. Finally, she could get to a working phone and contact her mother.

Jane headed on. When her feet hit the beginning of the bitumen road her high-heeled shoes began to click on its hard surface. How grateful she was just to hear that noise, it was the sweet sound of normality. Looking up at the street sign she read its name in her head, *Law street*.

The first few houses were quite different from each other in style. As Jane began to walk further down she noticed that the numbers of the houses did not run in sequence as they normally would.

"Look Oliver, this is strange," she yelled out through the rain.

Oliver did not know what she was meaning, he was struggling to hear her, "What is?"

"The numbers on the houses are not running in the correct order."

Oliver walked past the first house wondering if he had heard her correctly. It was a small villa which was number 72, there were no lights on inside. The second was a beautiful cottage which resembled a country bed and breakfast, it was number 10. This street seemed empty, it appeared that both houses were dark and lifeless. The next house, number 22 was surrounded by a large brush fence. As they walked past together Jane peered in through its huge gates to see a woman on the front porch in a swinging-chair. Jane's heart leapt for joy.

"Hello there! Hello, can you please help us?" Jane waved.

The woman was in her late thirties, she could not see or hear Jane. Instead she continued to rock in her swing, her face motionless staring into the night.

"Please hello!" Jane called louder.

Eventually Jane was able to get the woman's attention as she ran closer towards her. The woman greeted her with a beautiful big smile, but the woman did not get off the swing, nor did she stop swinging. Jane realised that she was now being sheltered from the rain, looking up she saw the houses amazing old veranda. A small relief for her cold aching body.

"Excuse me, we desperately need your help!" Jane asked as she wiped the wet hair from her eyes. "We have been in an accident and our car has broken down not far from here."

"Hello there," the woman said softly. "You look wet my dear, why don't you come in and have some hot chocolate, that will make you feel better."

The woman seemed vague as she turned forward continuing to watch the rain fall. Oliver had made his way up the porch also, he was just behind Jane and the look on his face told the story well. He was worried. Maybe this stranger would not be the saviour they were looking for. Jane bent down next to the woman making her stop her rhythmic swinging.

"Please do you know where we are?"

The woman thought about it for a little while, "Well, we are all in Limbo my dear."

"Where is that, where is Limbo exactly?" Jane questioned her feeling anxious.

The woman giggled a little as if it were comical, "I don't know where we are, I don't know. Limbo is here, you are here. This is Limbo." Moving her gaze from Jane and back to the falling rain she continued, "it's just so beautiful when it rains, such happiness and sadness all in one. Tonight, the rain feels sad."

Jane looked out over the rain that fell off the bull-nosed veranda trying to understand what this woman was saying to them.

"Do you have a working phone that we could use?" Oliver interrupted.

"Oh no, phones don't work here!" The stranger gave Oliver a quick look, "no phones work in Limbo." She appeared surprised that Oliver did not know that. The woman began to start rocking on her swing again which forced Jane to stand up and get out of her way.

Jane was annoyed by her vagueness, they had already had one hell of a night and she was just about over it. Oliver walked over towards the front door of the house and noticed that it was open, so he entered.

"Hello, is there anyone else here?" he shouted, "Hello!"

Oliver walked in feeling uncomfortable that he was leaving dirty marks over the clean wooden floor. Jane followed him inside the quaint old homestead. It felt wrong to leave the woman outside while they entered her house. They had no choice, they needed to find a phone.

The house inside was full to the brim of stuff, in a good way. Family photos covered the walls and there was a hypnotic aroma coming from the kitchen. Jane went over to the oven and bent down looking through its window, she could see it was home-made cookies.

28

Instantly her mind was flooded with childhood memories, she thought of Alex. Her anxiety grew deeper.

Alex! I have to get home to my son.

"Hello!" Jane called out in desperation.

The house was so warm inside, Oliver was enjoying how comfortable the house made him feel.

"Who the hell are you and what do you want!" A man yelled out causing the both of them to jump.

He had come out from behind a wall near the kitchen, he was holding a shotgun and he had it pointed straight at Oliver. Oliver raised his hands to the air as quick as he could.

"Oh shit!" Oliver squealed, "We mean no harm we are just lost, we need help!"

Jane was frozen.

"Please," Oliver begged. "We were in an accident and our car needs repairs, we just want to go home."

The man with the shotgun saw the fear in Oliver's eyes, he had not seen these two around Law street before. He lowered his gun down slowly curious as to who they were.

"I'm sorry," the man said. "There are some dodgy characters around here that I need to keep an eye on."

Oliver was relieved by the man's quick submission. Jane moved to Oliver's side to feel safer, he put his arm around her pulling her close.

"We spoke to the lady out the front on the swing, we thought she might be able to get us to a working phone. Maybe even tell us where we are, but she couldn't," Oliver told the man.

"That's my wife," the man began as he leaned the shot gun against the wall. "Cindy is her name, she...well she's not always the Cindy I used to know, if you get what I mean."

"Oh, I'm sorry to hear that," Oliver said honestly.

The man seemed broken, he was unshaved, and it looked as though he had not showered in days.

"Please," Oliver begged. "We have had the worst night ever and we just want to go home. Is there anything you can do to help us?"

"Please," Jane added.

The man looked over Oliver in his Tuxedo and Jane in her evening gown, both dripping wet and looking sad and sorry. He smiled, he knew exactly what they had been through. He wanted to help them.

"One hell of a night you say. I understand, I really do," the man said as he looked at the time on his wrist watch. "Honestly, the best thing I can do for you right now, is to tell you to keep walking up this God forsaken Law street. You *will* come across your very own house. Then when you do you can settle in for the night. Have a good night sleep. When you wake up tomorrow feel free to come back and have a chat and a nice cup of tea with us. I'm Sam."

Sam went to shake Oliver's hand, but Oliver and Jane just stood there confused. A second passed as Oliver apprehensively shook Sam's hand,

"I'm so sorry, but I don't understand what you are saying to us," asked Oliver.

"I know it sounds crazy, I do! But I'm telling you that you can just walk further down the street and you will be home."

Jane could not take any more of this nonsense.

"I have to get home to my son!" Jane stepped forward becoming angry at his unwillingness to help, "we need to use your phone."

"Look, there's no telephone's here lady, I'm sorry to tell you. Like I said, if you just keep walking down the street you will find your house, I promise you."

Jane looked past Sam to see an old phone sitting on a table next to him. It was connected into the wall and it reminded her of her Grandmother's house.

She ran over to the telephone unafraid of what Sam might do. When she lifted the handset to her ear awaiting to hear it's dial tone she heard nothing. She began to press down on its old-style clickers to try and reset the phone, but it was dead.

Sam just stared at her, "Like I said, there's no working phone's here."

The air became thick between them and Oliver felt like they had over stayed their welcome, "Come on Jane, let's go."

Jane just stood there staring at Sam, he stared back. She was upset with his lack of compliance.

"Why won't you help us!" she began to yell at him. Oliver grabbed Jane's arm from behind and started pulling her backwards towards the door.

"I'm sorry," Oliver said to Sam.

Sam just nodded as he watched the two of them back out of his front door. Oliver and Jane were once again standing on the front porch of the homestead while the woman, Cindy, continued to swing, watching the rain fall.

"What is going on with you people? Why won't you help us?" Jane screamed at her.

"Jane!" Oliver squeezed tighter on her forearm and gave her a hard stare, "stop it!"

He pushed her in front of himself and let her arm go motioning for her to head towards the street.

"Don't touch me!" she screamed at him.

Jane charged off into the rain and back into Law street, the rain was just as heavy and as cold as it was before. The street was long and well lit up, so she began to walk on quickly hoping to find another sign of life. The time was getting closer to midnight and Jane could feel the sense of pressure on her chest. She knew that Grace would not worry if they were late, they had been late home before. But, at this rate it felt like this night was never going to end.

Oliver ran quickly to catch up to Jane. He was annoyed by her constant fiery attacks, it had been happening more often lately and it was getting hard for him to ignore. He chased her down grabbing her arm making her spin around to face him.

"What the hell was that, what is your problem Jane?"

"I just want to go home!" she said pulling from his grip.

"You think that screaming at people is going to help, well it doesn't! They were trying to help us."

"Help us, are you insane? That wasn't help, they are crazy."

"Why, because they're different? That's bullshit Jane and you know it! Seriously what is going on with you?"

Jane just looked at him, he was saturated. She could see how angry he was, but she could no longer look at him. This was the first time they had argued in a very long time. They had their disagreements in the past which seemed to easily resolve themselves, they made sure that they never went to bed angry. But Jane could not let it go. The feelings she had after the run in with Giselle tonight were not allowing her to forget, she honestly believed that Oliver was lying. He had to be.

"How could you?" Jane said to him. "How could you do that to me? I never ever believed that you were like that."

Oliver with no hesitation answered as he pointed at her, "How could you even think that of me? It hurts Jane. Why, what happened, what happened for you to think this way?"

Jane just stood there shaking her head, she was so confused and angry, her mind was spinning out of control.

He's lying. He loves you. He's cheating. He loves you. I don't know, I just don't know! Who is telling the truth?

Her breathing became fast and uncontrollable, the pressure of this situation was bearing down upon her. Anxiety took hold. These episodes in Jane's life had started out small and rare a few years ago, to now being a part of her daily life. They had been her secret. But it was becoming too hard to hide them, especially from Oliver.

Oliver grabbed her and held her tight, for the first time in his life he saw his wife vulnerable and losing control. It broke his heart.

"We will get home, I promise you."

Jane began to cry hard into Oliver's chest she had never felt so low in her life. There was no control anymore, she felt powerless and alone. Her mind felt like it wasn't working properly, and she had become paranoid about everything. She loved Oliver and she knew he loved her, but her mind would not let her be free.

They had been through a lot in the last few hours, things were not as they seemed. The rain began to soften until it slowly stopped, that alone was a God send. Jane could feel Oliver's grip around her lessen until Oliver let her go. She looked up at him. He was staring down the street in a daze.

"Jane," he started. "Jane…"

Jane turned to look and see what he was staring at, what she saw froze her to the core. They both stood in the middle of the road as they looked upon the next residence in the street. It was the strangest thing they had ever seen.

"Am I seeing this?" Oliver slurred his words.

"Yes," she answered him.

They were looking at a unit, but it wasn't a block of units where there were units on the ground floor and then the units on the top floor. This was just one unit, the top unit on the right-side hovering in mid-air, all by itself. The stairs going up to it seemed to float from the ground all the way up to this isolated dwelling.

This vision caused Jane to look at the next house in the street. It was a two-storey attached town house, but there it was in front of her, split in half and not attached to anything. The left side which should have been another residence wasn't there. It was all alone. The sight of the unit and the townhouse was eerie and confusing. The unit was numbered 12c and the split town house was 42A. It made absolutely no sense at all what they were looking at.

Oliver sent both of his hands through his hair just holding them there on his head unable to believe what he was seeing. Jane looked up at the sky. Was this all just a dream, it felt so real. The two of them stood there helpless.

This cannot be happening, we are asleep, this is not real. It's not real, I have to get out. Please I have to get out! I want to go home. Wake up Jane, wake up!

Jane abruptly reached over to Oliver and pinched him hard on the arm.

"Ow!" He screeched holding his wound.

It must be real!

"Oh God why is this happening, why?" Jane screamed.

"I don't believe it!" Oliver pointed into the distance. "Jane look, look!"

Jane turned. It was like a mirage. There, further down, stood her beautiful home, it was lit up just as glorious as it was when they had left it earlier that evening.

"Home," she muttered under her breath.

Tears formed in her eyes and ran down her cheeks. Her tight lungs relaxed and filled with air.

Oliver grabbed her hand as they both ran towards the welcoming sight, they were excited even though it made no sense to them. They arrived at the front door, strangely it was unlocked. As Oliver opened the door Jane looked up and watched the entrance clock hit midnight.

Everything went black.

CHAPTER 4

When every day seems the same, it is your own choice of thought that brings joy or heartache.

Jane slowly opened her eyes. She noticed that she was staring up at the ceiling of her bedroom. Sitting up quickly her heart started pounding.

It was just a dream! Thank God it was just a dream!

It took her a moment to focus. Her body felt strange, her feet were tight and uncomfortable. Pulling the covers off she exposed herself seeing that she was still fully dressed in her evening gown. Her black high-heeled shoes were suffocating her feet.

Looking over at Oliver, she saw that he was fast asleep on his side, his back facing her. Lowering the sheet down, Jane revealed his tuxedo jacket. How odd it was that they were still in their clothes from the night before. The last Jane remembered they were both soaking wet from the storm, now she was dry and fresh.

Spinning to the side of the bed she slipped off her shoes, giving her toes a wiggle. Up she stood. Jane made her way down the hallway to Alex's room excited to see him, all she wanted to do was to hold him, and never let him go.

She slowly opened the door to his bedroom, peering inside. There was his bed, beautifully made and not slept in. Jane pushed open the door entering the silent room.

Where could he be?

Suddenly she felt strange. The walls of Alex's room began to look different, somewhat fuzzy instead of solid. They were moving. The motion was back and forward like the ocean waves. Jane was unable to clearly focus on them, it was like they were there, but they weren't.

Although shocked Jane cautiously walked towards one of the walls, needing to touch it to know that it was real. Her fingers could feel it's hard surface, but they were also indenting into it. Then she heard a child laughing in the distance, it was coming from inside the wall.

"Alex is that you?" Jane apprehensively asked the wall, "Alex!"

She pushed her hand further into the wall watching her whole arm disappear inside of its soft flowing texture. Feeling around she strangely thought that Alex was stuck inside the wall somehow.

"Alex!" she screamed again.

There was a loud boom of a sound which pushed Jane backwards onto the floor. She realised that the walls strange movement had abruptly stopped, the child's laughter had disappeared. Jane was left in the middle of the room, the space feeling empty and cold. Something was wrong. Up she stood quickly. Frantically she began to feel all over the wall again with both hands. It felt hard like a normal wall. She pressed her ear against it hoping to hear the child's laughter once again. There was only silence. Jane began banging on the wall's hard surface as she began to scream.

"Alex! Alex, where are you!" Jane slowly backed away from the wall looking at her hands.

This is it Jane, you have lost your mind. It's time for the looney bin for you.

"No, no!"

Jane ran from Alex's room searching the house for him, screaming his name. Down the stairs she ran hoping to find him in the kitchen, but he wasn't there. He wasn't anywhere.

"Alex, where are you baby?"

Leaving the kitchen, hands on her head Jane made her way to the front lounge room. Looking out of is large grand window, she saw a view that made her sick to her stomach. Across the street was a lining of tall green forest trees. She was still in Limbo. Slowly backing away from the horrific sight, she screamed finding herself being grabbed off guard by Oliver. He looked past her at the haunting forest, he knew where they were.

"Alex isn't here, neither is Mum," Jane told him in desperation.

He did not know what to do, he didn't even know what to think.

"What are we going to do?" Jane begged, hoping that Oliver would have an answer, but he just shook his head.

Oliver checked through the house once again, he had to. This was their house and it was exactly the way they had left it. There was even left-over spaghetti and meat balls in the fridge, the meal Alex and Grace had made for dinner the night before. Alex's favourite chocolate chip cookies that Grace had brought over were sitting on the kitchen bench, half of them were eaten.

Jane could not accept the fact that this alter reality was happening, it made no sense, surely it was impossible. Both of them stood in the kitchen confused, Jane afraid.

"I think I am going crazy Oliver."

"If you are going crazy then I am too! We are both here together, we are going to find out what the hell is going on, I promise you."

Oliver leaned over the kitchen bench noticing that is was 8.30am in the morning. The sun was shining brightly through the window, the sky was clear, it looked like it was going to be a beautiful day. A change to last night's nightmare.

"Maybe your mother has taken Alex out to the park or something like that," Oliver tried to be reasonable, but his words seemed stupid as he was saying them.

"Oliver, why would the trees be opposite our house instead of the Leeman's house. Where are all the other neighbours and friends in our street gone? It's just crazy! Where is Alex? I'm scared."

Oliver thought for a moment, he remembered Sam and Cindy. He decided that he had to go back and talk with him, it was his only option. Although their first encounter with them had been a bit sensitive, Sam had known things. He had assured the both of them that they would find their family home further down Law street. Sam knew a lot more than they did, so it was the obvious thing to do.

"He was going to shoot us last night!" Jane was hesitant.

"I don't think so," Oliver said shaking his head.

Oliver believed that Sam would not have hurt them at all. Maybe he was trying to understand this situation just as much as they were.

"I'm going over there, I have to. He is the only one that we have seen living here so far, he has to know something about what is going on."

Although Jane did not like the idea she knew that he was right. As Oliver set foot out of their beautiful home, Jane watched through the lounge room window as he walked down the front path. They shared a quick glance, Jane smiled trying to show support. She was scared that he would not return, but she could not go with him. It was too embarrassing to return after the way she had spoken to Sam and Cindy last night.

Oliver began his way down the street, he stopped for a moment looking back. He noticed in the lightness of the day that there were another two houses further down the street from theirs.

One was like a beach house which was right next to their home, and then there was a government housing home. This home also did not have the other side attached to it, it should have had an adjoining home connected to it, but it didn't. Oliver's mind just took it all in, unable to explain what he was seeing. The street then went on for miles but with no more houses to be seen, the forest which was opposite the houses that lined the right side of the street, also went on for miles.

Oliver continued on to Sam's house. Slowly he walked past the neighbour's, which was the strangely looking two-story town house that did not have its other half. It looked new and modern, but it looked strange to not have the attached residence which would have made it whole.

Next there was that floating unit. Oliver had to stop and really look at it. There it was in front of him, this one lonely top floor unit hovering in mid-air with its own balcony, the balustrade coming down all the way to the ground, it was an eerie sight. He looked up at the front window and saw a young man staring back down through his curtains at him. Curious, Oliver thought that he might talk to him later if things did not go well with Sam. It was refreshing to know that there was another sign of life in this odd place.

Oliver continued walking down the street until he reached Sam and Cindy's brush fence, as he walked into the property he saw Sam sweeping down the front porch. Sam looked up and saw Oliver still in his tuxedo and he smiled a gentle smile.

"I hope that's not the only outfit you had in your wardrobe boy, otherwise you are going to be very uncomfortable here."

"Good Morning Sam," Oliver said returning the smile.

"I thought you would be back," Sam stopped sweeping and instead sat down on a chair which was closer to the edge of the porch, "take a load off if you want to."

Oliver sat in the chair next to him and just continued to look at Sam not knowing which question to ask him first. Sam felt sorry for him, he knew what he was going through.

"What's going on Sam?" Oliver's question was a desperate plea trying to understand. "There's a bloody top-storey unit hovering in mid-air with a man living in it, and a two-storey town house without it's other half. Where are we?"

Sam took a deep breath and looked around. He leaned back into his chair.

"I wish I could answer all of your questions for you Oliver, I really do, but I can't. What I can do is tell you what I know."

Oliver nodded in appreciation of that.

"It's probably best if I just tell you our story and how we came to be here in Limbo."

"Please Sam, anything you can tell me would be helpful," Oliver was intrigued to know how Sam and Cindy also ended up here in Limbo.

"A long time ago, in the real-world I will call it. I can't remember exactly how long ago, it could be days, or years, or even decades, I just don't know. My wife Cindy and I had just been told that she had lung cancer. The doctor said it was probably caused from all of the chemicals we used on the farm that we lived on. We had decided to use these particular chemicals on our crops, because this you-beaut new company had come up with a way that allowed us to no longer have to worry about pests destroying our crops. My wife Cindy, was thirty-seven years old at the time and she had never been a part of any of the spraying, but I guess the wind carried it into her lungs. She started coughing occasionally until it was non-stop. Finally, she coughed up blood and we both knew then that it was bad."

Oliver and Sam had a small moment of silence.

"Anyway, we were told that she only had about four weeks left to live, which really made me mad. We have five children, ranging from sixteen to five."

Oliver bowed down his head in sorrow, "I'm so sorry."

"I looked into this company and their products and realised that they had lied to us about their chemicals being natural and organic. I remember this one guy, he looked me straight in the eye and promised me on his children's lives that his products would not harm us in anyway. He was the big guy, the boss. But I found out that he was using products that he was trying to dispose of from one of his other companies. They were toxic chemicals, and he was selling them to me as organic insecticides. I believed him. Ah, so stupid, I just believed him.

"So, instead of disposing of this toxic waste appropriately he sold it to us farmers instead. I also found out that he had no children. The anger inside of me was something I couldn't even begin to describe to you. I took my shot gun, I got into my ute and I was going to drive to this man's house and I was going to take his life, just like he had taken my wife's. He had given her a death sentence. There was also the possibility that it would eventually affect me and the children also, there was no certainty for any of us anymore!"

"What happened?" Oliver asked.

"Cindy came running out of the homestead and I thought she was going to stop me, but instead she got into the ute without saying a word and we drove off together. In a way I was hoping that she would stop me, but she didn't. Her mother was living with us at the time, so I knew that the kids were in good hands. I also knew deep down that Cindy wanted to watch me do what I was planning to do, so we both left. Now don't get me wrong Oliver, we are not some murdering country hillbillies that go around taking the law into our own hands."

"Sam, I don't think that at all!"

"We were angry, and I mean angry, everything was taken from us. Even our crops were doing things that were not normal, but we sold the final products knowing that things weren't quite right with them. The guilt of that alone haunts me every day. It even makes me feel just as guilty as that company selling me those chemicals. But living off the skin of your bones and having five kids to feed makes you do things you wouldn't normally do."

Sam began to tear up a little and he needed a moment to compose himself. Sam was not much older than Oliver and Oliver could relate to him quite easily. He would do anything to make sure that Alex and Jane were taken care of. Cindy came outside onto the porch holding a plate, she was so happy to see Oliver.

"Oh, hello there, would you like a cookie?" Oliver did not know what to do, he was feeling hungry, so he happily took one. They looked amazing. Sam took one and thanked his wife.

"This is really nice!" Oliver mumbled as he chewed.

"Well I'm glad you like them," said Cindy and off she went inside humming happily.

"She's a good cook that one, I'm so lucky to have her."

Oliver smiled at the love and affection Sam showed towards Cindy, his heart loved Jane just the same. Oliver adored that woman, her feisty actions and her compassionate heart made him smile. But Oliver was still intrigued about how and why they were all in Limbo.

Sam continued, "On my way to the city with Cindy in the ute with me and my shot gun in the back, I started to have second thoughts. I started thinking about when Cindy dies who will be there for the kids if I am in jail. Cindy knew that I would back out, she insisted that she would be the one who would bring justice to this man and take the blame. I couldn't let her do that! We ended up having a fight. I would not let her give up her last moments of her life for these animals, she needed to spend it with her kids. Cindy was so angry, she wanted to make him pay for the lies that he had told us. I pulled the ute over refusing to go any further. Cindy began screaming at me, she got out of the ute and ran off into the woods that were nearby. I tried to look for her for a while. I finally found her in a clearing on her knees with her hands over her face crying. I comforted her as best as I could, but we still didn't agree. When we finally decided to return to the ute we couldn't find the road. Instead we kept ending up here at the entry sign to Limbo, from that moment on we have never left."

"Why have you not left?" Oliver asked.

Sam began to laugh until he coughed, he found it hard to explain to Oliver where he was and what the rules were.

"You can't leave Limbo," he said staring intently at Oliver. "I don't even know how long it's been since I've seen those kids of mine. God, I miss them! All I know Oliver is that for some reason we are here, God has sent us here. Cindy is alive here. She is still sick, but the disease has not become worse since the day we arrived. I will count that as a blessing. Every moment I spend with her is a miracle."

"If you were in your thirties when this happened then how long do you think you have been here for? I ask because you look the same age, not older."

"We don't age," Sam continued, "not here. Cindy and I have been here for so very long. The memories I have in Limbo it could even add up to be a couple of decades. We are the same age, that has never changed, and Cindy's health is exactly the same, but it has been such a long time. Sadly, I have missed my children grow, that is something I can never get back."

Oliver was stunned as fear began to creep in. Was Sam saying that he had not seen his children for over twenty years. He did not understand at all. Sam could sense that Oliver was overwhelmed, he was not the best one at explaining things to people, he sat forward in his chair.

"We're all stuck here Oliver! You, me, everyone in this street! We live everyday over and over, and there are rules, that's why it's called Law street. I don't know why, I don't know the answers. All I can tell you is that I have spent every day for the past two decades waking up on Law street unable to get out. Oh, how I can tell you that we have both tried with all our might to get out of here, but you just can't. Cindy's mental health is failing more now than ever, she is not coping knowing that we may never leave. It's been so long I think she has finally given up. We both miss our kids so much. Cindy is lonely, and I don't blame her. The people here can be more like enemies than friends at times."

"How many people are here? Should I be worried?"

"Look don't misunderstand me Oliver, they are nice people here. We like most of them, but things have happened, unspeakable things. We try not to socialise as much as we used to anymore. I understand that you can be driven to do things you wouldn't normally do. Limbo can do that to people."

Oliver's mind was racing. At that moment a man in his late twenties walked past Sam's property with a cigarette hanging out of his mouth, he looked in as he walked past. Sam became agitated.

"There's that punk from the unit, that little shit needs to get some manners!"

Oliver stared over at this man who had looked in at the both of them. The man pulled his sunglasses down from his head and covered his eyes ignoring them.

"You watch out for that one Oliver, he has no soul."

"Why do you say that?" Oliver asked.

"I've caught him many times snooping around other people's properties, he has never spoken a word to us since he got here. I just don't trust him."

Oliver decided that it was time to leave Sam and return to Jane. It was going to be a hard conversation trying to explain what Sam had told him. He stood up shook Sam's hand and thanked him for his kindness.

"Don't worry Oliver you will work it all out, just like everyone else here."

Not believing in Sam's encouraging words he smiled and left. He walked down the street and as he did he turned and watched the back of the young stranger walking the other way, towards the entrance of Limbo. He wondered where he was going and why. The sun was making him feel hot and uncomfortable in his tuxedo and he longed to get out of it.

What was Oliver going to do with the information that Sam had just thrown at him. Could it be true, that they may never be able to leave. There was no room whatsoever in Oliver's mind for such a final outcome. There had to be a way back home, there just had to be.

CHAPTER 5

*Don't hide behind a false exterior. Being who you truly are, all of
the time, is allowing people to love you unconditionally.*

While waiting for Oliver to return, Jane kept watching
the clock. It was starting to feel like he had been gone
forever. She began to bite her nails unable to resist. As
she sat on the couch staring out onto the thick forest
from the front lounge room her thoughts taunted her.

*What if Oliver never returns? I should never have let him go
alone, that was just stupid! I don't want to be left alone here.*

She stood up and went to the fridge wanting to feed her emotional
appetite, but the fridge did not have much to offer. She wondered if
inside this delusion the food that she had ordered would still be
delivered today. She didn't have her hopes up that's for sure.

Looking over past the refrigerator door there on the bench sat
those chocolate chip biscuits her mother had brought over for Alex.
Jane reached into the packet noticing that six were already gone.

*How many biscuits did you let Alex eat before bed last night
mother? Or was it you, sneakily eating them after putting Alex to bed.*

The thought brought a smile to her face. She knew that they would
have had a wonderful time together, they always did. Jane took a biscuit
out of the packet and began eating it. Halfway through she began to
cry. This situation was unbearable to her.

Oliver startled her as he came in through the front door. Jane quickly wiped her eyes, concealing her sadness. He walked into the kitchen thinking about how he could start the conversation. For a moment they just looked at each other. Jane was desperate for answers.

"What did they say?"

"It appears we are in a place called Limbo, and you can't ever get out," Oliver shrugged.

It wasn't the best way to present it to Jane, but it was all he had in the moment.

"What does that even mean?" she asked him.

Oliver pulled out one of the stools from the kitchen bench, he took off his jacket and he sat down. He rubbed his forehead to relief the strain, his head was starting to hurt.

"Sam has a similar story to us. He says that he and Cindy have been stuck here for around twenty years."

"Twenty years!" Jane screamed.

The thought of being stuck inside this nightmare for more than a day was like hell to her.

"I don't know! I don't know!" Oliver began. "I think I am going to look around and talk to a few more people to try and understand this place better. Nothing makes sense. I feel like we must be dreaming, but we are here in it unable to wake up."

He was right, Jane felt the same. It felt like a dream, but it was as real as life itself. While looking out of the kitchen window onto their beautiful yard Jane tried hard to hold back her tears.

"Where do you think they are, Alex and Mum? Do you think they are okay?" she turned and looked at Oliver upset, he got up and came over to hug her.

"I'm sure they are just fine, they are together."

"Won't they be looking for us?"

"I hope so," Oliver said, praying that Grace had called the police and already had a search party out for them. "Let's just stop for a minute and try and work this out. Let me get out of this stupid monkey suit and have a coffee before a migraine kicks in."

Jane was uncomfortable also, she was well and truly over this black dress. Oliver only got migraines when he was completely stressed which didn't happen that often. Although he seemed cool and calm this was Jane's indicator that he wasn't coping.

Oliver took an aspirin before the two headed upstairs. He changed into some cargo pants and a t-shirt while Jane put on some jeans and a nice casual top. When Jane looked into the mirror she was surprised to see her make-up beautifully done and her hair immaculate. After all of that rain she had been in last night and sleeping on it during the night, it was as though she was all ready to go out again.

They allowed themselves a moment to have a coffee. They were both hungry, but they only ate a banana each, the two pieces of fruit left in the fruit bowl. It was now 11am and the delivery of food shopping that was supposed to come from 9am to 10am had not turned up. Jane did not think that it would, but she had hoped. She had ordered a new product, it was a dark block of chocolate wrapped in chards of peppermint. She was disappointed, her emotions would have appreciated some chocolate.

The doorbell rang, Oliver looked at Jane, "I'll go."

He headed from the kitchen towards the front door, but Jane was curious. She followed him, but instead stood at the bottom of the stairs, still able to see but slightly out of view. Oliver looked through the peephole and then back at Jane, he opened the door to a woman with long curly blonde hair. She was in a bright cerise shirt and white three-quarter pants. To Jane she looked to be in her late fifties.

"Why hello neighbour!" the woman happily sung as her eyes caught sight of Oliver. "I'm Mary and I am from the beach house next door, it's so very nice to meet you."

She was so over excited about meeting Oliver, but Oliver seemed to think that this was the way Mary was all of the time. She grabbed his hand and shook it quickly.

47

"I'm Oliver," he said as Mary pushed her way through the door and into the foyer of the house.

"I couldn't help it! I just had to come over and introduce myself to the lovely people that live in such an amazing house."

Mary spun around in amazement of the house and took all of its beauty in. Her eyes roamed the walls and then the ceiling, then the floors. Oliver was taken back by her flamboyant personality.

"It's just magnificent!" she squealed.

Mary looked over and caught sight of Jane standing on the first step of the stairwell.

"Hello," she said moving over to Jane. She shook her hand, "I'm Mary."

"I'm Jane, nice to meet you Mary."

"Well my dear, you have caught yourself a handsome fish in this one, haven't you?" Mary said as she pointed at Oliver. "And this house, you two must have spent years building this thing!"

"Oh yes," Jane began, "it took some time to design and build it."

Mary continued to happily look around lapping up the joy it brought her to be standing in such an elegant piece of real estate. Oliver and Jane looked at each other and were captivated by Mary's confidence.

"Oh, silly me!" Mary said to them, "look at me just taking over here. Well, you two must be absolutely confused about what on earth is going on."

Oliver smiled and nodded, "Yes, we are."

"I understand, all of us in Limbo have been through what you are going through right now, it is so very daunting. Maybe I should ask everyone over to my house tonight so that you can meet the people in the street. It might give you a better understand of the rules here. Maybe even get to know the neighbours and ask them whatever questions you want. Yes, that's a great idea!"

Oliver was unsure of the invitation. It seemed overwhelming, but Mary interrupted before Oliver could say anything that could stop her from changing her mind.

"Yes, you must both come over for dinner tonight, I insist! It has been so long since anyone new has popped up on Law street. How does six o'clock sound?"

Mary walked back out the front door and patted Oliver's cheek on the way out. Oliver's jaw dropped and when she got a few steps away from the front door, she turned around.

"See you at six. Oh, I'm so excited!"

Off she went heading back to her quaint little beach house next door.

"Mary, wait!" Jane ran quickly after her.

Mary stopped halfway between their house and hers looking back at Jane. She waited for her where she was standing.

"Please Mary! My son Alex, he's eight, he doesn't know where we are, and we don't know how to get back to him."

Mary was saddened by her plea and grabbed her hand, she knew personally what it was like to live without family.

"Oh, Jane my dear, don't worry. After all the time I have spent here in Limbo, I honestly believe in my heart that all the people we have left behind are safe. Alex is safe. We will all come together tonight, and you can talk to all of the residence. You can hear each of their stories. Maybe it will help you to understand Limbo better."

Jane nodded, and Mary smiled at her, "I will see you tonight and we will talk."

Jane allowed Mary to leave and return to her home. Mary waved at Oliver as she did. Jane watched her every step, even up until the front door closed behind her. Although Mary's words were comforting, they still made no sense. What did she mean by leaving people behind. Jane walked back to Oliver at the front door.

"She seemed a bit full on, didn't she?" Oliver stated.

"Yes, she was, but hopefully she knows more than what Sam told you. I need to get the hell out of here and I hope that someone in this place has an answer."

"What scares me Jane, is if they had an answer on how to leave Limbo, then why would they still be here?"

"Don't say that!"

"I'm sorry but it's true isn't it?"

There goes Oliver pointing out the dark truth of it all, Jane was trying to be optimistic. They both walked back inside the house. Jane's hopes were that when the time came to have dinner at Mary's, it would be the very engagement that would give her the knowledge to leave this horrible place. All she cared about was getting back to Alex. These people had to know something, any information would help her right now. It was comforting in a strange way for Jane to know that there were more people living in Limbo. At least they weren't alone.

It was an odd situation they were finding themselves in. Oliver and Jane were waiting to head to Mary's house for the six o'clock invite. It felt like forever, waiting around. Jane had stewed over it for most of the day, pacing the lounge room.

Oliver passed the time by trying to operate any electronic device he could find inside the house, but nothing worked. There was no signal at all. Clocks worked, the fridge worked, but items that created a sense of connection to the real-world didn't. Items like televisions, telephones, iPads were useless. It was all so strange and confusing, the rules to existence in Limbo seemed to counteract each other.

"I feel like we are just sitting around doing nothing," Jane said frustrated.

Oliver was concentrating so hard that he barely heard what Jane was saying. He had been sitting at the dining table for hours.

"Stupid bloody thing!" Oliver finally threw his mobile phone through the air, it hit the wall and then came crashing to the floor. The aggressive launch made Jane jump. She saw the phone fall to the ground after it pounded into the wall. There was now a large dent on the wall, with crumbled pieces of gyprock that had fallen to the floor around the phone.

Jane was angry with Oliver's outrage, he had damaged their beautiful home.

"Why did you have to do that! Now how are we going to fix it?"

Oliver said nothing. He knew that what he had done was going to annoy Jane. But Jane's anger was put on hold as they both watched closely while the damage on the wall miraculously began to start healing itself. It's slow magical reversal had the two of them watching in awe. They both moved closer to the apparition hoping to maybe touch its beauty.

"Are you seeing this?" Oliver was excited, but he tried not to talk too loudly, just in case it disrupted the process somehow.

"Yes," Jane whispered.

Every piece of gyprock that had fallen to the ground pulled itself back. The crack smoothly disappearing, the wall was eventually healed. Oliver touched it, it was like he had never even damaged the wall at all. It was perfect again.

"What does this mean?" Oliver said stunned.

"I have absolutely no idea," replied Jane as they just looked at each other.

CHAPTER 6

Maybe things are not exactly as you see them, there is always another side to every story.

The afternoon was moving slowly. Even though Jane felt uneasy by the surroundings, she wanted to go for a walk to clear her mind. Walking always made her feel better. Oliver was apprehensive, he would have no form of communication with her after she left. He did not want her going out there alone. Jane was adamant that she would be fine, and Oliver knew his wife well. It was best to let her go.

Jane grabbed her sunglasses and headed out the door, giving Oliver a gentle smile before leaving. The air felt so pure and fresh, she couldn't remember the last time she went for a walk outside. It was usually a 6am rise and straight onto the treadmill. Breathing deeply the cool air filled her lungs with a gentle peace.

Jane was enjoying the suns warmth upon her face. It made her feel disappointed that she had neglected her bodies connection to nature for so long. She walked back up towards the top of the street and peered into Sam and Cindy's house as she passed by. There was the rocking chair sitting out the front on the porch. Jane quickly walked on while no one was there, she was embarrassed by the way she had behaved the night before.

Jane then walked past the cottage and the villa as she had done previously the night before. Still there was no one in sight. Jane was relieved that she did not have to talk to anyone, she just wanted to be alone.

Moving past the street sign for Law street, Jane decided to head back down to where the car had finally given up. As she grew closer to the 'Welcome to Limbo' sign she could hear rustling in the distance. Jane decided to head off the open road and move into the thick forest for cover.

She weaved her way slowly through the forest, heading towards the noises. There was somebody close by. Making it to a point where she could peer through the woods, she saw a young man near their abandoned car. He was in his mid-twenties. He had somehow unlocked their vehicle and was now rummaging through it.

"What the hell," Jane spoke softly to herself as she watched as this man looked through their belongings.

He was a medium sized dark-haired man with a body that was very well worked on. He wore denim jeans with a white singlet and an opened navy shirt with rolled up sleeves. He sucked on a cigarette while he went through the glove box. It seemed to Jane as if he had done this before.

The man came around to the driver's side to yank the bonnet open, he proceeded to lift the bonnet and check out the engine within. He peered over his sunglasses as he began to tinker inside the cars lifeless heart.

Jane knew there wasn't anything of value inside the car. It annoyed her that this man thought that it was fine for him to violate her possessions. As the wind blew, the man's shirt gently lifted from side to side. Jane saw a glimpse of the handgun that was shoved in the back of his pants.

I need to get out of here!

Jane grabbed for her phone until she realised that she did not have it. This was not the position she wanted to be in. Slowly she crept back into the darkness of the forest trying to not make a sound, but it was so hard with all the fallen branches and the debris from the trees. She got far enough away that she felt comfortable to walk normally but in doing so stepped on a branch that echoed a big snapping sound.

Frightened she hid behind the trunk of a tree and peered out from behind it. The noise had reached the ears of the strange man. He stopped what he was doing and looked intently into the woods.

Fuck!

It didn't take long before the man returned his attention back to the car. Jane's heart was beating so fast, she was scared but relieved that she had not been spotted. Continuing through the forest away from the stranger, Jane headed in the direction of her house.

There were many tracks formed throughout the trees. She followed one happily looking around at the beauty that was in front of her. It was so peaceful with just the creaks of the trees and the birds happily chirping.

There was so much to explore. Jane began to get lost within the enchantment of the forest. After about ten minutes of walking she came across a steep hole in the ground that looked like its fall was endless. It was intriguing to Jane. There were rocks sticking out randomly from the sides of this giant gaping abyss within the earth. It was so dark, the bottom invisible.

She grabbed a good-sized rock and threw it down the hole watching it hit from side to side. Some of it crumbling away from the impacts until it disappeared into the darkness. She heard it hit the bottom and realised how dangerous this drop was.

Backing away carefully from the edge, Jane made her way towards the direction of where she thought the house should be. A noise in the distance stopped her, it was faint, but it was the sound of a car starting up, it was her car.

"No way!"

The stranger had managed to get the car started and in Jane's mind he was probably about to drive freely out of this horrible town. There was no way she was going to let that happen.

Jane ran as fast as she could through the trees to return home, when she finally hit the sunshine and the asphalt road she found herself to be further down the road than she had expected. She was way past all of the houses in the street.

"Damn it!"

Jane pushed herself hard until she made it back to her front door. Gasping she swung the door open.

"Holy crap, you scared me Jane!"

Oliver began to brush off the small dribbles of coffee that had fallen onto his pants as he sat at the dining table.

"Quick!" Jane ordered. "There is a man going through our car, and he has somehow got it started. I think he is going to use it to get out of here!"

Oliver's cup made a damaging sound upon the expensive table as he raced off with Jane. Together they ran as hard as they could down Law street. In the distance they could hear their car being revved up as if the stranger was testing its capabilities before using it to leave.

As they finally got around the corner they could hear the door close on the car. Jane was tired now, she was finding it hard to breathe. Oliver continued strong and could see the car being reversed and turned around in the distance.

"Hey! Stop! Stop!" he yelled.

Just before Oliver reached the car, the man inside floored it and started racing off down the dirt road.

Dust flew up into the sky and it slowly crept up around Oliver consuming his lungs with is dry grainy air. Jane finally made it to him, the pair struggled to get their breath back. Oliver coughed as the dirt tried to escape his lungs.

"Who was that?" Oliver questioned Jane.

"Just some young guy, jeans, opened shirt, mid-twenties. I saw him rummaging through the car and then he lifted the bonnet. He had a gun stuck in the back of his pants, so I left, I never thought he would be able to get the car started."

"I think I know who you are talking about," Oliver remembered the young man walking down the street when he was talking to Sam.

Jane was angry, "How are we going to get out of here now? What about Alex, Oliver? I can't stop thinking about him, I don't know what to do!"

Oliver moved towards her feeling helpless, what could he say. He had no ideas about how to get out of here. Jane moved away from him, she was in no mood for sympathy.

"Look, let's walk." Oliver tried to offer a solution. "Let's just keep going and see if we can make it out somehow. I don't care how long it takes, there has to be a way out!"

Jane agreed, she was tired of all this insanity, this road had to lead them to somewhere. They walked for so long, it felt like hours, there seemed to be no end to this crazy nightmare. As they continued to walk Oliver became confused.

"Wait," he instructed, they both stopped in their tracks. "These trees are looking familiar, this one has the bark ripped off, I'm sure I have seen it before."

Jane thought he was going crazy. He's seen the same tree before, she nearly laughed at his comment, but hell after what they had been through anything was possible.

"There is a sign!" Jane's eye caught sight of another sign, maybe they had made it to another town.

She began to run closer to it, but Oliver did not run, all he did was slowly look around the eerie forest that surrounded this never-ending road. As Jane grew closer her heart sank, it couldn't be. The words on that sign were like a knife stabbing into her heart, welcome to Limbo.

"No!" she screamed as she started kicking into the sign.

"No!" she yelled again unable to stop the flow of tears that streamed from her face. Falling to her knees she sat there in the dirt.

Why is this happening? Please God why are you doing this to me?

How could they have walked for so long only to end up at the very place they had begun. Had they died in that car accident last night

56

and were now faced with living in this life of Limbo for the rest of eternity.

"We're in hell, that's what it is!" Jane whispered to herself.

Oliver stood beside her, he was exhausted. He wanted to pick Jane up and hold her in his arms, but he didn't. He was afraid of her rejection, she had pushed him away too often. To Oliver it seemed as though Sam was right, there was no way out.

He stood there a broken man. His wife thought he was a selfish cheat, he was unable to see his beloved son, his life as he knew it was over. Oliver left Jane sitting in the dirt by the sign, saying nothing he walked back towards Law street.

Oliver walked past the villa, then the cottage and as he passed Sam's house he was like a zombie. Sam noticed Oliver and was about to wave at him from the porch, but instead watched Oliver walk down the street emotionless.

Sam was filled with sadness. He knew that look. Oliver had realised what he had once realised long ago, that they were never going to leave. Limbo had consumed them all, forever.

"Ah, poor thing!" Sam muttered as he shook his head.

Oliver returned home, he went straight to the cupboard and pulled out his top shelf scotch. He grabbed a glass, poured himself an oversized portion and threw it back without a thought. He then went to the freezer and put some ice in his glass, grabbing the bottle he headed outside. He sat on the outdoor couch under the veranda and settled in for the afternoon. Looking out over the yard he sat there, and he drank.

When Jane came home she saw Oliver outside drowning his sorrows. She let him be. Making her way upstairs she grabbed a photo of Alex that was hanging on the wall. Jane went to Alex's bedroom where she collapsed onto his bed clutching the image of her son. That's where her exhausted body stayed until she cried herself to sleep.

CHAPTER 7

Pretending to be happy is harder than choosing to be happy.

Mary had invited nearly all the neighbours to her house for dinner tonight. Why wouldn't she. Nothing new really happened in Limbo, so it was exciting to have new arrivals to chat with. Mary knew that it was a bitter sweet event to have new people turn up in Law street. It was difficult telling them that no one here had found a way out, no one except one.

Colin was a sports teacher from a senior college. He loved to inspire kids in their teenage years, the years where sometimes they go off the rails. It was his passion. He had invested his whole adult life into training and guiding boys and girls into becoming the best that they can be.

Mary enjoyed her long conversations with Colin. Even though there were those times where she had to pick him up off the floor after a drinking binge. His heart was of gold, but his mind could not deal with the entrapment that Limbo had offered him.

Mary will never forget the day when Colin disappeared. To this day she still didn't know how he had left, or if he had just passed on. He had come screaming to her one afternoon smelling of booze, crying with happiness.

"I've found it, I've found it!" he told her, "meet me tonight Mary and let's leave this place together forever."

Mary thought he was just drunk and talking crazy, how could she believe him. She was also a married woman; how would that look. So, that night she never met him. Instead she allowed him to sleep off his hangover and she would wait until the day reset. She went to check on him in the morning, but to her surprise Colin and his humble little caravan had disappeared from Law street and from Limbo.

Her heart broke not knowing where he had truly gone. She missed him so and prayed every day that he was in good hands, whether alive or dead. The rain had poured down hard that night. It only ever rained in Limbo when someone new appeared, now she knew that it also rained in Limbo when someone left.

CHAPTER 8

It's easy to judge, but not so easy when being judged.

Jane woke on the bed in Alex's room unsure of where she was. She could feel the residue of her old tears mixed with her mascara dried upon her cheeks. She was still tightly holding the photo of Alex against her chest. The sleep had surprisingly refreshed her. The clock was reading 4.55pm and Mary had invited them over for dinner at six.

Before her nap Jane could think of nothing worse than having to mingle and talk to strangers, but now she felt energised. These people knew more than she did about Limbo, and it was up to her to find out how she was going to get out of here. She was a journalist and a bloody good one. It was time for her to do some digging. She was going to get out of this horrible place, even if it killed her.

Cleaning up her face she made sure that she looked decent. She wanted people to feel comfortable around her, to trust her. This was going to be her chance to understand what kind of world she had fallen into. Although it seemed like a bad dream, it was time for her to use her skills to start finding answers to all of the questions she had.

On the way down the stairs her thoughts went to Oliver, she wondered what had happened to him. When she got to the kitchen she looked out the window noticing the sky getting dark. Oliver was outside still passed out on the couch. The scotch bottle was lying next to him three-quarters empty, he had done a good job at trying to finish it.

Instead of getting mad at him she grabbed a rug and covered him with it. He was exhausted and broken just as she was. But Jane wasn't going to let Oliver stop her from going tonight, instead she would tell Mary that he wasn't feeling well. Jane left the house with a new sense of purpose inside of her, she was a woman on a mission.

As she walked down the front stairs and headed left towards Mary's house next door, Jane was compelled to turn and look back down the street. There was music blasting from the strange lonely unit that hovered in the sky. The music so loud that she could feel it's beat pounding throughout her chest. Thank goodness she was not heading that way, the unit looked creepy and lonely there all by itself in the sky. Knocking on Mary's door that feeling of uneasiness fell upon her.

Oliver should be here with me, supporting me. How am I going to do this all by myself? Oh God I can't do this! Turn around and leave Jane, just go quickly!

The door flew open, surprising Jane.

"Hello, my dear, thank you for coming!" Mary looked around a little and then focused on Jane, "you're alone?"

"Oliver's not feeling well."

"Oh," she said as if she was unsure of the truth of it, "you mean he's hung over?"

How the hell does she know that?

"Um," was all that Jane could manage out of her mouth. Mary just smiled a great big smile at her.

"It's okay Jane, we have all drowned our sorrows with alcohol since being here, me especially! Please, come in and let's get you settled."

Mary had this ability to make Jane feel better about the situation, she was very comforting and approachable. Mary's husband Daniel was excited to meet Jane after everything Mary had told him about her.

"Jane, I'm Daniel, Mary's husband."

"Nice to meet you."

They shook hands, Jane couldn't help but notice how soft they were. Daniel was a lovely fellow, very chirpy. Jane thought that it would be rare that you would find him without a smile on his face or trying to please somebody. He was a bit like Santa Claus but without the beard.

"Thank you for having me over, I really do appreciate the effort you have gone to."

Both Mary and Daniel shook off the compliment, they loved to entertain, it really was their thing. Daniel decided to go off and finish whatever he was doing out in the backyard. Mary motioned for Jane to go through to the lounge room. Jane walked through straight into the open lounge, dine and kitchen area. It was huge and beautiful, Mary really had a flair for design.

"Oh Mary, this place is just lovely," Jane couldn't stop looking around.

"Thank you!" Mary beamed. "Now Jane I have invited some people from the street here tonight. I have asked them to come at six-thirty because I wanted you to get comfy before being bombarded by everyone. Don't worry they are all lovely people."

Jane was nervous about meeting the people that lived in Limbo, but she knew it was her only way to gaining more knowledge. It was unbearable to be here without Alex, she wanted to go home. The only way she was going to do that was to understand how Limbo worked.

"Would you like a drink Jane?"

"I'd love one thank you."

"I've just opened a white wine is that something that you would like?"

The house was so open and big, just one huge room, such a great holiday feel to it.

"Yes, anything is fine."

Jane was happy to drink anything at that moment as long as it had alcohol in it. Hopefully it would calm her nerves. Mary went over to the kitchen bench and poured Jane a glass and refilled her own.

"Come my dear, sit on the couch with me," she gestured to Jane as she returned to the lounge room.

Jane sat next to Mary on her light-yellow coloured couch. The colour softened the room and make it feel pleasant to be in. She would never have thought to use yellow, especially in a couch, but it was perfect. The two girls smiled at each other as they took a sip from their glasses, Mary placed hers down on the coffee table nearby while Jane held hers tight within her grasp.

"Just a quick warning," Mary started, "everyone here in Limbo is very different and they all have a story. We try to allow people to be who they are and leave it like that, does that make sense?"

No!

"I'm not quite sure what you are asking from me Mary?"

"Oh, nothing my dear! All I am saying is that the people you meet tonight are all very different and they have had a great deal to handle in their lives. I just want you to know that even though we are a small community here we try and stay out of each other's business. Like Otto for example who lives in the unit in the sky. I invite him to things all of the time, but he has never accepted in the whole time he has been here. Most people think he is dark and strange, but I just think that he is a man that likes to be left alone. I believe that we all get along so well here in Limbo because we just allow everyone to be who they need to be."

Jane did understand what Mary was saying, she nodded in agreement. She had better be subtle about how she interviews the guests tonight. Things were so different here. It would be interesting to know how each person reacted to being thrown into a life inside of Limbo.

One by one they arrived, and Mary introduced them to Jane. Firstly, there was Camilla and her son Frank who lived at number 72 in the small villa at the beginning of the street.

Camilla was an older lady at the ripe age of eighty-one years old and her mobility came from a wheelchair. She was a dark-skinned southern-style woman with beautiful curves and a voice to match. Camilla sung choir in church every Sunday when she was in the real-world. A loving mother figure to everyone she came to meet.

She had five daughters and two sons, but Frank was her only child who still lived with her. The others moved on with their lives getting married and having big families, but Frank was different.

As Mary informed Jane, Camilla had gone through a great deal with her husband when he was alive. He was a narcissist who believed that Frank was consumed by the devil and had to be saved.

Although Camilla was a strict religious woman, she could not see her son in that way. Instead she believed that all Frank needed was some motherly love and compassion to get his mind and his decisions back on track. The reason for this rift between Camilla and her husband was because Frank liked men over woman.

Although Frank had felt this way his whole life, only once had he given in to this sinful urge to be with a man. Strangely it was the same night that Camilla and Frank found themselves inside of Limbo.

Camilla knew exactly why they were both there, because of their sins. For herself she had in her past done something unthinkable. For Frank she knew it was because he had chosen to go against God and be with another man. Her heart bled for her son. She could not allow him to run away with someone who would cause him to go against God. This choice would send him straight to hell, she knew that unquestionably.

Here inside Limbo Camilla accepted that this was a second chance for both of them. A way to redeem their selfish ways. Camilla had to fulfil her punishment for the sins that she had committed, and Frank was to change his ways. That was how Camilla saw Limbo. Mary was seeming to be a great source of information for Jane.

Frank's appearance was tall, slender and he was starting to bald. Looking to be in his late forties maybe early fifties. He was a quiet person but not in a weird way, instead he had a peaceful feeling about him. Jane actually liked him a lot. She judged him to be the kind of man who would like his own company, one who wouldn't involve himself in any drama. But there was a sense of division between himself and his mother.

When Jane had Frank alone and talking he graced her with such a beautiful and loving vision of life. Her conversation with him made her positive. He was inspiring.

In Limbo Father James was living in the quaint little cottage next door to Camilla and Frank, number 10. Yet another sign to Camilla that God was testing them to see if they would change their ways.

Father James visited Camilla and Frank three times a week where they could privately confess their sins to him. This was so that God could see how much they had changed, to know how very sorry they were. But was Camilla and Frank truly confessing their sins or was it all for show. Camilla knew that she could not divulge the information she knew deep within her heart, and Frank had no intention of letting Father James in on his secret of being gay. They were both afraid of the judgement.

Father James was an older man in his late sixties and he knew what he was talking about. He was structured, well-groomed and loved being the one that people in Limbo could turn to in their time of need. He enjoyed saying grace before anyone ate dinner and knew that for most of them here, he was the connection they all needed to heal the pain that most of them were suffering. They all had a story.

Jane could see that all of the families here tonight were just trying to do the very best they could at making a life for themselves here in Limbo. But Although Jane was enjoying the night, she had no interest whatsoever in staying. Limbo was not going to be her new life.

Sam and Cindy soon turned up and Jane felt embarrassed to see them. How rude she had been the last time they had met, she was hoping to apologise to them both. Sam came straight over to her and shook her hand.

"We meet again Jane!"

"I'm so sorry Sam, I was so horrible to you both the last time…"

"Stop Jane, please don't, we know exactly what it is like the moment you enter Limbo. It is a confusing and scary place and I don't blame you at all for your reaction to it," Sam was such a loving and kind man.

Cindy just stood there looking at him as if even she was entranced by his loving ways. He was looking different tonight, well-groomed and clean. He was quite a handsome fellow.

"Oh, Jane I'm sorry too. I know that sometimes I'm not quite with it, this place really is hard on me. I've left all of my children behind and it's killing me," Cindy told Jane.

Jane looked down as she felt her heart hurt knowing that Alex was somewhere far away from her.

"I miss my son so much too," Jane said to Cindy.

Cindy could not help herself and the two women embraced. Both girls felt a connection between each other which made Jane even more guilty about how she had treated them. Cindy was a completely different person this evening, it was refreshing to be with her.

"You must come over for dinner one night, the both of you, or lunch or breakfast. Limbo only allows us to eat what we had in our house at the time we came here. You can't take food from house to house. Luckily for us we grew most of our own fruit and veggies. Being farmers, we always had a good supply of food on hand. Mary also has lots of different food, she loves to entertain," Cindy told Jane.

"I have absolutely nothing in my cupboards so that offer is like gold to me! Otherwise Oliver and I will be eating biscuits and meatballs for the remainder of our time here."

They all giggled together. No matter how odd Limbo became it was nice to be able to see the funny side of it.

"So, where is your old man?" Sam asked.

"I'm disappointed to say that he did not have a good day today and he is passed out on the couch."

"Exactly where I would like to be," Sam joked.

"Stop that!" Cindy scolded as she slapped him on the shoulder.

"Is he all right Jane?" Sam asked concerned.

Jane did not know what to say, "I don't know."

"He seemed pretty angry when he walked past the house today. I have seen that look in people's eyes before, I hope that he is doing okay. Limbo has this way of getting under your skin, if you know what I mean?"

"I sure do," Jane agreed with Sam.

Jane was happy that Sam and Cindy were so open towards her, everyone here had been that way. There was something wonderful about Sam and Cindy though, like when you meet someone for the first time and you know that you are going to be friends forever. Sadly, it was the second time they had met.

Next, Jane got to meet her neighbours on the other side of her house. The ones who lived in the two-story town house that had been split and missing its other half. They were two seventeen-year-old school girls. One was gothic looking; dark haired with dark eye make-up and black lipstick, but with light skin and green eyes. Her name was Alana.

The other girl named Stacey was stunning. She appeared to be like the high-school prom queen with her long flowing blonde hair, perfect teeth and her clear blue eyes. She was very well spoken but not at all ashamed of throwing a sly comment your way, just to have a dig at you. A little bit bitchy.

The two girls were the complete opposite to each other. Jane found it hard to believe that they were even friends, living in the same house together before entering Limbo. Their body language told the story that they were only just bearing the company of each other.

"They are sisters," Cindy whispered into Jane's ear.

"Sisters?" she questioned.

"Yes, by marriage. They were arch enemies at school for years. Alana's mother and Stacey's father met one day while being pulled into the Principal's office for their kid's bad behaviour. It ended in them getting married six months later. Alana and Stacey were of course devastated and made many threats to their parents. I think the threats made their parents get married even sooner."

Cindy found the story she told humorous, Jane gave a little smile also.

"They barely tolerate each other and it's quite fun sometimes to see how they react. What else can you do in Limbo than to get along, or spy on those that don't."

Mary's house was filling up and it was surprisingly a lovely environment to be in. She was right, although the people here were all quite different, and in the real-world it would be rare to see many of them spending time with each other, here they were enjoying themselves.

For most of them Jane was like a celebrity. Having questions thrown at her from every direction because she was the new kid on the block.

The last people to arrive for the evening were the family from the very end of Law street. It was the government housing looking home. In walked a young girl named Mandy. She was a twelve-year-old with brown wavy long hair and deep brown eyes.

Her mother Louisa was a petite woman who looked perfect in every way, it was obvious that her perfection was attained with many body enhancements. Mandy's step-father Jason, was a giant of a man. He looked tough, as his tank-top exposed his tattoos and enormous guns. They appeared to be a really nice family, even though Mandy looked to be a child who was introverted, maybe even a little sad.

Jane wanted to talk to the young girl, it was her motherly instinct. She missed Alex, so the conversation would be comforting for her to have.

"Hello there, I'm Jane," Jane said as she approached Mandy.

Mandy gave her a small warm smile. She held out her hand for Jane to shake it, but as they did, it was like they gave each other a zap. It was different from the little static zap you would normally get when getting out of your car. It was so much more real. Maybe not like electricity either, but instead like lightening. They were both stunned by the quick scare and had to laugh about it.

"I'm Mandy, it's really nice to have someone new to talk to in the street. I know that it isn't nice for you to be stuck here now, but still it's nice."

Jane smiled. It was lovely that Mandy thought it was nice to have her there, even though she didn't know her at all. Jane felt comforted to have a child around her again, she missed Alex so much.

"So how long has your mum and step-dad been together?" Jane asked.

"Too long!" Mandy cursed as she rolled her eyes.

"Oh, I'm sorry, you all look like you get on so well."

"Sure, we do! Until, well…until things get out of hand."

Jane half-smiled not sure what Mandy was trying to say to her. Mandy glanced over at her parents her face giving away exactly how she felt about her step-father. She was not a fan.

"Are you all right Mandy?"

"Yeah, don't worry Jane."

She appeared very mature for her age and Jane felt a connection to her straight away.

"So how has your time in Limbo been Jane, it's not the most pleasant place to be in, is it?"

Jane found it hard to reply, "Well, all I can say is that it is very different. It's hard to accept that you have left so many people behind."

"Well, I guess that is what happens when somebody dies isn't it? They leave everyone else behind."

Jane was fascinated by Mandy's analogy, they had all just disappeared like through death. The thought brought a great fear with it.

"Dead. Maybe we are all dead!"

Instantly Jane felt bad after she had said this, she was speaking to a child and should never had said something so final and scary.

"I think your right Jane," Mandy whispered as she turned to look at the residents of Limbo mingling at the party. "I think some of them here have been dead for a very long time. Even when they were living their lives in the real-world."

From the corner of the room Father James was intently watching the conversation the two girls were having. He didn't seem comfortable as he sipped on his beer and munched on a warm mini pie. Mandy grinned at him and Jane could sense that Mandy was teasing Father James in some way. He was a small man, even a little peculiar looking. He appeared fidgety, like he was annoyed.

"What is his story?" Jane asked Mandy.

"Oh, Father James just wants to save everyone, the problem with that is that most people here aren't worth saving."

Mandy was more than just an intelligent pre-teen girl, she seemed to know everyone in Limbo very well. Jane was interested to see how much she really did know. But there was also an anger inside the girl that saddened Jane's heart. Jane wondered how much she had gone through in her young life.

"I don't trust anyone here Jane, but your different I can feel it."

Jane was happy that Mandy felt safe around her. Camilla then wheeled herself over towards Jane wanting to be the next to interview the newest recruit.

"Speak of the devil," Mandy said under her breath as she moved away from Jane. "Hi Camilla!" Mandy happily sung.

"Hello Mandy, get me a soda would you dear, please."

"Sure," Mandy did as she was told.

Jane could feel that underlining act of pretend between them all. Although everyone was happily getting along, Mandy was showing her another side to this story. It would definitely be something she would look into, Mandy was going to be a very interesting individual to know.

70

CHAPTER 9

Death is a transition not an end.

Oliver woke and found himself outside on the couch with the rug draped over him. He could hear faint laughing coming from next door at Mary's house, but he could also hear pounding music coming from the opposite direction. His head hurt, and he was feeling a little sorry for himself. Staggering inside he squinted to see the clock reading nine o'clock.

"Oh shit," he muttered to himself.

He knew that he was missing out on the invitation at Mary's house. Inside his home was dark, except the small lamp in the lounge room corner that was on. Jane was not home, she must have gone to Mary's on her own. She was going to be pissed at him.

He was still a little uneasy on his feet. After Oliver composed himself he decided that he would go next door to support Jane. He slowly put on his jacket expecting the outside night air to be cold. Leaving, he shut the door behind him.

It was the blaring music from down the street that caught his attention first. He was taunted by its presence and felt the need to investigate where it was coming from.

Heading in the opposite direction, he decided to move towards the sound of the heavy metal music instead of Mary's house. Oliver felt like the volume of it was disrespectful to the rest of the community.

The base was so heavy, it's pounding bounced the very blood inside of his veins.

Noticing that the horrendous noise was being hurled out from the small unit that was alone hovering in the sky made him angry. Oliver knew that the same man who lived there, the one he had seen peering from the window, was the same man that had stolen his car. Jane had described him perfectly. He was also the man that Sam had told him to look out for.

Oliver's anger grew. This loser thought that he had the right to do whatever he wanted. He had made Sam fearful in his own home, he had stolen their car and now he was playing music like he was deaf. How disrespectful.

Oliver stormed up the street towards the unit ready to tell this guy exactly what he thought of him. He was sick of this place and if he was going to have to stay here forever then things were going to have to change.

The alcohol that was still roaming through his body was not making his choices clear, Oliver would never have been so confronting normally. He was protective and strong, and he stood up for what was right, in the real-world this music would never have bothered him.

Oliver got to the bottom of the stairwell and stood there uneasy. The stairwell was just there, unsupported by anything structural that he could visually see. How were these stairs even going to hold his weight?

This was not the strangest thing that he had seen in this place. So, he slowly eased himself upon the first step and found it to be just as stable as a normal stairwell. He made his way up holding onto the hand rail feeling more at ease with the strength of the structure. The music was louder here, he began to yell, even before he reached the top of the stairs.

"Hello! HEY!"

It was dark and hard to see. All of the windows at the front of the unit had the curtains closed. The window to the right of the front door had the curtain stuck on the couch, which allowed Oliver to peer through and look inside. He leant against the window with his hands cupping his eyes. The kitchen light was on inside and he saw the young man sitting at the table drinking. Oliver left his view from the window and began to bang on the front door.

"Hey!" he repeated over and over again.

Oliver went back to the window to see that the young man had not heard him over his music, so instead he started to bang on the window. Oliver was convinced that the guy inside was deaf.

This was getting Oliver even more frustrated, the man inside the unit had no care at all for the rest of the neighbours in this street. The music's vibration was almost making him sick, his heart was pounding.

Oliver watched on as the man at the kitchen table continued to drink down his scotch, the sweat running off his forehead. He was sitting there like he was in another world, a world deep within his mind. For a moment Oliver stopped banging on the window, he just stood there staring at him. This guy reminded him of himself a few hours ago, drinking away his sorrows. Suddenly he began to feel sorry for him, it was this place. Oliver wondered how long this guy had been stuck here.

This town called Limbo, whatever it was meant to be. This street of handpicked people would surly send anyone mad if they were doomed to be here forever.

Then that's when it happened. The man sitting at the table finished his drink and realised that the bottle itself was finally empty. He dragged something from down the table that was out of sight from Oliver until now, it was a revolver.

"What the hell!" Oliver gasped under his breath.

He was frozen in time unable to move an inch. Within a second of Oliver sighting the gun the man had shoved the end of it into his mouth and pulled the trigger.

BANG!

"NO!" Oliver screamed as he watched the man's brains being splattered all over the unit's walls like a precisely layered piece of abstract art. He covered his mouth with his hands and did not know what to do.

"Shit, shit, shit, shit!" he tried to open the front door tearing at the rounded handle, maybe he could kick the door in. Should he call someone, the police. There were no working phones in this place, what was he going to do. He didn't even know if there was any authority here.

He quickly looked back in through the window to see the same mess he had seen two seconds before. But something strange was starting to happen. Oliver's eyes opened wide in disbelief as he watched the incident start to reverse itself in slow motion. Every chunk of flesh and blood that had found itself decorated upon the walls and floors of this unit slowly began to creep its way back towards the man's dead body. The exposed blood now erasing its red trails. Every piece of human tissue making its way back inside the man's brain as if dancing to a slow love song.

The room was eventually clean and incident free. With a huge gulp of air making its way back into the man's lungs, his body heaved forward. Sitting up and opening his eyes the man sat awake in his chair alive and well.

"What the fuck!" Oliver screamed.

The man from inside the unit looked straight up from the kitchen table at Oliver standing in the window. Eye to eye they both stared at each other. The man bellowed out a laugh that was so loud that it even voiced itself over the music. Oliver was filled with fear and all he wanted to do was run.

Run! Run! the voice inside his head screamed.

He stepped back away from the window, scrambling across the walkway trying to get down the stairs as quickly as possible. His heart was pounding out of his chest, sweat pouring from his arm pits. He tripped here and there unable to judge the stairs with his grip on the rail constantly slipping.

Every now and then he looked back up at the door to see if the man was going to chase after him, but the door never opened. He finally hit the street and as he began to walk back towards his home he watched as the curtains in the front room of the unit opened. There stood the man looking down at him with no emotion on his face at all. Closing the curtain, the house became dark and quiet.

Oliver stopped in the street just staring back up at the unit's dark and empty window. What had he just seen. He had watched that man blow his brains out, and then he watched as his body mended itself back together again.

"What the hell am I going to tell Jane?" he asked himself. Nothing, he would tell her nothing.

This place, this life that he was inside of could not be real, it must be some kind of a dream. Oliver found it hard to walk straight, he was shaking. He continually wiped his hand over his mouth still unsure of what he had witnessed.

He walked on towards Mary's house where the lights were on and he could hear all the people inside, but he could not go in. He backed away and instead headed home, was he the one going crazy.

Oliver decided that Jane definitely did not need to know about what he had just seen, hell he didn't even know what he had seen. He went into the kitchen and went through all his cupboards, pouring out all the liquor that he could find down the sink. His hands were still shaking. Turning on the tap he rinsed his face by cupping the water with his hands. He was starting to lose it. He began to cry unable to control his feelings of uselessness. He took a deep breath in trying to gain control.

Emotional and scared Oliver could hear the neighbours talking out in the backyard of Mary's home. It made him stop and walk outside to listen to the conversations being had. He heard Sam's voice which was comforting to him. Standing there for a moment alone Oliver realised that he had to find out what was going on here in Limbo. He needed answers, and he wanted them now. Maybe it was a good idea to get to know all of these people who lived with them in Limbo, or at least find out more about the man in the unit. Oliver decided to head to Mary's house.

Mary was thrilled. Although Oliver did look a little under the weather as he stood on her doorstep, the added smell of booze coming out of his pores. She herself had taken to the bottle many times to help relieve the stress that Limbo brought. But there was something more, he was shaking.

"Oliver, are you feeling well?"

"Oh, yes…I am fine, I just wanted to find Jane."

"Come in. She is out the back. Do you need anything, a coffee maybe?"

"No, no!" Oliver was agitated.

"I will show you where she is."

"Thanks!" Oliver said as he followed Mary outside into the backyard.

Suddenly it was like a bunch of seagulls all trying to scab the last chip. Many of the guests flocked around Oliver excited to meet this new man that Jane had been telling them all about.

"Come on people back off!" Sam moved in and shook Oliver's hand pulling him to the side. He was able to get Oliver to himself.

Oliver took in a deep breathe, "It is so good to see you, Sam!"

Sam smiled, "It looks like you have had a hard day today Oliver. I hope things are looking up!"

"Not really."

Sam could see that Oliver was shaken up, "what's wrong mate?"

"Something just happened at the unit which has really freaked me out! I would really appreciate if we could talk about it at some stage."

"Of course!" Sam was concerned about Oliver.

Sam knew that Otto who lived at the unit was a real piece of work. He didn't trust him at all, especially after he found him inside his own house one night. He had broken in and was snooping around until Sam scared him off.

Sam tapped Oliver on the shoulder to ease his worries, it showed Oliver that he really did have someone he could trust here. Jane came over and kissed Oliver on the cheek which surprised him.

"Oliver, you're shaking."

"I'm fine Jane, just a result from the alcohol I decided to fix my problems with earlier. I am feeling a bit better now though."

"I can smell it on you!"

Cindy called Sam over leaving Jane and Oliver alone together. He grabbed her and pulled her close to him, so close that Jane found it hard to put up with his strong breath.

"Jane promise me that you will never go near that unit, or that strange guy that lives in it."

"The one that stole our car?"

"Yes, promise me that you will leave him alone."

Jane was stunned by his adamant nature towards this subject, "he stole our car, he's a thief. Why on earth would I want to go anywhere near him?"

Oliver relaxed and let go of Jane's arm, she backed away slightly and could see how distressed he was.

"What's going on Oliver, what's happened?"

"I think I should go," Oliver felt confused and unsure of his decision to come to the party.

"Stay, please, I need you here," Jane begged him.

It had been hard getting over-run by so many people at once. Being the newest person to arrive in Limbo Jane felt like she needed some support from Oliver. He needed to stay and meet all these people that were now going to be a part of their lives. They held the key to the both of them understanding how they could finally get out of Limbo once and for all. She needed Oliver to focus on what was important, and that was getting home to Alex.

For Oliver, Jane wanting him to stay made him feel like she wanted him around. It was a nice change from what he had become accustomed to, so he agreed to stay. He was finding it hard to focus on the conversations he was having with all of his new neighbours. It was overwhelming.

Meanwhile Mandy's step father Jason was hitting the alcohol hard. Mandy knew that it was going to either be a night where he would just pass out on the couch, or he would become the raging bull that she had come to hate about him. She couldn't believe that Mary was still offering him alcohol, sometimes Mandy thought that she did it on purpose, because of Colin. Mary wasn't the only one who missed him.

Mandy's mother Louisa had also decided to have a few drinks, she found it amusing to flirt with Oliver. Proudly she made no attempts to hide the fact that she found him quite attractive. Enjoying any moment to touch his arm and laugh at what he said.

It was normal for Jane to watch on as other woman threw themselves at him. There he was oblivious, as usual, to these women longing for his attention. But Jane noticed that Oliver wasn't being himself. Usually he would be the life of the party and always accommodating to everyone else's needs, but tonight he looked awkward and anxious. Something was wrong.

Oliver was in no mood to have Louisa continuously talking to him about nothing. He wanted to leave. His look over at Jane every minute or so was him begging for her to help him. Jane decided that she had tortured him enough. She began to move towards Oliver to save him from Louisa's clutches, but she wasn't quick enough to notice what was happening in the background. Before she could do anything, Jason came storming up to Louisa. He ripped Louisa's hand from Oliver's arm, pushing her to the ground with such force that she hit her head onto the ground. Her drink was sent flowing all over her.

"You slut!" Jason yelled at her, "as soon as there is some other man here you throw yourself at him. You're nothing but a dirty little whore!"

"Jason please," Louisa begged as she lay on the floor embarrassed.

"You leave my woman alone!" he turned and yelled at Oliver.

Oliver just stood there blank not knowing what to do. Jason took his finger and began pointing it and poking Oliver with it into his chest.

"You listen here, you scrawny little piece of shit, if you ever go near my woman again I will wipe that smirk off your face so quick…"

"Okay."

Oliver raised both of his hands up as if to surrender, he didn't even know what Jason was talking about. His mind was not even on the conversation that he and Louisa were having, instead it was on the trauma from watching that man blow his brains out.

"That's enough!" Sam yelled as he stepped in between Oliver and Jason, "I think it's time that you call it a night."

Jason just stared into Sam's eyes and he backed away. He looked down at Louisa on the ground and spat on her before he turned and left Mary's house. Cindy helped Louisa to her feet, who had now become timid and embarrassed by the ordeal.

"I'm so sorry Mary," Louisa started to tear up.

"Don't be silly dear, you don't have to apologise. Maybe you should go home too, sort this out with him."

Louisa just nodded and grabbed her stuff. She pulled onto Mandy's arm to acknowledge that they were both to leave, and that is what they did.

"Are they going to be safe going home with Jason, he seems so angry, what happens if he hurts them?" Jane asked Mary.

"Now this is what I was talking about earlier," Mary approached Jane slowly and calmly took her by the arm taking her inside.

"We all have our own things to deal with here in Limbo and we must respect each other's privacy. That's why we just let people deal with their own problems, not get involved. They will work it out dear, they always do, you understand?"

Jane did not understand. She was truly scared for Louisa and Mandy's life after how Jason had behaved. He was so violent. But Mary was calm, and she appeared to know what she was doing. Things were different in Limbo and Jane had to accept that Mary had done the right thing.

Jane went back over to Oliver to make sure he was all right, but he wasn't. She sent him home, but Jane didn't want to leave just yet, she wanted to have some time alone with Mary.

CHAPTER 10

Life is about being the best YOU that you can possibly be, it is not about pretending to be someone else.

M any of the guests at Mary's house left due to the carry on. It had been a lovely night for most of the time, but for Jane reality had sunk back in. After meeting Mandy Jane's heart missed her son, she wanted answers.

Mary and Jane sat outside together on the outdoor furniture and Mary poured Jane another wine. The time was now about eleven o'clock. Daniel saw the last of the guests out as they happily retreated back to their homes. Daniel then excused himself from the two girls and decided to call it a night.

"Goodnight my dear," Mary said as Daniel leaned down over her for a kiss.

"Goodnight ladies," Daniel said as he left.

Jane thanked him for such a wonderful night. She was very happy to have met everyone, although bitter sweet. There were so many lovely people here, but she was not interested in staying in Limbo and getting to know them better. Everything now was about trying to leave.

"How are you my dear?" Mary questioned Jane.

"Confused mostly," she answered as she put her wine on the table and lifted her legs up next to herself on the couch. She felt so very comfortable here, "so, let's get down to the nitty gritty, shall we?"

Mary giggled, she had been waiting for Jane to start asking her questions.

"What the hell is going on here, please just explain it all to me!" Jane begged.

Mary smiled her welcoming smile and began to tell Jane what she wanted to know.

"Welcome to Limbo," she started. "One day, just like you, all of us have magically turned up here. The why is unknown, but there are some things that I can tell you that seem to be common with all of us."

"What's that?" Jane asked.

"Well," Mary began as she thought hard about her words. "After speaking with everyone here over time, I have noticed that one of us from each household can remember a moment before arriving here. That single moment in our lives when we felt a shift. Where something happened. Where we were so low that we begged for something greater than ourselves to save us from our own lives."

That was a huge beginning statement for Jane. She sat there as the memory of herself sitting in the toilet cubicle at the awards night, when she was having a panic attack. She sat there trying to breathe as she begged to be set free from her emotional pain. There was a shift. She had felt it. For that moment she drifted to a place of peace. In that moment she felt free, until she was shocked back into reality.

"You know it don't you?" Mary asked, noticing Jane staring into the nothingness of the night.

"Yes, I do!"

"It's okay Jane! We have all been where you have been. Lost would be the best word to describe how we were all feeling in that particular moment. When I had mine, I felt a wonderful peace flow over me, like everything was going to work out. But I also knew that it wasn't going to be easy. Peace would come to me if I learnt how to let it in."

"And how do you learn to let peace in?" Jane was desperate to know.

Mary giggled, "Oh Jane, I have this realisation that I myself have not learnt that yet, hence why I am still here in this place of being stuck."

Jane was disappointed by Mary's answer and Mary could see that.

"Look Jane, what I do know is that we have all come here to experience and learn something. It could be the same thing, or it could be something completely different for all of us."

"How do you know this?"

"Let's just say, it's what I feel in my heart from experiencing this place for so long."

Jane was feeling that the information that Mary was giving her was just sending her in circles. She really didn't know much more than she did to begin with. It was disappointing.

Jane shook her head, "I don't want to stay here forever! Surely someone has left here."

Mary sat back into her seat uncomfortably and Jane noticed that she had hit a soft spot.

"So, someone has left here then, haven't they?" Jane pushed her.

"Yes, of course they have," Mary answered.

"But why does everyone seem to think that they can't leave, that makes no sense at all!" Jane was getting frustrated.

"Let me explain. A little while ago a man named Colin lived in a caravan on the land where you are now located, right next door to me. We all got on very well until one day he was gone. He vanished. His van and himself were never to be seen again."

"But how?" Jane was confused.

Mary squirmed in her chair feeling uncomfortable about the conversation. It seems that she may have to come clean about how much she knew. She stood up and slowly peered through the sliding glass door making sure that Daniel had definitely gone to bed, then she sat back down again. Jane sat forward on the couch knowing that what she was about to hear was going to be interesting.

"Jane listen to me, I am going to tell you what actually happened. I have told this to many people before, but it all went south pretty quickly. I chose never to talk about it again."

"Tell me," Jane begged.

"Colin was a teacher and he was the most wonderful man…" there was a pause as Mary started to think about Colin. Jane could tell by Mary's expressions that she truly cared about him.

"Were you in love with him?"

"No, no!" Mary appeared to be a little shaken by Jane's question.

Sadly, Mary looked into Jane's eyes, she took a deep breath and released it slowly.

"Yes dear, I loved him ever so much."

Jane smiled at Mary's honesty, Mary smiled back. Jane knew that this information would be controversial, especially in Limbo where there were only a handful of residents. Jane also wondered how she would have kept her love for this man a secret, especially from Daniel.

"You are the only one who has ever asked me that question Jane."

Jane reached over and held Mary's hand for a moment before she continued. She could sense that Mary was feeling comfortable talking to her. That is exactly what Jane wanted.

"Colin and I were very fond of each other. Daniel of course is my husband and I would never do anything to hurt him, as he would never do anything to hurt me. I stuck with my marriage because that was the right thing to do. That is what Daniel and I agreed to. We have both given up a lot in our lives, but it is what we have chosen to do for each other, and I wouldn't go against that trust."

"Are you happy?" Jane could see how hard it was for Mary to talk about Colin.

"Daniel is a good man. He has taken care of me all of my life, but I have never been in love with him. My parents pushed me into marriage, he is more like my best friend. We have never had a spark romantically and let's just say we both knew it from the start. I found magazines one day in a locked drawer of his, they were magazines of other men. Since that day I have known that he was gay," Mary took a small pause before she continued.

"Actually, I honestly believe that in my heart I have always known. I think that my parents wanted me to marry him to please their friends who were Daniel's parents. They were afraid that he was a little different and so they forced us to marry. When I found those horrible magazines, it was the day that I had my moment that we were talking about before. I was so upset. It's strange, I don't know why I was so angry, like I said before, deep down I always knew Daniel was gay. Finding those magazines somehow cemented for me that I had given up my life. Wasted my life. I ran from the house in tears with Daniel chasing me. The next thing I knew we both ended up here," Mary looked up to the sky with tears in her eyes. "It's my punishment I can feel it!"

"Please don't say that!" Jane said.

"When Colin arrived in Limbo a little while after Daniel and I did, there was this instant attraction. We got on so well and we all became very close friends."

"Why didn't you leave Daniel to have a life with Colin?" Jane asked her.

"I couldn't, Daniel was my safe zone as I was his. I felt guilty because we are taught that marriage is forever no matter what, in God's eyes we must stick it out."

Jane was sad that both Mary and Daniel had not chosen to be themselves in their lives. It was though they had stayed in their marriage through fear, fear of judgement, fear of displeasing others, fear of displeasing God and the fear of losing something that was comfortable.

"Every day Limbo resets at midnight," Mary began. "When the clock hits twelve o'clock all will go black. When the morning comes you will wake up the same every single morning here, just as you did this morning Jane. The food that was in your fridge will return, the clothes in your cupboard hung back the way they were. Any mess made throughout the day cleaned and back to normal. You will wake in the same clothes when you became lost in Limbo every single morning."

Jane seemed a little confused, "I don't understand."

"How did you wake up this morning Jane?"

Jane thought about it as she remembered, "I woke up in my black evening dress, my high heeled shoes were on while I was asleep in bed. When I went to look in the mirror my hair and make-up were perfect."

"Everything that was at the time that you had that moment, what you were wearing, your hair, the food that was in your fridge or cabinets at home, everything will reset back to that moment every time at midnight."

"But why?"

Mary shrugged her shoulders, "I don't know why, all I know is that nothing changes. I have tried to lend things to the neighbours, give them food for the next day, but you just can't. Once again in the morning when we wake up it has all reset itself back once again."

"Oh no," Jane was now upset.

"What is it?"

"We have no food in our cupboards. I ordered shopping for delivery the next day because we didn't have barely a thing. It never came."

Mary smiled, "You can come here anytime and eat my food, as long as you eat it in the house that you got it from. If you try and take it elsewhere it just disappears, right in front of your eyes. So strange! Sometimes we go up to Sam and Cindy's because they grow their own fruit and vegetables and they also have chickens. Camilla the sweet thing, she likes to eat different foods and because she was having her meals delivered every day she is in the same spot as you."

Knowing that Jane would have to rely on other people to help her out with food was disturbing her, she never liked to rely on anyone for anything in her life.

The question still remained about Colin, "Would it be fine if we talked about Colin again, I would love to know how it came about that he left Limbo."

"Of course, as you now know I could not leave Daniel for Colin because every night Limbo would have reset, which means that every morning I would have woken up in bed next to Daniel. How could I do that to him, it would kill him. He feels so alone already. Daniel means so much to me, I love him, he is my best friend and I can't lose that."

"But don't you feel lonely *with* him, don't you feel like you are missing out on so much in your life?"

Mary paused for a moment.

"I'm sorry! I've gotten too personal."

"No, no Jane that's fine!"

Mary was not offended at all by the question. "You are right, there has always been something missing in my life and of course it is because Daniel could not give me what I, as a woman needed and still need."

Mary was thinking so deeply; the conversation had stirred up many feelings inside of her. It was hard to talk about the life that she had endured but she felt comfortable talking to Jane. It was a relief to release so many thoughts and emotions after so long.

"You know he came to me that night," Mary told Jane.

"Who did?"

"Colin did," Mary turned to Jane.

"He was drunk, and he smelt like an old boot. He had been hitting the bottle more and more, this place got to him so badly. I had just let him down by telling him that I was going to stay with Daniel. I had to, I felt obligated to him and I was scared to leave. Colin was yelling at me this night, in a good way, begging me to leave Limbo with him. He was sounding crazy. He told me that he knew how to leave, but I didn't believe him."

"What happened?"

"I told him to go home and sleep off his drunkenness, I knew he would wake up fine in the morning because Limbo would reset. I guess that is one good thing, you never wake up with a hang over the next morning. But anyway, he told me to meet him in an hour at his caravan, but I didn't."

"How did he know how to leave?"

"I truly have no idea," Mary said. "I told him that I didn't believe him, but I think what scared me most was that I did. I could see it in his eyes."

Jane was shocked, "But if you believed him, why didn't you go?"

"When I looked into his eyes, beyond all of the alcohol I could see that he was telling me the truth. He could not stay in Limbo any longer, it was killing his heart. He knew how to leave, and I was too afraid to go with him. I was afraid to go to a life that I had always dreamed about, but I had no clue how to live. I was afraid to leave Daniel behind, I felt guilty so very guilty. Now every day I wonder what it would have been like if I had just met him. That night when I didn't meet him at ten o'clock, I waited, I waited for the rain…"

"The rain what do you mean?"

"It rains in Limbo whenever someone arrives or whenever someone leaves."

Jane remembered last night, how it was raining heavily. The rain had been pouring down welcoming them here to Limbo.

Mary continued, "I woke up at 11.55pm that night to the sound of a thunderstorm, it was so heavy the rain. That's when I knew that Colin had gone. I snuck outside and ran into the rain to see with my own eyes that it was true. There was only a vacant block of land where he used to reside. He had left me after waiting until almost midnight for me to come to him, but I never did. The next day everyone else noticed that his caravan was gone, and we have never seen him again."

Jane did not know what to say, emotionally she was trying hard not to cry for Mary, she had endured so much in her life.

"I'm so sorry Mary, I really am sorry."

"It's okay dear, my love life is not your worry," they both giggled through their tears. Mary was able to lighten even the hardest of moments.

"You miss your little boy, don't you?"

Jane's heart broke from Mary's words, she was finding it hard living without Alex.

"I don't know what to do, if there is any way for me to somehow get back to him I will try it. Thank you so much for telling me your story about Colin, it gives me hope that one day I will see my son again."

"I pray that you find what you are looking for Jane and I hope that you get back to your son quickly. Everyone else here who knew that Colin found a way out has sent themselves crazy trying to find the answer that he finally found. I have watched Cindy suffer terribly mentally. Please don't do that to yourself. I want you to of course try and find the answers you need, but don't let this place get to you. I've seen what it can do to a person. People can change into something that is not good, do you understand?"

Jane nodded. She could see that Mary had witnessed a lot since living here in Limbo. Jane needed Mary to be that person who she could trust and rely on in times of need. She was a valuable friend to have.

It had been a very long night and it was getting close to midnight.

"Goodness me dear, look at the time, it is two minutes to midnight!"

"Shall I help you pack up?" Jane was happy to clean up.

"Oh no Jane, all of this will be gone in the morning. One of the perks to living in Limbo is that at midnight everything will reset, and all these dishes and all the rubbish will be gone tomorrow. Back to where it all started from."

Jane got up to leave, "thank you so much for having me. I best be getting home."

Mary smiled as she watched the clock, the hands drew closer to midnight. Mary did not get up to see Jane out, she knew that Jane still did not quite understand how Limbo worked. Instead Mary spoke her name making Jane turn before she went to go through the back door to leave.

"Jane, thank you for listening. I'm so very happy that I got to talk to you tonight," Mary skulled down her glass of wine and made a loud ah sound as she swallowed it. "Goodnight dear Jane."

With that the clock struck twelve and Jane heard the bellowing noise it made. Mary began to become blurry in front of her eyes. She tried to rub them to make her vision clear again, but it didn't work. Mary was nothing but a dark shadow and then the darkness of the night swallowed them both, Limbo was resetting itself.

CHAPTER 11

I's okay to be angry, but it's not okay to hold onto it and never let it go. Anger will eat you alive.

Oliver felt uncomfortable. He tossed, and he turned not knowing why. He thought about the alcohol he had drunk yesterday, but he did not feel hungover. He felt quite good, he was just uncomfortable.

When he finally woke he realised that he had once again woken up in bed still dressed in his full dinner suit. The jacket had twisted around his body while he slept, and his tie was slightly choking him. He sat up taking off the bed covers and turning to sit on the edge of the bed. He tore off the tie and threw it angrily across the room. He undid his jacket and slowly took it off. He did so with his shirt, shoes, socks, belt and pants, leaving it all in a pile on the floor near the bed.

He looked upon Jane looking immaculate as she slept. He gracefully rummaged under the covers to take off her high heeled shoes. A small grin rolled from Jane's face while she slept, she turned over in bed and continued to sleep.

Oliver missed how they used to be together. They were a great team, but it was slowly falling apart. If only he could somehow prove to her how much he loved her. Oliver had originally planned to slip back under the covers and return to sleep but the disturbance had now made him feel wide awake.

He stood up and looked out the bedroom window, he gazed out on the street and at the forest of green trees that lined it. A big breath released from his lungs as he realised that once again he had woken to the nightmare that was Limbo. How would he struggle through another day without holding his precious son in his arms. Limbo was taking its toll.

He was anxious from last night's haunting memories. Oliver had never seen anything like it before in his life, he did not want Jane going anywhere near that guy from the unit. There was no way that he could tell her about what had happened, it would scare her. With the both of them not knowing how long they would be stuck here for, he did not want to turn the atmosphere so quickly into something fearful. Jane needed to have hope.

Oliver headed for the shower, when he stepped in he allowed the heat to ease the strain that he felt in all of his aching muscles. He had never felt so useless as a man. In the past he was always strong, not just physically, but emotionally and mentally as well. He was now a battered man. His wife accusing him of the greatest sin, he was unable to see his son, and he was in a place that seemed like a mental asylum. *What have I done to deserve such a punishment?* he thought. The heat from the shower was a perfect temperature as he enjoyed the peace.

The bathroom door flung open and Jane stood there hopping about.

"Morning!" she said as she tried to rip off her evening dress before she peed her pants. Although the task was difficult she won.

"Good morning," Oliver replied in a weak and tired tone.

"How are you feeling? Jane asked, "things seemed to get a little heated last night."

Oliver opened the shower door slightly, so Jane could hear him clearly.

"It wasn't me you know, I had absolutely nothing to do with that guy losing his shit!"

"I know, I know" she said believing him.

92

"Also, I don't want you going anywhere near that young guy that lives in the unit either, he's not right that one."

Jane was curious because Oliver had already warned her about this man. She herself had seen him break into their car and drive it away, so she knew he was trouble. She finished what she was doing, washed her hands and stood there by the crack in the shower door in her underwear peering through to talk with Oliver.

"I know he is bad news, I've seen that with my own eyes. Why are you so pushy about this guy, did something happen last night?"

Oliver was stuck in knowing what to say to her. He continued to run his head under the warm water with his back to her as she held the door open.

"Nothing happened," he answered, "he was playing loud music last night and it just pissed me off that he thinks he can do whatever he likes without a care in the world."

Jane smiled, "Yes, we could hear the music last night from Mary's house."

Jane closed the shower door and let Oliver enjoy his shower.

"Mary told me last night that she knew a guy who actually found a way to get out of here," Jane had spoken a little louder to make sure that Oliver heard her clearly over the running water.

"What?"

Oliver opened the shower door again, peering out like an inquisitive child. Jane was tying her hair up for the day in front of the mirror and she spoke to him looking at him through the mirror.

"His name was Colin and he lived in a Caravan right here on the spot where we have our house. He told Mary the night before he left that he had worked out how to leave Limbo and he asked her to go with him, but she didn't."

Jane walked over to the crack in the shower door again.

"Really, so somebody has actually left from here?" Oliver could have cried.

Jane looked him straight in the eyes and with a big grin she said, "Yes!"

Oliver smiled also, and he reached through the shower door to plant a big, wet kiss on her cheek.

"You bloody beauty!" he cheered.

They both had a laugh and Jane left the bathroom heading to the robe to get dressed, she felt like going for a run today to clear her head. Oliver had his spark back. He knew what this meant, that there was a way to get out of this prison and return home again. They may not know how just yet, but they were going to do everything in their power to make sure that they did.

Jane got changed into her running gear, going for a run always helped to clear her mind. After all the information Mary had told her last night it would be a great way for her to get some fresh air to help process it all. She hoped that it would stir up some ideas about Colin and how he worked out how to leave. She was a cleaver woman, she was determined to understand.

While eating breakfast together at the kitchen bench, Jane went through and tried to explain to Oliver everyone she had met who lived in Law street and what they looked like. This helped Oliver to remember. She also discussed their personalities and their stories to the best of her memory. She knew that Oliver had missed out on most of the stories, he was quite amazed by what Jane had to say.

"Sam asked about you before you arrived last night. He was worried about you. He said you looked angry."

Oliver smiled at Jane and shrugged as he threw back the last sip of coffee, "I was angry."

He had never tried to hide his weaknesses, he just let them come and go. Acknowledging his emotions is what made him such a strong person. This is why this place was getting to him, because how could he just let things go here, there was no way for him to escape.

Jane felt the need to comfort him, but she just couldn't. There was still that pain inside of her that maybe this wonderful man had done something unspeakable behind her back.

94

Why can't we just sit here and talk about it?

There was a distance between them. Usually Oliver would cuddle her and kiss her constantly, but she could see that he was deflated and unwilling to show her affection. Their relationship was constantly changing from hot to cold. All the unsaid crap was weighing them down and Jane's thoughts were constantly changing.

Maybe I have pushed him away that he is now too scared to come near me. Should I forgive him so that we can move on? Or maybe he no longer loves me, or he loves someone else. Is it my fault that he fell into the arms of another woman? Of course not! You should be angry at him! How dare he do that to you! It is not your fault.

Oliver found it hard to know how to behave around Jane. It was killing him. How much longer did he have to put up with her accusations and her belittling of him. He was too tired to try and understand how to fix everything.

"You know you get angry too Jane. I'm not the one who yelled at Sam and Cindy the first time we met them," Oliver didn't know why he had said that. Maybe the guilt of not being at Mary's partly for most of the night had him acting defensive.

Jane was tired of all this crap. She was trying so hard to understand this place, she had gone out of her way to meet everyone last night because her heart was aching for Alex. Why couldn't Oliver have just kept it together so that he could have gone with her last night. To support her. Jane started to blame Oliver for them being stuck in Limbo. He was not trying hard enough to help find a way to get them back home.

"It would have been better if you had come with me last night, instead of getting drunk," Jane had her dig.

"I'm sorry I was going to come, but…. well by the time I woke up it was late."

"I know, it just would have been nice to have you there with me at the start. It was hard trying to talk to all of those people by myself. It was uncomfortable!" Jane started out calmly, but the tone in her voice began to show her anger. "We have to remember that it isn't about us, it's about getting home to Alex. Next time just try and take your problems out some other way instead of drinking so much that you pass out!"

"I'm sorry!" Oliver yelled at her from across the counter. Jane stepped back in shock.

I didn't deserve that! How dare he speak to me like that!

"What the hell is your problem?" Jane defended herself.

Oliver looked up at her and began to shake his head in disbelief.

"What's my problem?" he returned her question.

He could feel his anger growing within himself, how much more could he possibly take, especially from Jane. It was like her life now was focused on how much she could torment and blame him.

"I will tell you my problem Jane, we are stuck in this shit hole, unable to leave. I can't see my son and my loving perfect wife believes that I am a cheating prick and won't come near me. That's the fucking problem Jane! I'm tired so tired of all this bullshit."

There was silence between them as Jane did not know how to respond to his outburst.

"I'm going for a run," Jane said quietly. She collected her jacket unable to deal with Oliver's rude behaviour. Her unwillingness to participate in the argument frustrated Oliver.

"Oh, that's right Jane you go ahead and leave without us talking about it! Go and create some more crap in your head and see how that goes for you!"

Jane stopped abruptly and turned around to face Oliver, but she had no words to say to him. There was never a time in her life that he had ever spoken to her like that, even when they did argue.

"How dare you!"

"Excuse me! How dare I? You have some nerve Jane. You sit there on your high horse accusing me of horrible things that aren't true. You're like a time bomb to be around. I'm sick and tired of this!"

"Well then don't be around me then!"

There was a sickening silence between them both. Oliver's guilt got the better of him, "Jane, I'm sorry…" Oliver moved from the kitchen towards Jane, but she stepped back.

"God, you are driving me crazy!" Oliver threw up his hands into the air. "I don't know who I am anymore! I don't know what we are anymore. Your treating me like a criminal one minute and then like your husband the next. You can't keep doing this Jane it's just not right!"

"I'm sorry but I don't trust you anymore, I can't!"

Oliver felt her words like they were daggers to his heart. Jane saw the reaction in his face. Even though his sadness made her feel bad, she could not allow herself to back down. There was this overwhelming voice in her head telling her that she had every right to treat him this way, he deserved it.

"After all these years this is what you think of me?" Oliver was gutted.

"I'm sorry but I need time, time to process everything that's going on. Right now, I just want to go home, that is what is important."

"Why?" Oliver laughed. "Why on earth would you want to go home to Alex and be this person. We can't be a family, we just can't. You have been treating me like this for months, it's not just about your thoughts with Giselle it has to be more than that. I think your just coming up with ways to blame me for things, so that you can leave."

"What?" Jane was shocked.

How dare you blame me for this! Our marriage failing is your fault not mine.

Oliver continued, "If you wanted out of this marriage Jane, you shouldn't make up lies and excuses so that you can blame me. You can't blame me for everything!"

There was a deadly silence between them. In some way his words frightened her, maybe they were true. But she would not let him see that he had caused doubt in her mind.

"Why not," she said softly but angrily as she left slamming the front door behind her.

Jane's blood was boiling, she was so upset. Oliver and her rarely fought. She started to feel like maybe she was the one that was causing this rift between them. Maybe she was the reason why they were both stuck here.

I don't know what is real anymore!

Feeling suffocated she tried drawing in the morning air to help calm her nerves. Her emotions began to erupt like a volcano inside of her stomach and she knew that it wasn't going to be long before she broke. Not just emotionally but mentally as well.

I have to get out of here!

Jane ran hard off towards the forests dark cover. She was in no mood to talk or see anyone feeling this way, especially a bunch of people she hardly knew. She wanted to hide. The coolness of the forest air hurt her throat as she breathed in and out deeply. She tried so hard to keep it together, but who was she kidding she was losing it.

You can fix this, you can fix this!

She felt lost and completely out of control. Never in her life had she ever felt like wanting to be out of this game called life, until now. This very moment she wanted to die. She was desperate for peace. Her thoughts were jumbled and confusing. She couldn't focus. Voices and memories flew in and out of her mind. Breathing harder and harder she was trying to contain emotions that were uncontainable.

CHAPTER 12

Strangers are just friends that you haven't got to know yet.

It had been so long. So long since Jane had wrapped her arms around her beautiful son Alex and told him how much she loved him. She missed him so much that it was painful. The emotional state of Jane's mind was dangerous and cramped. Nothing seemed real anymore and she could feel herself losing the battle over her sanity.

She continued to run. She ran as far as she could through the forest and then along the road that had brought them here. When she ran she continuously found herself back to where she had started from. In front of that ugly sign, welcome to Limbo. She wanted to burn it to ashes.

"Piece of shit," she muttered under her breath.

Although she knew that no matter which path she took, it would return her to the sign she kept trying and trying, hoping there was a way out. Tired now of the road she ran through the woods again, at least the view was more stimulating than an endless road.

Stopping to finally take a breath she found herself not far from that hole that was deep within the forest. The long lonely drop in the earth that she had found when they first arrived here. She slowly walked over to it, standing at its edge as she peered down. It was long and deep with the bottom unclear, the size of it was grand. While in a trance she could hear her mind remembering her thoughts from when she first saw this endless pit.

Surely no one could survive if they fell into this hole.

So many thoughts passed through Jane's head as she stood there staring...wondering.

I'm the reason we are here! I'm the one that causes all the fights. I accused my husband of being a lying, cheating excuse of a man. This is my punishment for all the horrible things that I have done to my family. I will never see my Alex again because I don't deserve him. It's all my fault.

At this very moment in her darkest of hours each answer kept coming back to Jane choosing to finish this nightmare once and for all. It could all be over if she chose for it to be. This place was not her home. It was filled with strangers, even Oliver was a stranger to her. There was no comfort, just pain and suffering and she had had enough.

I can't do this anymore! I just want the pain to stop.

Unaware of her body creeping closer and closer to the holes dangerous edge, she was distracted by the noise of rocks falling into the deadly abyss. Looking down Jane saw a small portion of the earth crumbling away from under her feet. She had never ventured this close to anything before. There was a sureness, a confidence in her that took away all of her fear.

Jane, Jane, come closer, come closer!

The voices that called to her from within the long deep tunnel were actually coming from inside of her diminishing mind. How much more could she take; how much longer could she endure the pain. This was a prison to her and it was killing her, slowly one piece at a time.

It's time Jane, to make it all stop.

Feeling no fear but instead intrigue she wondered if this earthly trap could be her way out. Would Oliver even care if she were gone. It didn't even matter anymore, nothing mattered except being free. Free from this pain and endless suffering. Oh, how she longed to be set free.

She closed her eyes as she felt her sweat drip down from her forehead over her eyelid. Her breathing slowed.

All I want is peace, no more of these unbearable games.

The trees hummed with life inside her ears and the birds seemed so happy.

I just want to be happy, that's all.

It was like she had wings. Without even acknowledging her choice she allowed her body to fall, head first into the hole of freedom, hands by her side. Relaxed her body free-fell until it hit the edge a quarter of the way down. There was a large cracking sound inside of her body.

As she fell, her body mangled itself against the tunnels edge over and over again. The pain was intense, but Jane found that her peace did not falter. There was still no fear even though her body was being crushed with every impact. Keeping her eyes closed she could only see cracks of light through those moments her eyes flickered quickly. Jane knew that there was no turning back, she was falling to her death.

Feeling her body being torn and broken, the life inside of her began to dim. Her head rolled around uncontrollably from her neck being shattered from the beating. There was nothing left for her to do but to meet the bottom of this dark endless hole.

"Aarrgghh!" she screamed as she hit the floor with a great force. All the air that was left within her lungs had been thrusted out. There was silence.

Am I dead yet?

At the bottom of this deadly grave Jane's body lay lifeless and ruined. Her skin torn off in chunks and its remains left on the rocky walls. Her bones broken so much that most of them had turned to powder. Her arms and legs twisted in places where they should never be able to rest. There she was, her story finally over and her freedom given to her. But her mind continued to wonder, to talk, to think. Her pain was so incredibly real as she lay there unable to move, but somehow, she was still present. She was still alive.

Thinking she was finally going to take her last breath something began to happen. There was an energy that filled the air around her, and without her permission the event that just occurred began to rewind itself.

Jane felt her body lift away from the dirty floor as she opened her eyes. The choice she had made to end her life was not being allowed. Instead somehow, she was returning to the top. Every hit, every knock, every injury that she had sustained inside of that hole was being reversed, just as it had originally happened. She felt the pain of every piece of skin that had been torn off be returned to her body. Every bone crushed was being repaired. Floating back slowly to the top she re-enacted her committed suicide backwards. It was being erased.

There she stood at the top of that hole once again looking down upon it as her feet pushed crumbs of soil down into it. With her eyes wide open she lifted her arms out in front of herself inspecting them. They should have been full of horrific injuries, instead she found herself perfectly intact.

This can't be happening!

Jane let out a deafening scream, the birds in the trees flew away in fear. She screamed again realising that this place of unending misery, had not allowed her to take her own life. She had now lost all control. The thought of having to stay inside of this nightmarish world forever was crippling.

Falling to her knees, grasping the edge of the hole with her hands she screamed, "What do you want from me?" but all she heard in return was her own question echoing back, unanswered.

She collapsed to the ground holding herself in the foetal position rocking herself uncontrollably. Her tears mixed within the dirt that had covered her face and she felt it's crunch inside her mouth. Finally, she allowed herself to release all the emotions that had overcome her for years in this single moment. Sobbing and sobbing she lay there unable to stop.

There was no death, there was no life. She could feel that the energy that had not allowed her to pass over would never allow her to leave. Only an eternity of Limbo.

Turning to lay on her back her sobbing eventually stopped. Jane felt that she had nothing left inside to give, emptiness was all that she felt. She lay on her back with her arms and legs out like a star fish and she just looked up through the trees that had grown all the way up to the sky. The leaves crunched underneath her whenever she moved and small twigs that had fallen from the trees stuck mildly into random places of her body. There she laid looking up.

"This dream feels so real," she whispered to herself as she closed her eyes. Her body aching from her emotional pain. In the distance she strangely could hear a nursery rhyme being whistled, then it stopped.

"Well, I don't think it's a dream, but I can tell you it's all pretty fucked up, whatever the hell this place is!"

Jane sat up quickly after hearing the male voice talking to her. She turned to see the man who had stolen their car, he was sitting quite casually on a nearby large hollow log lighting up a cigarette. They sat there for a moment just staring at each other.

Jane was filled with fear. This man was bad. His odd calmness was creepy to her. From what she had seen so far, he was not a person to be left alone with in a dark forest. She quickly got to her knees and then to her feet. Looking around she hoped that there was some help around somewhere, anywhere. She was in the forest in Limbo, who was she kidding, there was no one else here.

"You're the chick from the big double storey house, yeah?"

"Yes," Jane answer trying to back away slowly. The man smiled at her as he sucked on his nicotine stick, he could see that she was uncomfortable.

"Your husband paid me a visit once, he was a little angry at me."

"You stole our car."

The man laughed again, "I didn't steal it!"

"So, where is it then?"

The man looked at her intently and he realised that Jane really did not know much about Limbo at all.

"Look, my name is Otto. I have been here probably about three months longer than you, but time here is different, we really don't remember exactly how long we have been here for. In the real-world I don't even know what year I am from. I know that I am twenty-eight years old, but I cannot for the life of me recall what year I was born. Back when I had a life, I was a cop."

Jane did not know whether to believe him or not.

"Real-world?" she asked him.

Otto could see that she was still afraid of him.

"I'm sorry! I have tried everything to get out of here. When I saw your car, I thought that maybe I could get it going, that maybe I could leave. I have to try everything."

"What happened then?"

"That fucking Limbo sign!" Otto laughed as he shook his head, taking another drag, "That fucking sign!"

Jane laughed, she couldn't help it, she felt the same way. Otto was happy that she had released some tension between them. He put his cigarette out and went to shake her hand. Jane stepped back quickly afraid that he was coming at her. She realised her mistake and moved forward and shook his hand.

"I'm Jane."

"Nice to meet you Jane," Otto sat back down over on the log. "I'm sorry, but I did happen to see your attempt at trying to see if that big gaping hole in the earth has a bottom to it."

Jane was humiliated, she looked down unable to look Otto in the eyes.

"Hey, don't worry about it! I've blown my brains out at least five times since being here. I rode your car into a tree before it vanished into the nothingness that is Limbo, I get it, we've all done it."

Jane face was blank, so Otto tried to explain, "As soon as you die here you get reset. You can damage yourself as much as you like, and you will retain that injury for the day until midnight. But, now here is the cool part, if you die Limbo will instantly reset you."

That made sense to Jane after what she had just experienced.

"So, the car is gone?" Jane asked disappointed.

"Oh yes, it only stays for exactly twenty-four hours and then when a reset happens after that it disappears. I thought that seeing you both arrived the night before I had until the next night to see if I could use it, but it didn't work. I kept on ending up at the beginning, at that sign, I got so angry that I rammed the car into a solid looking tree. I got thrown a good hundred metres, broke a few bones including my neck. Luckily, I eventually died and then, shazam, I'm whole again. Hurt like hell though. I'm glad I didn't have to lay there all day with my injuries waiting for tomorrow to come, that would have been shitty."

Jane took a deep breath, although she did not know Otto, and Oliver had portrayed him as did others here, as a bad person, she was not feeling that vibe from him. All she saw was a desperate man trying to do exactly what she was trying to do, get back home.

Jane walked over to the big log and sat at the other end of it. She left a good distance between them to feel safe, but also enough to show confidence that she trusted Otto. Feeling embarrassed she tried to brush off the dirt that she felt was over her face and mouth. She wanted to know more about Otto and what he understood about Limbo.

"How do you know all of this?" She asked him.

Otto shrugged his shoulders, "Experience I guess, I watch and learn."

"But, you don't talk to anyone here, why is that?" Jane asked him.

He smiled and looked down.

"People judge Jane, they took one look at me and decided that I was a bad guy. They have seen me drink, get angry, lose my shit, and I get it. I haven't been the best roommate in Law street, but no one else is trying to leave, they all just seem complacent here. I must leave, I don't understand why no one else is trying. That's my focus every day. I can't stop! I won't!"

"I know it's like they have all given up. I understand that Sam and Cindy have been here for a long time, as many of them have, but I have a son, Alex," she looked over at Otto. "They have children too, but I can't just give up on seeing my son again, I can't, but they have."

Otto was nodding to what she was saying,

"Don't blame them Jane, they may have been here a lot longer than us, who knows. I have a newborn daughter, I miss her and her mother so much."

Otto stopped as he began to choke up. Jane felt bad for him, "I'm so sorry."

Otto nodded, "I agree, there has to be a way to get out of here. When I saw you today I finally realised that maybe I have to stop trying to do this on my own, it's turning us all crazy."

There was a pause between them.

Otto wanted to tell Jane his ideas, "I have this theory." Jane was listening so Otto continued, "the word Limbo in the dictionary means to be in an intermediate state or in a waiting period. Intermediate means to be between something or in the middle. So, to me Limbo does not mean forever, it just kind of means stuck."

Jane's heart jumped, he was right. Limbo was like a waiting period.

"Also, we live on Law street, right?" Jane nodded in agreement with him. "Is this a clue that we are in some kind of a test, we need to find the law, the law of Limbo to leave."

Jane's smiled as her eyes opened wide, this guy was definitely a cop. Otto had been taking in all the information around him and trying to analyse it to gain an answer.

"Wow," she replied, "that really is an amazing concept."

Otto smiled, he was glad that someone thought that his idea about this warped place could be something to think about.

"I wonder what is it that we need to do to get out of here. All I know is that only one man, named Colin, is the only person to have ever left."

"What?" Otto sat up straight, "there has been someone that has left?"

"Yes, his name was Colin, but I thought everyone else here knew him."

Jane was fascinated that Otto did not know. Otto just laughed and covered his face with his hands, "Jane, you have just given me the greatest gift that anyone has ever given me!"

"Mary actually told me last night at her house. How come you didn't know he had left, weren't you here when Colin was here?"

"Mary knows everything!" Otto was smug. "You are the only other person, that I know of that has come here to Limbo since I got here myself. Everyone else was already here before me. I have not been social about getting to know anyone else because they judged me as soon as I got here. Mandy was the only one that didn't judge me, she seems to be cool. We hang out sometimes when I'm not busy trying to get out of here or drinking myself to death. Mary was very open and kind at first. She is a tough woman, but I don't think Mary would like to know the things that I know. That's why I don't talk to her. She seems lovely, but I just can't face her. Now, she just thinks I'm an ass."

"Why? I don't understand. What do you know about her?"

"I know that her husband is gay, Daniel is his name."

"Oh that, don't worry about that Otto. She told me last night that he was gay, she knows," Jane reassured him.

"So, Mary knows about Daniel having an affair with Frank?"

"What? No, I don't think so! Frank, Camilla's son?"

Otto laughed, "I caught them out here in the forest one day when I first arrived in Limbo. They were so shocked and scared about me seeing them and what they were up to. Daniel begged me not to tell Mary. I agreed, and I just decided to stay solo and keep out of everyone else's business from then on in."

Jane thought about the conversation with Mary last night. Mary had been so sure with her decision to stay in Limbo instead of leaving with Colin, a man that she loved. She stayed faithful to Daniel as he was to her. Jane was thinking that Mary knew that Daniel was gay, but she did not know that he was having an affair with Frank.

"Mary doesn't know about Frank, does she?" Otto asked.

Jane looked up at Otto as if he had read her mind.

"No, I am sure she does not, and I also think that it will hurt her quite deeply. She gave up a love with Colin to stay here with Daniel. Mary thinks that they have a bond that couldn't be broken…Otto, why don't you just put all that aside and get to know everyone here? You must be lonely without being able to talk to people?"

"People form their own opinions which they have done about me Jane. I haven't been the best neighbour and I'm happy to be on my own. At least I can focus on what is important, and that is leaving!" He answered her.

"But if you just tell them that you are a police officer, then they may feel safer. It could reunite us all to try and find a way out of here together."

Otto looked down unable to face Jane, "Sometimes I think that I am that person they portray me as. Things did not go well from the beginning, but I must say that it was probably my fault, my anger does take over sometimes."

"We all get angry, especially here. I think that our anger has this ability to create a world inside our minds that isn't even real. We come up with so many stories of what if, that we forget about what is."

Jane smiled at Otto as he looked up, it suddenly hit home what she herself had just said. An overwhelming feeling told her that she was talking about herself.

Jane had tortured Oliver for this supposed affair that he had had with Giselle. Yet she knew deep down that Oliver would never cheat on her. Was it all just in her head. Was it her own insecurities feeding the voices that kept saying that he did it? Jane was disappointed in herself. It appears that she allowed her own judgment on herself turn to one on Oliver as well. He was an easy target to blame. It was time that everyone started working together and behaving with respect instead of judgment.

"So, you have no idea and I have no idea how to leave this place. We are stuck for now, but together maybe we can work it out. If Colin can leave then we all can," Jane said confidently.

"I may not know now, but I can tell you that I am going to find out!" Otto said determined.

Jane knew how hard it was for herself to be away from Alex. Otto had a new baby girl, his longing to go home and see his family must be unbearable.

"What's her name, your baby?"

"Her name is Stephanie, she is the most beautiful thing that I have ever seen. When I held her in my arms I would sing nursery rhymes to her until she fell asleep. She looks just like her mother, Kate."

Otto sat on the log just staring out into the forest in another world as if he was imagining both of their faces. Jane was sure that this man was not a bad man. She could see his compassion and the love that he had for his family.

Jane stood up and decided that it was time for her to return home. She was eager to see Oliver and finally talk to him about the affair that she had accused him of. Instantly she could feel her mind return to a balanced state, it surprised her how quickly it could change. One minute she could bear her life no longer, and the next she was determined to fix everything. Maybe she was crazy, but she didn't care. Energy swirled inside of her and she was excited.

"Well, I think I am going to head off now, you have given me a lot to think about," Jane said.

"It was nice meeting you Jane."

Jane smiled and went to walk off, she turned back towards Otto.

"Thanks, you know for making me feel better."

Otto smiled at her, he knew exactly what she was going through, he had been there many times before.

"Anytime Jane! Make sure you let me know if you come up with a plan. I'm in for anything!" he said as he lit up another cigarette.

"I will," she giggled, it sounded like they were agents on a secret mission.

Jane began to run towards her home. She was extremely happy that she had met up with Otto, he had definitely changed her perception on things. Everyone else here had portrayed Otto as some kind of an enemy, but to her he was quite a nice young man. Jane found it refreshing that there was someone else in Limbo that had not given up. As she ran she could hear that Otto was whistling nursery rhymes again, he missed his daughter. The song now stuck itself inside of Jane's head. It was soothing.

Jane's thoughts were now aimed at whether or not she should tell Oliver about this meeting, she knew that he had warned her not to go anywhere near Otto. She didn't know why, because Oliver had refused to tell her. Otto did say that Oliver had gone to see him. Maybe Oliver had talked to him about the car and the conversation didn't go very well.

Jane decided that she would keep her guard up, even though she was very good at judging people's character. She had to trust Oliver. Although Otto did not seem in any way that he was the kind of person to take advantage of someone, she acknowledged that she had only just met him. Oliver's encounter with him obviously was not all roses, but there was something unique that Jane was drawn to with Otto.

For Jane to her this new person in her life had suddenly given her hope. He had dragged her from the depths of defeat and given her the thoughts that maybe, just maybe, she could find a way out of this prison and back to Alex.

CHAPTER 13

Forgiveness to others brings not just forgiveness to yourself, it also brings you freedom.

Jane thought about all the things that she had accused Oliver of. Although at times she felt betrayed and unloved, she wondered if it was all just lies that she had told herself, unproven lies that she had chosen to believe inside her mind. There had been many times over the past year that she wondered about Oliver, it wasn't just the one time with that woman in the rest room. Oliver was a people person, and many took advantage of that. He did not realise when women flirted with him, and it hurt Jane that he was so naive.

The mothers at Alex's school couldn't keep their hands off of him. This definitely made Oliver uncomfortable, but he was always too kind to just tell them to piss off. For some reason these women in the past hadn't bothered Jane, but Giselle was different. She came across as a powerful woman and could take whatever she wanted. Maybe it was the confidence that Giselle expelled. Maybe Jane had just become tired of Oliver not standing up for himself and being man enough to shoo the attention away.

Jane entered the house and saw that Oliver was in the kitchen drinking a coffee. They looked at each other. The both of them were no longer angry. Oliver was ashamed that he had behaved so horribly.

Jane sat down on the couch exhausted, she was covered in dirt, "I'm just so tired!"

Oliver had slowly watched his beautiful wife change over this last twelve months into someone who was insecure about everything. Jane had lost her spark and love for life. Oliver felt scared that Jane would still attack him, but he tried once again to make things right. He moved into the lounge room and he sat next to her on the couch.

"I'm so sorry Jane, for everything!"

"For what?" She asked feeling she was to blame.

Oliver took in a deep breath and shook his head, "I feel like this is all my fault, you have lost all of your trust in me. I've let you down. I've been away too much and thinking about my own career while you have been home taking care of Alex. I've been selfish."

Jane was moved by Oliver's apology. Tearing up from his words she knew that it wasn't all his fault, something was happening inside of her that she just could not explain. It was nice to hear Oliver acknowledge that she had given up a career that had meant a lot to her. Doing what she loved made her feel alive, her writing, her ability to create, travel and explore. She loved being a mother, but she had chosen to give up everything that she loved doing to support Oliver in his life and with his career. There was only enough time for one of them to shine.

"It's okay," she said to him. "It's just getting to me that I'm losing control. I'm lost inside Oliver and I feel like I am losing everyone that I care about. I thought I had lost you, I thought…"

"I love you Jane!" Oliver stopped her. He began to understand Jane's thinking. It wasn't that she blamed him for everything, it was her defence to feeling that she was losing him somehow. "Nothing in this world will ever change that, it just couldn't. Together with you is when I feel whole. When we are not I only feel empty. There is absolutely nothing that could ever fill that hole Jane. Please understand that I would never betray you!"

The honesty in his eyes was compelling. Jane began to cry. She heard and trusted the words from his mouth and was saddened because she believed them. Now she knew that it was her own doing that had caused such a rift in their relationship. It was her constant thoughts of unproven jealousy and anger that had caused her to accuse her soul mate of something that was unthinkable. How could she have done that to him, to their relationship. Oliver embraced Jane and they both cried in each other's arms. It was the first time they had felt connected for such a long time.

Oliver although faithful, knew that he had purposely taken more time away with work than needed, due to the increasing tension at home. He found it difficult to deal with and working more was his answer. He loved Jane with all of his heart, but he was also a man who had no idea about emotions and how to fix what was happening to their relationship. He had let Jane down by not being around when she needed him, and he was sorry for that.

The fear that his absence had caused so much pain in both of their lives broke his heart. In that moment he vowed to himself that he would once again regain Jane's trust and be the husband and father that he once was. His actions had caused doubt in her mind and had allowed Jane to question her own self-worth.

They held onto each other for a long time. Although it felt like forever neither one of them wanted to break the embrace that both of them so desperately needed. This was the first time for so long they had trusted in each other. Their deep love began to heal.

As Jane's tears started to ease her emotions needed something sugary and chocolate.

"I'd kill for an endless block of dark peppermint chocolate right now!"

They both released each other and laughed at Jane's ability to let the tension go, allowing humour to fill the room again. That is exactly what Oliver loved so much about her.

"Only one block of endless chocolate?"

They looked up at each other smiling. There was this intense energy between them and they were able to just sit there in the moment together. The relief that the strain and confusion they had been experiencing for so long was resolved, had brought them freedom.

Suddenly something on the coffee table next to the both of them caught their eye. It was an image that started to appear and then disappear again. The pixels of the item were unclear as if it were a badly taken photograph. Slowly it's presence faded in and out growing in strength and sharpness. Back and forth the item came and went until it was clear and solid, it was a block of dark peppermint chocolate.

"What the hell?" Oliver was startled by the vision. "Are you doing that?"

Oliver stood unsure of what to do and continued staring at the strange phenomenon awaiting Jane's answer.

"I don't know! I don't think so," Jane said bewildered by the fact that the very thing she wanted was trying to create itself in front of her.

She slowly reached out her hand wanting to touch the magnificent object, but as she did the chocolate disappeared abruptly. Both of them let out a small sign disappointed that it had gone.

"Damn it!" Jane sniggered.

"This has to have something to do with Limbo Jane!" Oliver was excited. "You knew exactly what you wanted, and it was trying to appear for you, you created it!"

"But it disappeared, why?"

"I don't know why," Oliver said as he sat back down next to her wiping his palm over the table. "But it is one step closer to understanding what this place is all about. Maybe this is what happened to Colin. He knew what he wanted, and he got it!"

Jane just continued to stare at the table, maybe Oliver was right. If you realised how to leave Limbo maybe you could control it. Colin was able to control Limbo when he left, telling Mary when and where he would leave from.

"What were you thinking Jane?"

"All I know is that I felt relieved and at peace. In that moment all I wanted was to eat a piece of chocolate. I'm confused right now but I can tell you this, we are going to get out of here, I can feel it!"

Oliver smiled at her, he kissed her on the lips, "I know we will, I believe in you."

"I want to talk to Mary again, maybe even some of the others, we should be getting everyone's opinion about this place. I want to know why most people have given up. I want to know what they are afraid of!"

"I'm coming with you Jane!" Oliver did not want his wife alone while talking to these strangers, he had seen how some of them behaved. They decided to go for a walk past Mary's house. Jane wanted to talk to Stacey and Alana as well, but instead up ahead she could see Mandy sitting on the small wired fence that surrounded the front of her home. Jane smiled at her as she walked towards her. Mandy happily smiled back.

"Hello again."

"Hello," Mandy replied as she swung her legs allowing them to hit the wire fence as they came back down. It caused a rhythmic sound every time she did it. It reminded Jane of when she was a child, she loved to do things like that as well. Jane's attention was taken towards the front door of Mandy's home, there was shouting coming from the inside, it was her parents fighting.

"Are you all right sweetheart?" Jane was worried about her.

"I'm fine, it happens all the time," Mandy just smiled and then looked down at her feet as she swung them.

"Mandy do you know how long you have been here in Limbo?"

"No," Mandy just shook her head. "None of us really do, we feel that it has been a long time, but we can never keep count."

"We can't, why is that?"

"Limbo won't let us, it's like we know how old we are, but we don't know what year we were born. Time is different here."

115

Jane was fascinated with Mandy's answers because Otto had said the same thing. She herself knew her age was thirty-two but as she tried to remember her year of birth it was just too hard. She knew the information was there, but she just couldn't find it inside her brain. Oliver and Jane looked at each other, he shook his head and shrugged his shoulders, he couldn't remember either.

"Why don't we know this?" Oliver asked her.

Mandy became a little shy, she turned and looked at the front door. Jane felt like she was scared.

"My step-dad doesn't like me talking about this to anyone, he says I give false hope to people."

Jane loved how Mandy spoke, she was so much older and wiser than her age and she could see that there was a lot of information inside of Mandy that could help her.

"How do you know these things about Limbo?"

Jane could hear Mandy's step-father begin to call for her. The door flew open and Jason was standing there with a cigarette hanging out of his mouth, white sloppy singlet and dirty track pants on. The way he stood there leaning against the door frame made Jane feel uncomfortable. Jason nodded at Oliver to acknowledge him as he sucked on his cigarette. Oliver nodded back.

"Come inside for lunch Mandy," Jason ordered. "Hey Oliver, I'm sorry about last night, I was just a bit tanked and not myself, you get it don't you?"

"Yeah, I Understand." Oliver replied.

Mandy slowly jumped down from the fence and looked up at Jane. Oliver walked over slowly to have a chat with Jason, he wanted to make sure that things between them were amicable. Mandy gestured to Jane to come closer to her and so Jane bent down so that she could whisper in her ear.

"While I am asleep at night I hear a man's voice, it tells me all about Limbo."

"Really?" Jane asked as Mandy just nodded.

"Come on Mandy," Jason pushed again.

Mandy went and walked inside. When Jason moved aside to let Mandy through the door there behind Jason's big stature was Louisa in a rocking chair crying. She was holding a bag of peas wrapped in a tea towel on her face. When she noticed that Oliver had seen her she was embarrassed, and she turned away. Jason shook Oliver's hand once again.

"Hey, no bad vibes between us from last night, let's start over, shall we?" Oliver tried to be the bigger man.

"Why not," Jason smiled at him and then abruptly closed the door in his face.

The smell of alcohol that had poured from Jason's presence was overpowering. After what Oliver had just seen, he wondered if this man was an abuser. He walked up to Jane and she seemed happy.

"Mandy just whispered to me that there is a voice that talks to her every night, a man's voice that tells her about Limbo."

Oliver was distant and did not know what to say to her, "His wife..."

"Yes Louisa."

"I saw her in the background, she had a big mark on her face that she was putting ice on, she was embarrassed when she saw that I had seen her."

Jane looked back at the house, "Oh no, do you think that Jason did it?"

"Definitely," Oliver replied. "I don't know but I've seen a lot of wankers in my time and he is definitely one. Oh God, this place is doing my head in, is there anyone here that is normal?"

"I'm worried about Mandy," Jane said. "What should we do?"

"I don't know, there's no Law in place here, how do you stop it? I can say something to him but what will that do, who do we report it to?"

"Maybe I should talk to Louisa another day, girl to girl?"

Feeling helpless, they headed back to Mary's house. Maybe she would know more about Mandy and her family. Mary was warm and welcoming when she saw them on her doorstep.

Jason was intently watching Jane and Oliver's every move through the front window as he puffed on his cigarette inside. They were the new ones in town, he was not worried by them. His life here would not change just because some do-gooders had arrived. He had made sure that the people in this street keep their noses out of his business. Otherwise he would have to teach them a lesson.

CHAPTER 14

Sometimes leaving the comfort of what we are used to is the best medicine.

Mandy entered through the front door noticing her mother Louisa putting an ice pack onto her face. The large red mark was becoming puffy making her eye squish up, it looked like it was closing over. Jason had obviously hit her again in the eye, or close to it. Mandy was nervous as Louisa looked concerned, she knew this look on her mother's face.

Her mother pulled at her arm as she instructed her, "Go to your bedroom baby while Jason and I talk."

Mandy nodded and headed for her room. Jason could see what Louisa was trying to do, she was trying to let Mandy off the hook.

"Get back here you little shit!" Jason groaned as he latched the front door. "I'm sick of you two girls going against me, you both have been lazing around this house doing nothing! Just because you live in Limbo doesn't mean you can get out of doing your shit around here. This is my house, it's not free accommodation, do you hear me?" He moved closer towards Mandy.

Mandy just nodded as she tried to back away from him, she was young, but she wasn't stupid. She could smell the alcohol flowing from his pores. She had watched Jason guzzle his scotch down today without a care in the world. Jason knew there was no implications to his actions here in Limbo, whatever he did Limbo would just reset it. Jason wrapped his hand around Mandy's arm firmly.

"Don't you hurt her!" Louisa screamed at him as she rose to her feet.

"You shut up bitch, you're always protecting her. What are you going to do about it anyway? I will do as I please here and nothing or nobody can stop me!"

With that he drew his right arm back and swung the back of his hand across Mandy's face with all his strength. The pain that tore through Mandy was unbearable. The force knocked her to her knees and she was unable to hold herself up. Jason continued to hold her limp body by her arm and dragged her back to her feet. He had hit her so hard that he had broken her nose and her face was covered in blood. Mandy could not breathe through her nose, finding it hard to stay conscious.

"You are a fucking asshole!" Louisa screamed as she launched herself onto Jason's back, she wrapped her arms around his neck trying to choke him.

Jason was a strong solid man, he let go of Mandy's arm allowing her to collapse to the floor. He easily broke the hold that Louisa had on him and threw her to the ground. In her vulnerability he pounded a good solid right kick into her slender stomach. She screamed in agony.

Little Mandy lay on the floor feeling like she was broken. Her face was numb, and it felt like it was no longer there because she couldn't even feel it anymore. She started to lose control over her body as she began to shake. Laying on her side on the soft lounge room carpet unable to move, she watched as Jason continued to kick into her beautiful mother. Tears fell from her eyes as her pain became unbearable. She prayed to God hoping that he would allow them to die quickly. Mandy was not afraid to die for this was not the first time that Jason had killed them. She just wanted the pain to end quickly for them both.

Jason was so angry all the time and the alcohol would always take him over the edge, it didn't happen every day, but it did happen often.

120

Living in this household was like living in a prison. Constantly Mandy and her mother had to live with this abusive man who got his entertainment out of beating the life out of them.

Life in the real-world was like this also. Mandy could not understand why she had to live a life such as this one in the real-world and then be trapped here reliving it over and over again. Her mother always longed to be with a man, she was never satisfied with it being just the two of them. This confused Mandy and it made her feel like she wasn't good enough, she wasn't enough for her mother to be happy, but how was this being happy.

Her mother was supposed to protect her, to keep her safe and now, here in Limbo it was out of her control. There were days that Mandy could not forgive her for this. She had brought them into this world of constant pain and suffering, who was going to protect them now. Most of the neighbours knew what was happening, and of course they tried to help, but what could they do but pretend that it didn't happen. Limbo would restart itself every day which kept them inside this nightmare. Who would challenge a man like Jason, and when they did they were tortured by him also.

By now Mandy could see that Jason was just kicking into a limp corpse that used to be her mother. When he finally realised that Louisa was either unconscious or dead, he walked over to Mandy still full of anger. Mandy closed her eyes as Jason raised his big right army boot and stomped on her skull, crushing it.

The music she heard was soft in her ears and she knew that it was now the second part of this agonising process. The pain and the agony were complete and now it was the forgiveness stage. Her body had healed, and she opened her eyes to see her mother hugging her in her arms tightly as they both sat on the floor of the lounge room. Mandy heard the loud sobbing from Jason who was now sitting in the corner of the room rocking himself, unable to cope with his horrific actions.

"Mandy are you okay, answer me?"

Mandy looked up at her mother. There was no more blood, no more pain and her mother once again looked beautiful. But inside Mandy felt different, this time she would not forgive her mother.

"Please Mandy, I'm sorry!" Jason blubbered from the corner.

Louisa kissed Mandy on the forehead and then left her alone sitting on the floor. She left Mandy so that she could instead comfort Jason as she always did.

"Don't worry my love, we understand don't worry. It will all be better soon."

Mandy watched her mother console the man that had beaten her to the point of killing her, killing them both. How dare she. What would have happened if he had done this in real life.

She remembered the last moment in the real-world. She had locked herself in her closet crying. Her face buried deep into her hands, praying to be taken away, while Jason had one of his episodes. He had beaten her mother to where she had collapsed on the lounge room floor unable to get up.

They were becoming worse these episodes of Jason's; her mother had been put in hospital three times in the past and each time she ignored the help that she was offered. Jason had never touched Mandy before, but this time, this time he did.

When Jason opened the closet door where Mandy was hiding, he grabbed her by the hair and dragged her out to where Louisa was lying on the lounge room floor. He made her kneel in front of her mother. Louisa was gasping for air, covered in blood as she stared motionless at her daughter. Mandy had tears falling from her eyes, fearful that she would lose her mother forever. Jason began to slap Mandy, toying with her so that Louisa could see. He wanted Louisa to watch as he hurt her beloved child, the child that he believed got in the way of their relationship.

"Run," was all that Louisa could manage to whisper from the small breaths that she was taking as she lay helpless on the floor in her own blood. Mandy rose up against Jason and she ran. She ran as fast as she could through the front door, past the fence and into a strange forest. That was the last time that she remembered being in the real-world. Since then it has felt like she had been in Limbo forever.

She missed Colin, her only saviour here. He was the one that would camp outside of her home if he knew that Jason had been drinking. He was the one that had saved her so many times in the past. But he was gone now and this life of being tortured felt never-ending.

Mandy had endured enough. She knew that Limbo would reset itself tonight and tomorrow she would be forced to start this life again, here in this very house with her desperate mother and her abusive boyfriend. But today, today she chose to leave. She stood up, turned around and headed for the door. Louisa turned her attention from Jason as she saw Mandy leaving.

"Where are you going?" she questioned her forcefully.

"How dare you!" Mandy said in anger as she stormed from the house sickened by her mother's inability to see the truth. Why could she not see that she did not need Jason in her life, they were just fine without him. What kind of a mother was she.

Louisa hung her head in sadness as Jason continued to sob needing her to hold him. She knew very well that her daughter was angry at her, which she had every right to be, but she could not lose the only man she had in her life. Mandy would forgive her again, but a life without a man always seemed so lonely. It was a price she paid to have someone to take care of them. Yes, Jason had a temper, but he was always sorry for his actions afterwards.

Jason swung away Louisa's comforting arms and stood up as he wiped his eyes, his moods were sporadic. He lit up a cigarette and pulled out his drugs.

"Babe please..." Louisa begged, she knew that things with Jason were bad, they didn't need to get any worse.

"You're the one that makes me do this Louisa! You make me hurt you and Mandy, I don't want to, but I can't help it you get me so angry. Now look at me, I'm a mess."

Louisa was happy now that Mandy had left, she would be safer while Jason continued this destructive day. Things would be different tomorrow. Jason's bipolar disorder was hard to monitor especially without medication, it was a daily battle with him and it did seem like it was getting worse. Limbo could reset the body, but it did not reset the mind.

After Mandy had ran out of the house crying and slamming the front door, she stood there in the middle of the street. Breathing deeply, her body so full of anger, she didn't know what to do. She then let out a huge piercing scream. Louisa cringed inside the house from the sound of Mandy's pain and began to cry due to her guilt.

Shocked by this scary shriek Jane stood from Mary's lounge to look out the window. Watching Mandy in the far distance running into the thick forest crying disturbed her.

"What on earth?"

"What is it?" Oliver asked.

"Mandy has just screamed and run into the forest, she's so upset."

Mary placed her cup of tea onto its saucer, unmoved by the incident.

"I'm going to see if she needs help," Jane began to head for the door.

"Oh Jane, it's probably just another family issue they are having," Mary said playing the moment down. "It's best if you just leave them alone."

"What are you saying, that this happens all of the time?" Oliver asked.

"Well, Jason sometimes gets on the turps a bit, and when he does he becomes a little handsy with the two of them, like you saw the other day. He has bipolar and he is not medicated."

"Well what do you all do about it?" Jane asked.

"Do?" Mary questioned her.

"Yes, do! What do you do about it?"

Mary just sat there, "We do…nothing! What are we supposed to do, get hurt ourselves? Jane this happens every second day, to the point where we all just let it go. It's not our problem, not anymore."

"Not your problem," Jane was angry, how could anyone just watch on as a child gets hurt.

"Let it go, are you serious?" Oliver had his say. He was baffled by Mary's unemotional response. He got up from the couch and he headed towards the door to join Jane.

"This is Limbo things work differently here, I'm not going to get myself beaten everyday trying to stop something that will happen again tomorrow. We are old and tired, we are no match for Jason."

"Surely there is something else that we can do, Mandy is just a little girl, she needs our help," Jane begged.

"Jane forgive me but there is nothing you can do. Believe me we have all tried very hard to intervene but everything we have done has failed."

Jane's blood boiled, "Maybe instead of just sitting around all day pretending that things aren't happening, you should open your eyes and start seeing what's going on in your own life!"

Daniel raised his eyes from the book he was reading at the dining table. Jane could not believe what she had just said to Mary, she was so very angry, but she had gone too far. Mary was stunned and unsure of what Jane was intending but she did not appreciate her tone towards her after she had been so welcoming.

"Don't you raise your voice to me Jane," Mary seemed calm but forceful. "I have been living here a lot longer than you! I have given up a great deal for these people in Limbo and I don't need you telling me that I should be a better person. I've done enough, I'm sick of trying to do the right thing for everyone else."

"You're right, I'm sorry," Jane's voice calmed down. "But you need to start realising that things aren't as you think they are here. The people you trust are living their life whether you like it or not. You're getting left behind Mary."

Jane looked hard at Daniel who lifted his book ignoring her words. Jane wanted Mary to question Daniel's faith towards her. Otto had caught Daniel being intimate with Frank in the woods, Mary should know that she was honouring a relationship that was one-sided.

"How dare you!" Mary rose from the table, "are you accusing my husband of something?"

"No Mary," Jane said as she opened the door, "I'm not accusing him of anything, I'm telling you what is!"

With that both Jane and Oliver quickly left, closing the door behind them.

"What the hell was that all about?" Oliver asked.

"I will tell you later," Jane assured him as they both headed towards the forest. Oliver could see that Jane was becoming fiery, he loved it.

CHAPTER 15

Loving yourself is translated into not letting people treat you like a doormat.

A
lthough the forest was the stamp on knowing that you were in Limbo, it did have this ability to make you feel hidden when you wanted to be. Mandy was never going to return to that house again. When Limbo resets she would just leave through her window over and over again. It felt like she had put up with this abuse for decades and no longer could take it. She had lost count how many times she had been murdered by Jason's hands.

Mandy didn't know what to do, she was only a twelve-year-old girl who was torn between her mother and being alone. Her experience here in Limbo had made her grow up quicker than what she actually was, it was like living a full life mentally and never growing up to be an adult physically.

In the past she remembered how Colin would wait out the back of her house every morning while she snuck out of her bedroom window. He would hide her for the day between his caravan and Mary's house. Sometimes she would even go to the other neighbours if Jason was uncontrollable, they were all so helpful and wonderful when Colin was here.

It was the moment that Jason hurt Colin and Mary physically that ended her help from all of them. Jason had beaten them both, but they did not die straight away. Instead he left Colin and Mary for hours in the woods in agony until eventually they passed and reset. That very night was the same night that Colin left her and Limbo. Mandy thought about him a great deal. Maybe Mary blamed Mandy for Colin leaving and that's why she stopped helping her.

Colin begged Mandy and Mary to leave with him, but they couldn't. How could Mandy leave her mother here, she also did not know what she would be returning to. Mandy had told Colin all the secrets to Limbo, he was drunk but aware of what she was saying to him. She thought it was like a peace offering for how Jason had hurt him, or even a thank you for always protecting her. Instead Colin left.

That last moment in the real-world Mandy knew that her mother was dying. To think that she would return to a life without her was the scariest thing she could ever think about. Living with Jason alone was unquestionable. Would he even be convicted for his actions, or would she have to continue living in his care? There would be nobody that could protect her, surely, she would die in the real-world if she returned. Mandy thought about what could have been if she had agreed to leave with Colin that day.

Crying was her outlet, the release to allow all the emotions that were stored inside of her out. She had become a young adult early, almost taking over the role of parent a lot of the time. She missed her school friends, although there was only Angela and Boston that were her true friends. Boston was slightly older at fourteen, but he had always had a soft spot for Mandy. He was the one at school that would take care of her if anyone was bullying her.

They had been neighbours when her father was alive, and they had grown up playing together since they were born. The only time Mandy would see Boston after her father's death was when she went to school. Louisa had decided that they would both move in with Jason, at least she could still attend the same school. Boston was sad to see Mandy leave her family home that day, but what was her mother to do. She was a stay at home mum with no income, the welfare payments were not supporting them. Mandy knew that her mother found interest in men so that she would not have to work. She always had this thing that she needed to be taken care of.

It was when Jason made Louisa agree to disappearing. Overnight they forced Mandy to wake from her slumber, pack a bag and leave everything else behind. She had forgotten her favourite toy which was left warm in her empty bed. She never saw anyone she knew again. It was a new house, new school, new community. Mandy felt sad and lost remembering her friends.

Mandy looked up at the sky, she could not see much of it with all the tall trees of the forest covering it up, but she could see enough. It was nice having the trees hiding her, she felt safe. Looking up to the lost sky she thought of her father, Adrian in heaven, she missed him so. She was eight when he died. He was a strong fit man who was killed by a group of people who had broken into their house one night. Luckily Louisa and Mandy were not at home. Louisa was out with her girlfriends and Mandy had decided at the last minute to stay at a friend's house overnight. Her mother had never been the same, none of them had ever been the same.

Louisa let herself go after Adrian died, dealing with depression and anxiety. It was a shock to see such a healthy man die at a young age of forty-eight. They had both met later in life, Louisa had lived a hard life and Mandy's father Adrian had saved her from herself. They accidentally met one day when Louisa's car broke down.

Adrian was infatuated with her instantly, he never cared about her past or where she had come from. Her smile stole his heart and it never stopped being stolen. It was Jason that picked up the pieces for Louisa, making it easy for Louisa to return to the life she once lived before Adrian, it was what she knew. She had always thought she was never good enough for Adrian even though he loved her so.

Louisa had known Jason in their younger years. He was the main reason for all the bad things that happened in her past. Louisa felt like she would never find another man like Adrian to take care of her, so she returned to the next best thing. Louisa had no self-confidence at all. Jason had always wanted to take care of Louisa and he was angry when she left him for Adrian, but after ten years of being gone he was secretly happy that she needed him again. He felt like he could be even more protective and aggressive with her because in the past she had betrayed him.

Mandy knew exactly what Jason thought of her; some princess that was the love child of a relationship that he had felt deceived by.

She felt like every time Jason looked at her it reminded him of Louisa's betrayal, especially if there was whisky involved. What had Mandy done that had caused her to be in such a horrible place. Why did she deserve this punishment?

Mandy's thoughts went to her father, just thinking about him seemed to ease her pain. Her Papa Joe who was her father's father was now singing inside of her head the songs that he would sing all year round. It made her smile, they were like two peas in a pod and Mandy missed them both.

Jason did not allow Papa Joe to visit them or spend time with her because in Jason's eyes he was not part of their family, not anymore. He had made that clear when Papa Joe had tried to talk to Mandy at school and Jason found out somehow. He threatened her Papa Joe. Mandy did know that secretly Papa Joe was trying to win custody over her, but it seemed to take so long and in the real-world time had run out for all of them. That's when Jason made them disappear, so that Papa Joe would not find them.

There was a noise coming from behind her, cracking sticks. Mandy became afraid that Jason had come for her, she could see someone coming and she decided to run and hide.

"She couldn't have gone too far!" Oliver said to Jane as they hiked through the forest.

"Mandy!" Jane yelled as she cupped her hands over her mouth.

Mandy noticed that it was Jane and Oliver and she came out from behind the trees relieved to see it was them.

"Jane!" she yelled back as she ran over to her.

"There she is!" When Jane got close enough she hugged her tight. "What's going on sweetheart?"

Mandy burst into tears in Jane's arms and buried her head into her chest. When Mandy looked up at Jane fear quickly swept over her face. Jane looked up at Oliver. Mandy screamed with all of her might. Jason stood there behind Oliver with a heavy branch held up high over his head. Oliver turned seeing Jason just in time to raise his arms for protection. The blow hit him hard. The pain that was sent through his body was something that Oliver had never experienced before. He fell to the ground unable to control his fall, finding it hard to breath. The world started fading in and out.

"Oliver!" Jane yelled.

Jane began to run, pulling Mandy by her arm. Jason was just too big and too fast; the only way Jane could save Mandy was to stop and take on the giant herself. She picked up a rock and threw it at him, but he just knocked it away. Never had she confronted such an aggressive man before, she felt helpless.

"Run Mandy, run!" she screamed but Mandy did not want to leave Jane. Instead hiding behind a large tree.

Jason raised his hand to hit Jane, she quickly moved out of the way. Raising her two hands as fists, Jane prepared for a fight knowing very well that she was out-numbered in strength.

Suddenly Oliver came jumping out from nowhere grabbing Jason around his neck and holding him tight. He dragged Jason to one knee as Jason started choking for air. Jane moved in and kicked him hard in the nuts. Jason screamed in agony. Releasing his grip Oliver allowed Jason to fall to the ground.

Jason coughed as he gasped for air, "You are going to pay for that!" he croaked.

He breathed through his pain and rose quickly to both Oliver and Jane's surprise. Jason lunged at Oliver. Wrapping an arm around Oliver's throat he threw him to the ground hitting his head on a large rock. The noise was horrific sending him unconscious.

"No!" Jane screamed.

Jason looked at Jane and he began to laugh, "I am going to have some fun with you bitch!"

"Leave her alone!" Mandy yelled as she ran in front of Jane, blocking her from Jason.

Jason just laughed louder, "Oh what are you going to do little girl? Nothing, that's what you are going to fucking do!"

Jason just pushed her out of the way like a small insect slamming her small body into a tree. Her knee shattering from the impact. Mandy was struggling to move.

Jane tried quickly to get a punch in, but Jason just grabbed her wrist and twisted her arm behind her. He breathed heavily down the back of her neck and into her ear he whispered, "I'm going to have you all to myself you pretty little thing, your feisty, I like that!"

"Fuck you asshole, you're nothing but a coward!"

Jason pulled out his tongue and wiggled it into Jane's ear.

"Get off me you piece of shit!"

Jason spun her around and looked at her eye to eye gripping both of her arms tightly. She was so afraid of him. He was freakishly strong and full of drugs which was fuelling his rage. Jane could not give up. She whipped her head forward quickly head-butting him in the face. Jason let go of his grip on her as he dealt with the unexpected blow. Jane fell to the ground onto her bottom and Jason became even angrier. Oliver was starting to regain consciousness, but all he could do was watch on feeling hopeless. He could not focus himself enough to stand up.

"Aarrgghh!" Jason yelled like a savage animal, he stomped towards Jane ready to teach her a lesson as he flicked the blood from his eyes. He was going to do whatever he wanted to her and nobody was going to stop him. He knew he had so much power here in Limbo, and the drugs that he had just taken had given him the strength. Jason was unstoppable, he felt like a god.

Then there it was, a mighty BANG!

Jane did not know what had happened, but Jason just stopped in his tracks and fell to his knees. Blood began to pour from a hole in his forehead as he fell face first into the ground in front of her.

Jane looked up and saw Otto standing there with his arm raised holding his gun.

"Get up Jane!" he said.

Jane quickly got to her feet. Otto put his gun down his pants and headed over to Jason. Rolling him onto his side he started tying up his hands. The rope he was using was slipping and he was finding it hard to keep them tied tight enough.

The blood on Jason's head that had run down his forehead had already started making its way back to where it had started from. It was reversing itself, Limbo was resetting his body. As Otto struggled to tighten the rope around Jason's big hands he started to squirm back to life.

"Stand back!" Otto told Jane as he held out his gun and proceeded to shoot Jason in the head again. Jane let out a scream as some of his blood projected onto her pants.

Otto looked at Jane, "We have to tie him up before he wakes up again, otherwise he will just keep at it, he's on ice."

Jane held Jason's hands together and Otto made sure that this time he got the knot right. Jason started to come to and once again Otto got out his gun and shot him in the head. Jane jumped, she looked at him with another shocked look.

"Three left," Otto said as he smiled at Jane, it was like he was enjoying it.

Mandy limped over to Oliver and tried helping him to his feet. The pain in Oliver's head was intense. He held the back of his head as he felt the blood oozing from his injury. He was dazed but able to stand with Mandy's help.

Otto had Jason tied up well, he then sent his body rolling down a small embankment into the tree trunks below. He nestled his gun into his pants and encouraged them all to leave, "Let's go. Let's go."

"What happens if he gets out?" Jane asked.

"Don't worry, Jason isn't always like this, it's only when he does the booze and the drugs that he loses it. Tomorrow he will probably come over and apologise to you."

"What the hell are you talking about, are you sticking up for him?" Jane was so angry at Otto.

"No!" Otto replied. "I'm just saying this is not what he is normally like. This is Limbo coming out in him."

"Bullshit!" Mandy yelled at him, "this is him!"

Otto just looked at Mandy, everyone was stunned by the twelve-year-old's words.

"All right, all right he is an asshole, I get it! Come on we better go. Let him wear off all of his anger and substances for today," Otto suggested.

Otto walked the three of them back to Jane and Oliver's house, as he went to leave Oliver shook his hand.

"Thanks, I appreciate what you did for us today."

"No worries mate."

Oliver was thankful for what Otto had done but he still didn't completely trust him. He knew he was unstable and the fact that he had seen Otto shoot himself in the head was disturbing. Oliver now understood one of Limbo's laws, that there was no death here. There was still a tense feeling between Otto and Oliver, but it was time to start letting it go.

"No more shooting anyone in the head, not even yourself, okay!" Oliver joked.

Otto just smiled, tapped Oliver on the shoulder and he left the three of them.

Mary had watched from her window, the four of them walking down the street. They looked as though they had been in a small war.

"I told them!" she muttered under her breath.

She knew this would happen if they became too involved, it had happened many times before with the rest of them.

"They will have to learn how to mind their own business."

Limbo was nothing like the real-world. Mary knew that soon Jane and Oliver would understand that they would have to allow Jason to be who he is, no matter how dark. Mary remembered when Jason had hurt her, she could never go through that pain again.

At home Jane felt safe until tomorrow morning, but the fear of wondering what Jason would do when he woke up was overwhelming. Oliver began vomiting. He had an excruciating headache, so Jane wrapped up his wounds and gave him some medication.

"He will be fine tomorrow," Mandy told her.

Oliver went to bed hoping that the throbbing that was pounding inside his brain would hopefully stop. Jane heated up the spaghetti and meatballs for her and Mandy. Later, Jane then ran a hot bubble bath for Mandy after she requested it.

"I haven't had a hot bath for so long, we only have a shower at our house," Mandy said.

"You know you can come here anytime. I wish that things were different, I would have you here all the time if I could. I miss Alex and you are both so similar. Not that I think you are replacing him here, all I mean is that it is nice to have you around."

Mandy loved that Jane enjoyed her being in Limbo, she could see how honest she was. They smiled at each other as Jane looked at the red marks Jason had left on her neck in the bathroom mirror.

"I will leave you to it, just call out if you need anything," Jane said.

"Thanks for everything Jane."

Jane then allowed Mandy to sleep in Alex's room in his bed. When it came time, Jane tucked her in and kissed her on the forehead. Mandy smiled, she missed her Father doing that. For Jane it was as if she were kissing Alex goodnight. She loved having Mandy there, it made her feel complete again. There was an amazing energy flowing between them, it was unbelievably strong.

Suddenly there was that vibration noise again that echoed through Jane's ears. It caused her to stand up thinking that the walls were about to move, but they didn't. The noise abruptly stopped. Jane smiled thinking she was going crazy. As Jane went to leave the room, Mandy called to her, so she turned back.

"I trust you now Jane," Mandy said.

"I'm glad you do," Jane responded.

"Thank you, for helping me. No one has for a long time."

Jane looked at Mandy more intently, "we will work this out somehow, I promise."

"I know," said Mandy as Jane left turning out the light and closing the door behind her.

Mandy smiled to herself in the darkness of the room. Even though she knew that she would be waking up in her own bed tomorrow after Limbo resets, she saw that Jane was the answer. She too had heard the vibration that Jane had heard just moments ago, and she knew what it meant. That Jane was just like her, she was able to bend Limbo.

CHAPTER 16

Great things can come from adversity.

Every night when Mandy went to sleep she had the same voice talking gently to her over and over again. It sounded just like her Papa Joe, she missed him so very much. There were some days in the morning when Mandy would wake up and not remember anything that the voice had told her, but she knew that the voice had spoken while she was asleep.

The things that the voice would tell Mandy in her sleep were repetitive. Even if a night went past and she could not remember what the voice had told her, she still knew what it was trying to do. It was trying to make her leave. Although she was aware that the voice loved her and wanted her to find her way out of Limbo, there was nothing left for her to return back to. There was no guarantee to Mandy that she was even alive. The voice would tell her that if she left she would survive, but how could she trust a strange voice inside of her head. Maybe she was just crazy. What if Jason had broken her body beyond repair, how could she live life that way? How could she return?

In her heart she knew that in the real-world her mother was dead. She did not know the fate of Jason, whether he was still alive or if he had taken his own life. She assumed he was dead because the voice that spoke in her sleep had told her that everyone was dead in Limbo, everyone except her and Jane. This gave them both the power to bend Limbo.

Having someone that can bend Limbo gives the residents here the chance to become aware of the ultimate law of Limbo. The one law that would open the gate for them to leave and return to the real-world. Mandy could see that Jane was working her magic even when she didn't know what she was doing. One day she will understand completely, and this scared Mandy. For so long she was the only one that had this power.

Mandy had become talented at bending Limbo, sometimes she got so far that she almost transported herself back to the real-world, but at the last moment fear always stopped her. What would happen to the rest of the residents that she would leave behind? There was so much pressure on her. She would never tell anyone here all that she knew. She just couldn't. If they found out that she could help them leave, they would be so angry with her.

The voice had allowed Mandy the skills to leave whenever she wanted. Father James had told her that her role was to help the others here return to the real-world, to have a second chance at life. Father James also told her all of their dark sins, the reasons why they had been banished here in the first place. He hoped that this information would assist Mandy with helping the residents of Limbo to heal. But did these people deserve a second chance? Mandy was not convinced.

Mandy was torn. If she were to leave, then she would have to forgive her mother and Jason for all of the cruel things that they have done and still continue to do to her. She would have to allow all the others in Law street the chance to be forgiven and she did not know if they deserved forgiveness, or a second chance. They were here because they did not forgive themselves for the horrible things that they had done in their lives, so why should she.

Father James was the only one who did not fit in here. Mandy did not know his secrets like she did with everyone else. There was something about him that made her nervous. To Mandy he felt like a teacher that was always watching what you were doing, spying on you. He didn't seem like he belonged here.

In the early days she was trusted by Father James with everyone's secrets. He knew what Mandy was capable of and begged for her to follow what the voice had told her, to help everyone get back to the real-world. In Mandy's eyes none of them deserved a second chance. Knowing their sins was a lot for such a young girl to bear. Mandy had no forgiveness for those who created suffering, Jason had made her that way.

Mandy was not ready this morning, before she even had a chance to escape through her window Jason had barged into her room. He grabbed her by the hair and dragged her into the living room.

"Stop it! Stop it!" she screamed at him in pain.

Her mother must still be asleep, but she was quickly woken by the commotion. Mandy could not smell alcohol on Jason and he did not seem high on drugs. Most of the time if Jason was sober he was not a violent man.

Louisa came out of her bedroom surprised by the sight of Jason grabbing onto her daughter's hair. Mandy had started crying from the pain, although her life was full of pain it never got easier to deal with.

"What are you doing? Leave her!" Louisa shouted.

"This little shit left me to rot in the forest all day yesterday! Fucking Otto blew my brains out three times, tied me up and rolled me down a hill. Leaving me to lay there for the whole fucking day!"

"That's not Mandy's fault surely!"

Louisa grabbed at Jason's hands trying to get him to release his grip. Mandy punching at his arm made him let go. Mandy rubbed her head as she drove her face into Louisa's chest crying, she peeped out looking at Jason in fear.

"She saw him do it and she never told anyone that I was lying there all day. Now I'm going to do the same thing to her and see how she likes it!"

Jason walked over to Mandy waving his finger in her face, "I'm sick of you always using Otto to save you, well he can't help you now!"

"It was your own fault," Mandy screamed at him, "you were going to rape Jane!"

Everyone stopped, Jason looked at Louisa unsure of what she would do.

"What?" Louisa looked at Jason. She knew her man was violent, but she did not believe that he would do such a thing.

"She's lying!" Jason objected.

"Otto had to shoot him to get him away from Jane!" Mandy wanted her mother to finally see what kind of a man and life she had chosen for them.

This man was not loyal to her, he wasn't faithful, he was a sick horrible human being who cared about nothing but himself. Louisa stopped for a while and did not know what to think. Jason looked at Mandy with pure evil, he wanted to make her pay for what she had done, but it was important to him that Louisa always remained on his side.

"Baby I would never do that, I would never be with another woman," his voice had changed, it was loving and soft. "You know that she does these things to hurt us. She always does. Otto puts things into her head about me. They are all lies."

Louisa toyed with his words and looked hard at Mandy, "Are you lying to me?"

Mandy moved away from her mother, "No! Why would I do that?" her voice quivered.

"You are lying," Louisa confronted her daughter. "Why did you lie about such a thing? You are always doing this Mandy! Tell me the truth and tell me what really happened."

Mandy didn't know what to say, once again her mother had taken Jason's side. She was so oblivious to the truth. Mandy could no longer be a part of this, she had to let her mother go. It was killing her inside knowing that her mother could not love her own daughter enough to believe in her.

"You know that I would do anything for you and I have, because I love you!" Jason's words were like ice to Mandy but to Louisa they were all that she needed to make her heart flutter. They hugged and smooched together, and Jason offered to make her breakfast.

"Go on baby, go and have a nice long shower and I will make a special feast just for my girl," he smacked her right butt cheek and grinned.

"You are just too much," Louisa said as she headed back to the bedroom. She was still angry at Mandy for her deceitfulness.

"Now no more crap between you two, I'm sick of it! I want to have a nice peaceful day today. No alcohol…" Louisa said as she looked at Jason, "and no more lies!" she looked at Mandy as she shut the door behind her.

There was silence as Jason headed to the kitchen to start up breakfast, he had once again won the fight. He was good at manipulating Louisa into agreeing with him and going against Mandy. Jason couldn't help himself he loved to cause Mandy pain.

"Dry your eyes little princess your lucky that you are even here with us. If I had it my way you would have been gone a long time ago. If only things went to plan, I would have been happily rid of you."

"What does that even mean," Mandy frowned.

Jason thought about his response, he had accidentally told her more than what she needed to know. He was still pissed off at her for leaving him tied up like an animal all day yesterday. He had Louisa's trust over Mandy, and he could see that no matter what Mandy said to her mother she would never believe her. He shrugged his shoulders and smirked teasing her with his silence.

"I'm leaving here every morning and I am never going to be a part of this horrible family any longer, you can all go to hell," Mandy told Jason under her breath so that her mother would not hear her threats towards him.

Jason laughed, she had given him exactly what he wanted. He decided that he was going to tell Mandy a secret that he had kept from the two of them for years. It would be the very thing that would concrete what he had always wanted and planned. He continued in the kitchen cooking as he told her.

"Mandy it makes your mother very upset when you don't come home to us. That's why I had to beat the crap out of Colin and Mary that day because you kept hiding out with them. Your mother was so upset when you wouldn't come home. I don't like it when she is upset and so I have a problem. I would rather you never come home, but your mother has a soft spot for you, which is rather fucking frustrating to be honest with you. You were never meant to be a part of Louisa's and my life. I love that woman like you wouldn't believe but to me you are nothing but a piece of trash."

Mandy's heart dropped, no one had ever spoken to her like that before. She felt so unwanted and unloved even though it was coming from Jason it was still hitting her heart.

"My plan was to get rid of you and your stupid father, but you ruined that for both of us. You had to go out that night when your father was killed and ruin everything that I had planned."

Mandy's mouth dropped, was this Jason confessing his guilt to her over her father's death, "No…you didn't…"

"That's right," Jason continued as he clanged around the kitchen making lots of noise. "You ruined everything for me that night. Did you think that I was going to let your father get away with stealing my woman? A week before he died I saw your mother again, it had been years since I had seen her. I stopped her in the street and spoke to her for a little while. I realised then that she was still the one. I invited her over one night and well things happened. I suppose that your father was not giving her everything she needed in that marriage. I knew that she would be safe in my arms that night. So, while she was with me I sent a few of my mates over to your house to make sure that Louisa would never leave me again."

Mandy found it hard to move as if she was cemented to the ground, she did not understand what she was hearing. Jason just started to laugh his evil laugh.

"I'm going to tell her, and she will leave you, you murdered my father!"

"Do you think she will believe you, she never has, and she never will, just like now. I have had sex with hundreds of women while being with your mother, it doesn't mean that I don't love her. You are just a thorn in my side little girl and when you leave forever the better Louisa

142

and I will be together. So, fuck off if you want to, I don't care, and I never have. The only thing that hurts me is when your mother is sad and remember that I will do anything to make sure she isn't sad. Even if it means dragging your sorry ass home!"

Mandy had witnessed her mother's loyalty to Jason, her mother always took his side. Mandy had to leave, and she had to leave now. The world was closing in on her and she did not want to allow Jason the pleasure of seeing her tears. This man was her father's murderer whether he had done it with his own hands or not. She ran to her room slamming the door. Lying on her bed she cried unable to move with the pain that was now inside of her. This was a nightmare and finally she had realised that she was in hell.

They were all dead and this was the hell they had moved on to. What had she done that made her deserve such agony. All she wanted was to cry in the arms of someone who truly cared about her, instead she cried alone. She thought about grabbing some of her belongings and escaping out of her bedroom window and heading for Jane's house. She wondered if she would be able to even make it there, her heart had been crushed so powerfully.

Jason felt good about telling Mandy his secret. It was the first time he was absolutely sure that Louisa would stay on his side, even if Mandy tried to tell her. Jason had convinced Louisa that Mandy was a compulsive liar. Jason enjoyed how much pain he caused Mandy in that moment, she deserved it after the way he was dumped in the woods yesterday. To him Mandy was just Louisa's mistake. He had done all of these bad things in his life because he loved Louisa, maybe too much, she had always had a hold over his heart. Sex was just sex with other woman but with Louisa he always felt like he was actually making love to her. It frustrated him how much she was attached to Mandy, if Louisa could only see how much better their lives would be without Mandy then his world would be perfect.

When Louisa would cry and cry over Mandy not being home it would break his heart to see her in so much angst. He was in a prison already with the two of them, but he knew that one day, one day he would be free of Mandy's emotional control over the woman that he knew was his. Louisa was like a possession to him that he never wanted to let go of.

CHAPTER 17

Fear of moving on can stop you from experiencing some of life's greatest adventures.

J ane liked her early morning walks, it was something she had started up since being in Limbo. Strangely although it had felt like only days that she and Oliver had been in Limbo for, she could not keep up with counting exactly how many days precisely. It was not a nice trait of Limbo, forgetting how long you had been trapped for.

Clearing her mind through inhaling the beautiful forest air was exactly what she needed, it brought upon a gentle healing that Jane could feel was happening.

Alana was out the front of her house today and they both exchanged a hello. Alana appeared to be a nice girl, so did Stacey. It would be wise to catch up with the two girls later and get to know them better. Jane headed for the woods.

Today Jane steered clear of Mandy's house, she did not want to walk past and accidentally bump into Jason or Louisa. Mandy was on her mind though, there had to be a way that she could take care of Mandy without Jason knowing. He was like a ticking time bomb, Jane was so fearful in his presence. But Jane did not want to live every day in fear either. Instead she pushed the horrific incident in the woods aside allowing herself to be free.

Being honest with herself if she saw him again she was unsure of how she would feel, her body shuddered to think that she would have to spend forever with such an abusive individual. Deep down for some reason there was still compassion for Jason. Jane always believed that people could change, she had a big heart.

As Jane walked through the forest she turned back and decided to head towards Mandy's house. It was killing her not knowing how she was or what she could do to help her. Jane peered through the forests dark coverage, camouflaged as she watched the front of Mandy's house. It appeared peaceful and quiet which was a good sign. Jane hung around for a little while resting against one of the giant trees.

Jason came out the front door. He was dressed only in his boxer shorts and a gown that was hanging open. He walked up to the bush just past the front door, pulled out his penis and proceeded to urinate on it.

"Charming," Jane whispered rolling her eyes.

The smell of bacon and eggs started to waft from his house, it smelt amazing. When Jason was done he went back inside singing as he closed the door. Maybe Otto was right about Jason, maybe the way he was in the forest was not the way he always was. It was hard for her to believe that he was different.

It didn't take long before she saw Mandy climbing out of her side bedroom window, she looked so upset. Jane had never seen her like this before. Mandy couldn't even manage her backpack due to the tears pouring down her face.

"Oh no," Jane muttered under her breath.

Mandy was surely heading towards Jane's house. Jane began to quickly run through the trees, jumping over logs and branches until she was in front of her own house. She began to jog across the street and that is when Mandy raised her head from the ground and saw Jane heading towards her. Mandy stopped, dropped her bag and fell to her knees crying.

Jane ran as quickly as she could to Mandy. Passing Mary's house, she saw her curtains in the front window moving. Mary looked out and then closed them again. It frustrated Jane that Mary was not willing to do anything to help Mandy. But in her defence, she had been here a long time and Jason was a scary man to be around.

How many times had Jason hurt these people?

"Mandy are you all right?" Jane yelled.

Jane fell to her knees beside Mandy and held her tight. Her breathing was so sporadic that she could not even speak to Jane. Alana came up from behind and she also got down on her knees.

"Looks like Jason has been a dickhead again!"

"Alana!"

"Well it's true Jane, what kind of a father is he?"

Those brave words instantly made Alana think about her own past, realising that she herself had not been grateful for the father figure in her own life. Guilt hit her hard in that moment.

"Let's get you inside before he starts to look for you," Jane said.

Jane and Alana had to scoop Mandy from the ground using all the strength they had. They both carried Mandy to Jane's front door. Oliver noticed the three girls struggling from the front window and like a true gentleman went out and picked Mandy up into his arms, carrying her inside.

"Now that's a man!" Alana announced.

Jane couldn't help but smirk, it was true. She was happy that she had finally realised what she had in Oliver before she lost him. Mandy continued to cry uncontrollably. Oliver carried her upstairs and put her into Alex's bed, he watched on until Mandy finally cried herself to sleep. Oliver headed back downstairs.

Jane was devastated having to see Mandy in such a way. Alana was moved by Jane's wonderful motherly qualities, so kind and loving. She missed her own mother so very much. Alana started to fell emotional, being the proud person that she was she did not want to hang around and allow Jane and Oliver to see her vulnerability. There had been enough crying for one day.

"I'm going to go," Alana started to quickly head for the door.

"Wait!" Jane did not want her to go. "Please Alana you have been so wonderful, I don't know how to thank you."

"You kind of just did," Alana smiled at Jane as she let herself out.

If she had stayed any longer Alana was sure that her heart would not cope with the emotions that were welling up inside of her. She headed for the darkness of the forest and Jane watched through her window as the teenager disappeared into the coverage of Limbo's trees.

"Maybe she doesn't like us?" Jane said to Oliver.

Oliver came up beside her and put his arm around Jane, "don't be silly, she is just a teenager who has her own stuff to deal with."

Jane placed a hand on top of Oliver's which he had resting on her shoulder. They were in a trance just looking out the front window at Limbo's forest.

"Knock, knock can I come in?" A voice echoed through the slightly ajar front door. Jane and Oliver were surprised to see Father James was standing in their doorway.

"Sorry to scare you but thought it would be a good time for a chat."

"Of course," Oliver let Father James inside.

"My word what an amazing house!" Father James said as he entered. He had never been inside a house quite like this one before.

"Thank you," Jane answered proudly.

Oliver offered their new guest a cup of tea but instead found himself making him a strong black coffee with a swig of whiskey in it. Father James was a small man with a slight roundness to him, he was clean shaven and a happy soul that emanated joy. They sat at the kitchen bench on the stools which Father James found a little hard to manoeuvre because of his short frame. Jane insisted they go into the dining room, but Father James refused, the swivel stools made him feel like he was a kid again.

Father James enjoyed cracking jokes, "Laughter is a good way to cleanse the soul," he said.

Father James was refreshing and fun to be around. Oliver had never drunk whisky in his coffee before, although different he was sure he was going to do it again. Oliver excused himself and went upstairs to check on Mandy, his absence gave Father James a chance to talk to Jane alone. He had been looking forward to talking privately with her.

"So, Jane have you made yourself comfortable here in Limbo?"

"Comfortable?" Jane yelped. "God no!" Jane raised her hand to her mouth realising that she had used God's name in front of a priest. "Sorry!"

Father James enjoyed her quirkiness, "Sadly Jane, most people here have given up on themselves and on each other because there is no way that any of us can get out of here."

"Well, I don't believe that Father at all," Jane was surprised that a man of faith was showing absolutely no faith at all.

"You don't?"

"No, not at all. Things have happened that are showing me the very opposite."

"They are, like what my dear?" Father James sipped his coffee.

"Firstly, there is Colin, and secondly I feel like I am able to control small things in Limbo. The other day I really wanted a chocolate and I nearly made it appear on the coffee table in front of me. I was somehow able to bring what I wanted into Limbo." Jane listened to what she had just told Father James and it sounded absolutely insane, he must be thinking that she was a fool. Instead he smiled a big smile and tapped her on the shoulder.

"Jane," he started out softly. "We have all been put here for a reason, I truly believe that. I also know that each of us have secrets and reasons why God has chosen for us to experience this alternate world we know as Limbo. If we all just give up on ourselves and each other then we will definitely be stuck here forever. I'm proud of you for going against what the rest of the people here think. I thank you for trying to

149

make a difference in certain situations even when it seems like you can't."

Jane thought of Mandy and she did not know what to say, Father James' words were so kind and loving.

"Don't you ever give up on yourself or even those who seem like they don't deserve your forgiveness. Love is a strong emotion that has the ability to heal any wound. Like you and Oliver for example. It didn't take you long to understand that you no longer wanted to be living someone else's life. It's hard to pretend being someone you're not, isn't it Jane?"

Jane's mouth dropped, how did he know that she had been feeling like that in the real-world. That she had allowed herself to turn into a person that she no longer recognised. A person who had pushed the man she loved away and accused him of things that were never true.

Jane had started to understand herself more while being in Limbo. In some strange warped out way it was like she was taking a break from her constant life of misery. She no longer had to pretend to everyone in her life that she was perfect in every way, that she was happy and in control of her life even though she wasn't. Limbo had offered her time to look outside of herself. To recognise a life that she no longer wanted to be a part of. It was time for her to change and to live life as the real Jane instead of this imposter.

"What is he doing here?" Mandy's voice was firm. She was annoyed that she had found Father James talking with Jane.

"Mandy you're awake," Jane stood up and hugged her.

Oliver thought it was strange that Mandy was so forward towards Father James.

"Oops it seems like it is my time to go now!"

Father James slowly hopped off of his stool as best as he could. He grabbed his hat and cane and thanked Oliver and Jane for their hospitality. Mandy did not see him out. But as Father James was walking through the front door he tipped his hat at them all and looked straight at Mandy.

"Sometimes we have to believe in something bigger than ourselves. That is what faith is. Fear will only stop us from getting what we need." Father James smiled and left. He hobbled down the street with his cane whistling as he walked.

"What did he tell you?" Mandy interrogated Jane.

"Nothing! He just told me to never give up on myself and each other. I think he believes that we can all find a way out of Limbo. What has gotten into you Mandy?"

Mandy stormed back up the stairs towards Alex's bedroom. Jane and Oliver looked at each other, "I will go to her," Jane said as she headed upstairs.

Jane found Mandy crying into her hands while lying on Alex's bed. "Mandy I'm worried, please tell me what is going on." Jane was able to sit on the bed and turn Mandy over to face her, "Mandy, please you have to trust me!"

Taking in a deep breath she decided to tell Jane what had happen this morning. "Jason came into my room before I even had time to get up. He pulled my hair and dragged me out into the lounge room…"

"Oh my God!" Jane was devastated.

This man is a monster!

"He was angry that we had left him tied up in the woods for the whole day. He said that he was going to do the same thing to me. My mother made him stop but when I told her what happened, what Jason was going to do to you, she called me a liar!"

"I'm so sorry Mandy," Jane felt guilty that she had taken the brunt of Jason's anger for what had happened yesterday.

"She never believes me; my mother takes Jason's side all of the time. I can't take it anymore. When my mother went to have a shower Jason told me things, horrible things." Mandy paused. "He told me that he was the one who had planned the break in that night my father was killed. He said that I messed up his plans because I was meant to die that night as well!"

Mandy cried her heart out again and Jane could only hold her. Mandy was now faced with the fact that she was living with her father's killer and with a man who wanted her dead in the real-world.

Jane grabbed Mandy's face so that she was staring eye to eye with her, "I will not let this happen to you any longer, I just won't! I don't care what bloody rules this Limbo has we are going to break them!"

"I want to leave, I do but I just can't leave Jane, I can't. You don't understand!" Mandy was scared that Jane might do something altering without even knowing the power that she possessed.

Jane could not understand why Mandy was so afraid to leave. Limbo was like a living hell for her so why would she not want to get out of it. Nothing made sense. Jane just held Mandy tight unable to know the depths of her true pain. There was no way that Jason was ever going to lay a hand on her ever again.

Oliver stood by the bedroom door, he wiped tears from his eyes and he just nodded at Jane. He felt the same, he would do everything in his power to protect Mandy. This man had to be stopped.

CHAPTER 18

It is our own choice to believe in the truth or to believe in a lie.

Cindy was enjoying having Jane, Oliver and Mandy over for dinner. Jane and Cindy talked so much that Cindy could feel her mind being stimulated. Sam noticed the wonderful affect that Jane had on Cindy and he appreciated having Oliver to vent to, it had been hard here in Limbo. Mandy was the closest thing to a daughter they had here, and they had tried hard to protect her as best as they could. There had been many times she had used Sam and Cindy as a safe house.

Cindy's mind had diminished slowly over the time she had spent in Limbo. Although Limbo would reset every day, it did not reset the impact it had on everyone's mental health. Limbo knew how to send people crazy. Jane and Oliver thought that it would be a great idea to go out and have a night of normality. They were positive it would help Mandy to feel like a normal kid, even if it were just for the night.

Mandy enjoyed Sam and Cindy's company as well, she loved how much they treated her like their own. They too had tried to help her in times of need and they would always have a special place in Mandy's heart. Although Mandy wanted freedom for the both of them she was also scared to lose them like she did Colin. Besides Jane and Oliver, they were the only ones left who still helped her when she needed it the most. There was also Otto, he was trustworthy, but he wasn't always around when you needed him.

The conversation for Cindy and Jane had turned to Limbo. Although they loved talking about their own lives in the real-world the dream that they would leave and return to their families was still very much alive. Jane loved to see Cindy excited about seeing her family again, she saw hope in Cindy's eyes.

Cindy placed her hand over Jane's, she knew how hard it was for her not to see Alex. She still yearned for her own five wonderful children that she had left behind at their family ranch, but Cindy honestly believed in her heart that she had deserved to be in this place. Even though Cindy had not followed through with her plan to commit murder for revenge, here Sam and herself lived out their days over and over again.

All Cindy wanted in the real-world was to be well again so that she could grow old with Sam and watch her beautiful children grow. In some ways she got exactly what she wanted, her disease did not progress in Limbo and she was with Sam. Sadly they both had to live without their children.

"I will make you another cup of tea my sweet," Cindy tapped on Jane's hand. Heading over to the kitchen bench she began to heat up the old kettle.

Cindy stared out of the kitchen window into the darkness, wondering what it would be like if things were normal. Her thoughts were on her kids. She wondered if they had continued to grow up, had she missed out on all the wonderful milestones of their lives. Then she realised that she would have missed out on it all anyway, due to her illness. There really was no good outcome for her. How sad that was.

"Sometimes I just think that this horrible place is all in my head!" Jane announced to Cindy. "Sadly, I feel like I'm the reason we are stuck here. That I am the barrier that holds Oliver and myself trapped inside Limbo. Why can't I just let go? Why can't I just let go of all the shit in my head and be free?" Jane blurted out. "Oh god I don't even know what I am saying."

But something happened, Cindy froze. Her heart skipped a beat. "What did you say Jane?" Cindy turned and looked at her.

"Oh nothing!" Jane said shaking her head, "I just wish it were all a dream and I could wake up, maybe it is just a dream! I don't know I am just talking nonsense."

Mandy had stopped playing with the deck of cards on the ground. She was concerned about the things that Jane was saying. Watching Cindy analyse every word made her feel sick to her stomach. She wished that Jane would just stop talking about Limbo altogether.

Cindy turned back towards the stove with her back to Jane. So many thoughts rushed through her head. It was the first time in a long time that she actually could feel her brain firing. The kettle began to whistle, and it continued to whistle. Cindy was still thinking.

"Cindy," Mandy called to get her attention, "the kettle."

"Oh!" Cindy jumped.

Cindy made Jane another cup of tea, she sat down with her at the table, but she was distant.

"Are you okay?" Jane asked her.

"It's nothing. I'm just really missing the kids that's all," she smiled as she sipped her tea.

Cindy began to cough. The deadly illness still plagued her body, it never got better, and it never got worse. Some days were good, and some were bad. She pulled out her handkerchief and coughed into it. Blood had made its way from her fragile lungs onto the handkerchief.

Jane was upset, "My goodness Cindy. I am so sorry, we should leave you. I have been so selfish talking about myself and here you are with five beautiful children that you miss, and you are not feeling well. Can you forgive me?"

"Don't be silly Jane, we all want to get home. It's not like I'm not used to coughing up blood. At least it won't kill me here!"

Jane was adamant that it was time for Mandy, Oliver and herself to leave. Cindy tried to make them stay longer and finish her cup of tea, but Jane refused. As Jane said Goodbye Cindy hugged her tight.

"Thank you, Jane, for everything."

Jane smiled, "For what? I should be thanking you for the lovely evening."

"You will understand one day how much you mean to me. You have given me my spark back!"

Jane smiled at Cindy. What a beautiful thing to say. Jane hugged her again and they left.

Cindy closed the door behind them and as she did she just stood there placing both of her palms on the door. She began to breath heavily as she leaned her forehead on the door between her hands. Sam was talking to her casually, but she could not hear what he was saying. Cindy's mind was somewhere else, continuously replaying those very words that Jane had said. It was like an epiphany and she felt the shift those words brought her. It was the truth that she had chosen to blind herself from this whole time.

"Are you coming to bed Cindy?" Sam asked her.

Still Cindy did not move. She continued to stand there with her hands and her forehead leaning on the back of the closed door.

"Cindy what's wrong?" Sam began to worry.

Cindy spun around leaning back on the front door with her arms behind her back. She looked on over the world around her as she slowly walked through the lounge room. She stopped in the middle of the kitchen, lounge, dine area that was their home. Tears rolled down her cheeks as she began to smile.

"Cindy talk to me, you're scaring me!" Sam screamed at her.

Then the walls began to slowly move, they danced in a beautiful wavy movement. Then it was the floor, and then the ceiling. There was a loud vibrational noise, like a humming. It wasn't annoying, instead comforting.

"Cindy what is happening?" Sam was afraid, holding onto the kitchen table.

He had never seen anything like this before, but Cindy was so happy. She wrapped both of her hands around her mouth in disbelief.

Sam ran over to her unable to understand what was happening to the house. He grabbed her tight.

"We have to get out of here!" he yelled thinking that it was an earthquake.

Cindy reached out her arm over to the couch in front of her, as it also began to wave in motion. Her hand felt the couch, but it started to mould itself inside of the couch.

Sam looked on, his mouth wide open and almost touching the ground. "What is going on?" he yelled.

Cindy turned to him full of joy, "I'm sorry Sam but I know."

"What do you know Cindy?" he grabbed her and shook her. "You're making no sense!"

"I know how to leave. Limbo is not real, but we are."

Both Sam and Cindy just looked at each. Sam did not understand. Suddenly they heard a noise that they had not heard in so long, it was the sound of their children playing around them. The sounds were unclear, but they knew it was their children. A vision of the real-world began to focus in and out, as they saw glimpses of their beautiful kids that they had not laid eyes on for years, for decades.

"Cindy…" Sam chocked up.

His heart was jumping with joy just to have this small snapshot of his life that once was. The room then began to turn. The spinning motion worked its way faster and faster around them, but they were not moved at all, it felt like they were in the middle of a tornado. It was peaceful where they were, with sheer madness and confusion everywhere else. Their eyes could not see clearly or focus on anything anymore. The sounds of whirling winds combined with the sound of their children laughing danced around them. Then it just suddenly stopped, and all was black.

Cindy could not hear anything anymore, she was in complete darkness. Finally, she realised that she had covered her face with her hands, pulling them away slowly she found herself alone kneeling in a forest clearing. It was not the forest that she had known for so long, it was not Limbo. She knew exactly where she was. Rising to her feet she heard Sam calling for her in the distance. Running towards his voice they met and embraced each other like they hadn't seen each other in years.

"Cindy, you did it! How?"

Cindy laughed, "I finally realised that I had forgotten who I am!"

Sam had absolutely no idea what she was talking about, but he didn't care. They had both found themselves in the last place they had been before losing their way into Limbo. They walked through the woods embracing each other and as the trees cleared there in the distance was their ute. It was still parked off the road waiting for them, just as they had left it. Sam could not contain his emotions, he just cried falling to his knees. Cindy cried and bent down to hold him.

"Things are going to be different from now on," she told him.

Sam stood up and they both got into the ute. He noticed the shot gun sitting on the backseat of the car and he remembered where they were heading on that particular day. Cindy grabbed hold of his hand taking his focus away from the gun.

"Sam, let's go home."

Sam smiled at her and he turned the ute around with one swing of the wheel and he headed them back towards home. When they pulled up the driveway it was bitter sweet. There was this horrible feeling that they were still in Limbo even though the neighbouring houses were not there. They both slowly got out of the ute stepping down onto the very familiar red dusty dirt.

Cindy became nervous, she had longed to see her beautiful children. "Please God please," she prayed.

"Stop it Jeanette!" Marion yelled from inside.

"My babies!" Cindy whispered as she heard their precious voices.

Cindy ran from the ute up the porch stairs and flung open the door with all her might. There she stood staring at the wonderful chaos that played out inside their family home. Sam ran up behind her. Both of them were filled with such joy as they watched their household of five children being lived out. Cindy's mother Patty was happily cooking in the kitchen, she was helping Celia their ten-year-old daughter stir the cookie batter together.

Cindy ran over to Marion their sixteen-year-old daughter. She was sitting on the couch in the lounge room reading her school book, and Cindy embraced her tightly.

Marion was filled with fear with the long and loving moment and questioned her mother. "Mother is everything well? Do you know something more about your sickness?"

Cindy was saddened that she had scared her, "Oh no my darling I just wanted to hug you that's all!"

She patted Marion softly on her forehead and then joyously hugged all of her other children. Sam did the rounds as well, grabbing each child with all the force that he could. He embraced John who was thirteen, then Celia who had by now accidentally covered her father's top in flour. Then he lifted Freddy their five-year-old son into the air making him laugh. Cindy grabbed Jeanette who was eight and did not want to let her go. Finally, Sam and Cindy told them all to come in together as a family and just hug each other.

Patty was absolutely bewildered with the affection that was happening. "What on earth is wrong with the both of you, have you gone mad? You're acting like you have been gone forever!"

Cindy went up to her mother and hugged her again, Sam got in on the action and held her tight also.

"How long were we gone for?" Cindy asked her mother.

"For say twenty minutes!"

"I feel like everything is going to be just fine from now on mother," Cindy affirmed.

"Well if that is the case, get off me then!"

They all laughed, and Sam looked over at Cindy. Although he was over joyed in this miraculous moment he also knew that returning here meant that Cindy's disease would progress. There was no stopping the outcome, she was going to die.

As time moved on, Sam watched Cindy glow more and more everyday as she spent every moment with their beloved children. She baked, sang, danced, you name it she was doing it. It was if she was no longer allowing this life to become focused on the negative things. Where she once worried about her cancer and became a slave to it, now she was dancing with it.

There was never a moment that the two of them were not grateful for the time they now had with each other and their family. Within this time of gratefulness also brought on the thoughts of their much-loved friends that they had left behind in Limbo. They prayed every day before bed, that those who were still lost in Limbo could one day learn how to leave it behind, just as they had.

Months passed, and Sam had noticed that Cindy was no longer coughing like she used to. They both decided to return to the doctors to see how much the disease had progressed, with a small amount of hope inside.

This day was such an amazing day, the sun was shining bright and Sam was proud of himself. He had chosen that he would no longer farm his land. He had ripped out all of the crops knowing that the plants had been contaminated by the poisons that he had trusted in the past to be safe. The moment he disposed of the very last plant he was approached by a man who wanted to purchase his land.

Although Sam told him about the chemical spraying the man was not worried. Instead he wanted to hold onto the land for as long as he could, knowing one day the land would be worth a pretty penny. It was going to be an investment for his children. He was a rich man who wanted to divide the land into smaller pieces and build a house for each of his children when they had grown. At the moment they were only very young.

The generous man offered Sam more money than what he could refuse. The deal was done. Sam and his family could stay in the house for as long as they wanted, because it was the land not the homestead that this investor was after.

For Sam the sun shone brighter today, even though the fear of losing his beautiful wife was with him constantly. His body was slowly being released from the unbearable stress that had once taunted his mind. He no longer struggled to put food on the table. He no longer killed himself farming his land, and he no longer felt the guilt of selling a contaminated product to his consumers.

The doctor's office never smelt nice. Sam hated how so damn clinical it was, but Cindy was happy to be there. He did not understand why she was not nervous about what the doctor had to say.

Doctor Cunningham entered with a solemn look upon his face which was not a good sign. Instantly Sam felt like he was going to be sick. Maybe it would have been better if they didn't know at all. The doctor put his notes onto his desk in front of Sam and Cindy as he sat down. Clearing his throat, he was unsure of what to say next.

"Look, I don't want to give you any false hope, but your results are showing that your disease has reduced around fifty percent somehow."

Cindy grinned, "Thank you doctor, I guess we will be on our way then." Cindy rose out of her chair as she grabbed her clutch ready to leave.

"What?" Sam squirmed. "On our way, what are you talking about woman?" Sam wanted to hear what else the doctor had to say. Had the doctor just told them both that things were better, that there was hope.

"Please, please sit down Cindy I would like to chat to you about this," begged the doctor.

"What's to talk about doc?" Cindy stared at him.

The doctor leaned back on his chair, "Just keep doing whatever it is that you are doing Cindy, and report back to me in three months."

"I will, I promise!" Cindy smirked.

She walked right out of that room leaving both men still sitting in their chairs dumbfounded. Sam got up, thanked the doctor with a hand shake and then moved quickly to catch up to his wife. When he did he pulled on her arm to stop her.

"What's going on my love?"

"Don't worry Sam, everything is going to be just fine from now on. Do you believe me?"

The look in her eye was something that Sam had not seen since the day she told him to marry her before it was too late. He knew when she was being strong willed, and he loved it. He nodded, and they left. There was an aura now about Cindy, it was if she had this knowing, an unbelievable ability to understand what was going on. Sam did not know how Cindy was getting better, all he knew was that she was. He never questioned her again.

Every three months after that appointment they went and saw Doctor Cunningham until he finally told them to stop coming. Cindy was completely cured.

CHAPTER 19

Sometimes we have to let people move on so that they can shine their light to others.

As Oliver and Jane walked home down Law Street in the dark they held hands and Oliver drew her in close to him. They had had a wonderful night with Sam and Cindy. Jane felt closer to Cindy every time they spoke. It was so nice to have someone to talk to, to be able to vent your feelings to someone trusting was wonderful.

Oliver had begun to feel worthy again. He was safe to wrap his arms around Jane and to tenderly kiss her on the forehead. The trust she once had for him felt like it had returned. Her whole demeanour was changing. They were not happy about being stuck here without Alex, but they were trying to find the small joys instead of fighting all of the time.

Mandy loved seeing much they adored each other. It had been a long time since she had known what a real family was supposed to behave like. She missed her father so very much, and her Papa Joe also. Jane looked over at Mandy and then grabbed her, pulling her in close. Jane wrapped her arm around her neck while all three of them walked joined together, each revealing an authentic smile upon their faces. They were happy, even if it were just for this brief moment.

As they gracefully walked home arm in arm Jane felt a hard-single drop of rain hit her on the head. Then there was another one that hit her nose. Initially she didn't think anything of it, until she just stopped. Fear consumed her, it was about to rain in Limbo. Oliver allowed Jane to stop and he watched as she put her palm out feeling for the rain drops.

"Oh no!" Mandy looked towards the sky.

"So, it's raining, we can run home if you like," Oliver said.

"No!" Jane said. "It only rains in Limbo when someone is coming or if someone is leaving."

Jane's stomach began to hurt. Her instinct was to turn around and head back to Sam and Cindy's house. Oliver and Mandy followed her. There it was, that noise again. The same noise that she had heard twice in Alex's room, its high vibration stung her ears.

The brush fence around Sam and Cindy's house started to move first. It began its wobbly wave motion as the image of the house struggled to stay focused to their eyes.

"What's happening Jane?" Oliver had never seen anything like it before, not on this scale.

"No, they are leaving us!" Jane yelled.

"Jane, I don't want them to go!" Mandy knew that there was nothing they could do to stop them.

Mandy's heart began to burn, she couldn't lose anyone else. All of the people who meant something to her here were leaving. Standing there watching she broke down in tears, it was just another blow to her already painful world. Jane could not understand how this was happening. Cindy had not said anything at all to her tonight about knowing how to leave Limbo.

Jane reached out touching the brush fence as it moved in its wavy motion, this was the indicator that the house was soon to leave Limbo. She could feel the fences prickly harshness, but her fingers were strangely lost inside of it, like it was water. The rain began to pour as Oliver came up by her side, he was unable to comprehend what was going on.

164

The house began to fade more and more. It flashed, disappeared, re-appeared and continued to do so until there was nothing left but an empty block, it was completely gone. Jane began to cry, she had just lost her best friend here, the only trustworthy person that she felt she could rely on.

Oliver could not believe it, "I don't understand, how did they leave?"

"I don't know!" Jane desperately cried. "Why wouldn't they have told us if they knew?"

Jane grabbed onto Mandy as they tried to console each other. Otto came running up from his unit next door, he stood there beside them. The rain was now pouring down hard on top of them all. The noise of the rain was all that they could hear. But Otto was not standing there in misery and disappointment, instead he began to laugh. He laughed so loudly that it was pissing Oliver off.

"What the hell is your problem?" Oliver yelled at him.

Otto looked at Jane with a huge smile on his face, "Stop crying Janey, this is the proof that we need, we can get out of this place!"

Oliver went to go over and tell Otto to get lost, but Jane grabbed him to stop him. Her tears ceased while she thought.

"He's right!"

"What?" Oliver looked at Jane.

"He's right!" she spoke louder over the rain. "I'm sick of this crap, I'm not sitting around here anymore waiting for something else to happen. I'm not going to allow this life for me or for any of us. I want to go home! We all do!"

"But Jane you don't know where they have gone. They could be dead," Mandy cried.

"I'd rather be dead!" Otto shouted into the rain.

"I would rather be dead too!" Jane screamed.

They all stood there with the rain pelting down on top of them. Otto began to clap Jane's performance loudly. Mandy hated how rude he could be even though she knew he was kind at heart. He just didn't know how not to be an ass all of the time.

Now Mandy was afraid that Jane and Oliver would be the next ones to leave. If that happened, then she did not know what she would do. The rest of them here had given up on helping her stay safe from Jason. She didn't believe that Otto alone would be able to protect her. Off Otto walked back down the street to his unit next door elated, he turned to look at them again.

"Let's talk tomorrow Jane!" he yelled with sarcastic happiness though the rain. He pointed at her as he walked backwards towards the unit. A laugh once again bellowing from his mouth.

She nodded at him, it was time that they all finally learnt for themselves what Sam and Cindy knew.

"Jane, I don't trust that guy!" Oliver persisted with his feelings.

"He is a police officer Oliver, he saved us from Jason, that should be enough to trust him!"

Oliver was forced to break down the walls to Otto. Sam was a good friend and he had told Oliver to never trust him, but now Sam was gone. Otto was also able to protect Jane when he couldn't. It was hard not to start trusting him.

"He can help us, I know it!" Jane tried to convince him. They both watched as Otto climbed his wet stairs and disappeared into his unit.

"A police officer you say?"

"Yeah, a good one!"

Jane took one last look at the empty plot of land where Sam and Cindy's property used to be. She noticed a figure standing in the rain further up the road. It was Father James in his dark rain coat holding his walking stick. He weirdly stared at Jane nodding in approval giving her the faintest smile, he tipped his hat and he then returned to his house.

Oliver released a huge exhale of air from his lungs which brought Jane's attention back to him. Jane realised that things in this place were never as they seemed. Why had Sam and Cindy just left without telling them. Maybe they didn't even really know them at all. Who could you trust here. Everyone had their secrets. There in the rain she just stared at the empty piece of land.

Mandy had watched on as Father James acknowledged Jane. She could see how pleased Father James was with her. Mandy was now angry that Jane had lied. The two of them had been talking today, they had surly planned this together. Mandy realised that what Jane had said tonight to Cindy had trigger the truth about Limbo. Mandy decided that Jane knew what she was doing, she had assisted Sam and Cindy with Father James' help.

"What did he tell you!" Mandy yelled harshly at Jane turning on her aggressively.

Jane was taken back by Mandy's sudden change, "Who?"

"Father James, he's told you, hasn't he? He has told you about all of us and he has told you how to leave, that's what is happening! How dare you lie to me Jane!"

"That's not true…." Jane began. Father James had not told her anything, they barely knew each other.

"LIAR!!" Mandy screamed at her.

"Mandy! I don't know what you are talking about, please let's go home and talk about it."

Oliver watched on, he had no idea what was happening, "Mandy, please listen to Jane," he begged her.

Mandy was so angry. She walked backwards through the rain unable to believe that Jane had chosen to do such a thing to her.

"I would rather be beaten than to go anywhere near you! I won't go back, Jane, I won't. You can't make me, and neither can that stupid old priest!"

Mandy turned and ran in the rain back towards her own house, Jane watched on in despair as her silhouette began to merge into the darkness of the stormy night.

"MANDY!!" Jane screamed at the top of her lungs.

Mandy was gone. Jane was a mess. She continuously screamed into the nights frozen air. Oliver grabbed hold of her wanting her to stop. She was so angry.

"Jane listen to me! We are going to get the hell out of here I promise you. It's time we started thinking about ourselves and doing what we need to do to get home to Alex. I can't stand this place just as much as you and I won't watch the both of us lose our minds while we wait for something else to happen. I've seen some crazy shit here and I'm over it!"

Jane slowly become calmer, he was right. It was time that they stopped being side tracked from what was important and that was to go home to where they belonged, to their son. She nodded at his authoritative opinion and she realised that Father James knew more than what he was letting on.

"Why would Sam and Cindy leave and not tell us? Why does Mandy think that I was a part of it?" she said to Oliver.

"Maybe they had no choice, maybe it was just their time to go. I don't know. With Mandy, as soon as she saw Father James she turned angry, that has to mean something."

The rain did not move them, they didn't care about its pounding force that hurt when it hit their faces, they had felt it before. Jane looked from side to side unsure of what to do. Should she try to follow Mandy and talk to her so that she could understand why she was so angry. Or should she head towards Father James' house and get some answers out of him.

Otto was staring from his lounge room window, Jane hoped that Otto was not hiding anything from her. Sternly she moved towards Father James' house and Oliver followed.

"That's it!" Jane roared, "someone is going to finally fucking tell me what is going on!"

Oliver was excited. This was definitely the Jane from the past, the one that would not stand for any injustice. She was the one you would go to, to get the job done. They called her the closer, because no one ever really said much after she told you exactly what she thought.

"About time," Oliver whispered with a grin.

Jane headed for Father James' house adamant that this was the moment that she would finally understand all of this Limbo bullshit. Standing up tall she banged on his door and screamed over the rain for him to open up, but he did not answer.

"I know that you are in there, open up Father James!" Jane continued to yell.

Oliver looked around the house but saw no sign of life coming from the inside of it. There were no lights on, no movement, it was empty.

Why isn't he answering?" Jane moved to the window.

"I can't see anything from the side," Oliver told her. "It looks like there is no-one home."

"I saw him, we all did! He walked back into this house."

Puzzled they both left for home. Jane was steaming with anger and could not get her mind to focus on any one thing. Everything was just falling apart around them. As they drew closer to home Jane was relieved to see Mandy crying on the front doorstep, she ran to her and held her tight.

"Mandy, if I've done something to hurt you I am sorry!"

They all went inside and moments after it hit midnight and Limbo reset before they even had a chance to talk.

CHAPTER 20

Moving on from the past allows you to see a better future.

Alana was a kind soul that was hidden behind the dark make-up and facade of this gothic act, to keep herself from letting others in. It was nice to see Alana on Jane's early walk this morning, the two teenaged girls usually kept to themselves. Alana wanted to talk with Jane. She needed to tell someone how she was feeling, Limbo was suffocating her. After seeing Jane behave so loving and motherly towards Mandy she trusted her with her secrets.

As they walked, Jane tried to allow Alana to explain the relationship between her and her sister Stacey without interrupting. They had equally been detrimental to each other, both being each other's enemy for many years at school. It had been a shock for Alana to know that her mother and Stacey's father were even dating. The two girls felt tricked and unable to have their own individual say about whether or not they all wanted to live together as a family.

At school there were many students who found their situation humorous, many enjoying the agony it was causing both of them. The new sisters had become the daily gossip and the daily joke. It was harder for Alana who only had one friend at the school, where Stacey was so popular most of her class loved her.

Although both of them had their part to play in this unusual painful relationship, Stacey was definitely the one that was more open to calling a truce. She was tired of Alana's constant put downs hoping that one day she would eventually just let go and accept the fact that their parents truly were happy.

Stacey was a Daddy's girl. She had seen how much pain her father endured when her mother left after having an affair with her father's best friend. Never would she forgive her mother for what she had done to their family. She had torn them apart.

The moment her mother agreed that Stacey was to live with her father while she travelled the world with her new boyfriend made Stacey feel abandoned and worthless. Stacey told people that she no longer had a mother, she was dead to her. But she had her father, and she was grateful for that.

Growing up it was Stacey's father who was the one who changed her nappy, who cuddled her and read her stories at bedtime. Her mother was never able to make that connection with her, they say it was post-natal depression. Stacey was never interested in the term the doctors gave to explain why her mother could not love her. She longed for her father to find someone who would stop his loneliness and love him unconditionally as she did.

Alana's mother was compassionate, completely opposite to Stacey's mother. It was the day at the shopping centre when Stacey bumped into Alana's mum while the two parents had just started dating. This encounter completely changed Stacey's mind about her father being involved with her arch enemies' mother. Alana's mother treated her as if she already were her own daughter, buying her a coffee and chatting about boys. At the end of the time they spent together Alana's mother even bought her the book that she had been saving up to read.

"Shhh, it's our little secret," she told her.

This was the closest thing that Stacey had ever had to a mother figure in her life. Stacey felt respected and cared about. But sadly, Alana felt abandoned by her mother. She knew how loving she was, so accepting of others, it meant that she would have to share her. Even with the whole gothic stage she was going through, she knew that her mother would love her and accept her through any crazy idea she had.

It was hard for Alana to know that her mother had accepted her enemy, the one that had caused her so much pain and suffering during her high school years. That is why she could not let go of the fact that she wanted her mother to get a divorce and move out. Alana was tired of trying to pretend that everything was going to be sweet and happy. So, she did everything that she possibly could to destroy this happy little family.

Alana trusted Jane, she was just like her own mother so kind and open, easy to talk to. Alana had watched Jane walk past her house every day in the morning. Today Alana sat outside waiting to see her, she was so lonely and hoped that Jane could be that ear to listen to her about all the problems that filled her mind.

The pressure of being in Limbo was already hard enough to tolerate, but to only have Stacey here was a nightmare. Stacey behaved like she was in charge always shouting out orders. Do this, do that, it was so frustrating. Alana just wanted to be Alana. It was early this day and even though Alana was not a morning person she managed to be out and about just in case Jane walked past, which is exactly what she did. They continued to walk together.

"How is Mandy?" Alana kindly asked.

"I don't know, I want to go there now and make sure that she is safe. I fear for her." Although Jane was desperate to find Mandy there in front of her stood Alana, head hung low and sadness in her eyes. "What's going on?" Jane asked her.

Alana was apprehensive but deep down it was what she had been waiting for. "I know I'm always a bit dark and gloomy but really I just feel trapped here. I suppose it wasn't just here it was back home in the real-world as well. It's nice to actually talk to someone. My mum was an amazing person and now I feel like I took her for granted and maybe even pushed her to the limits. I miss talking things out with her, she always accepted me for who I was no matter what."

It was lovely that Alana felt close enough to talk to Jane while her mother couldn't be here with her. "I miss my son also. I love being around you girls it comforts me and makes me feel like I am being a mother," they smiled at each other.

"Do you remember what happened to you before you got here?" Alana asked Jane.

"Well, sure. I remember that we nearly had an accident in the car, but we veered off of the main road into an embankment and then we couldn't find our way back. Limbo was the only place we could find. I don't remember the year it was or the year I was born but I remember most things."

The two girls began to walk through the forest, Alana went quiet and Jane was worried she had said something wrong.

Alana stopped and looked down as tears filled her eyes, "I don't mean to be so horrible all the time. I feel as though this is who I am now and there is no way out."

Jane went to hug her, "Don't worry Alana, Limbo gets to all of us."

"It's not Limbo…" Alana started as she pulled away from Jane's embrace. Her thoughts and emotions were whirling around inside of her. "It's not just about being stuck here, it's about me, it's about everything. I remember the day that Stacey and I came here. I remember how I was feeling. I woke up and Stacey and I had had a huge argument the night before. The fight we had was all my fault, she was trying to make things right, trying to make the family work but I just couldn't. I just abused her and blamed her for trying to steal my mother away from me. I went and sat on my bed afterwards and just cried into my hands unable to stop. I wanted so desperately to forgive her, but I just couldn't let go Jane. She was so mean to me in primary school and it turned into such a war in senior college. She was my enemy and we have both done some really horrible things. She meets my mother and miraculously has a special moment with her and suddenly she becomes an angel. I just don't know if I believe her. At that very moment when I sat there with my face in my hands I felt like this was it, the moment that would change my life. If felt bad, like things were going to turn for the worst if I didn't change. It was the lowest moment in my life and I didn't know how to get out of it, I couldn't breathe."

Alana's story forced Jane to remember back when she had felt the same way. When she had locked herself into that toilet cubicle in the ladies' room the night of the awards ceremony. It was the lowest time in Jane's life and in that moment, she was unsure of how she could ever get out of such a sinking feeling. Jane could hear in Alana's voice that she wanted to see the good in Stacey, but there was also so much pain from the past.

"People do change Alana, maybe Stacey has realised that having a family is more important than all the fighting."

Alana looked at Jane and nodded, but there was still so much doubt. How could she ever trust Stacey, she had hurt her so much. How could she ever possibly forgive her for what she had done?

"There's something else," Alana said. "That morning something was wrong, I could feel it. There was a boy I knew, Thomas. He asked me to walk to school with him that day, he's kind of a freak like me. That morning I saw him waiting for me from my window and I told him to get lost and that was the nice version of it. I was angry, and I took it out on him. When I saw him at school later that morning there was this feeling in the pit of my stomach. It was sickening. The next thing I remember is Stacey and I running from the school and into the trees, then all of a sudden, we ended up here. Why am I such a horrible person Jane?"

Jane hugged her again as she wept, "Oh Alana, I'm so sorry that you feel this way. But I just want you to know that anyone can change. Let me tell you that sometimes we get these thoughts into our heads that just aren't true, believe me it's what I've been doing. Maybe you think that you have been horrible but really you are just being hard on yourself."

"No, no it's me," Alana repeated. "I want to trust people I do, I want us to be a family, but I just can't. How do I let it all go when I am so angry all of the time?"

"Sometimes Alana we don't see the whole picture, we make decisions on just part of what is really going on. I blamed my husband for having an affair on information that I was coming up with in my head. I had to trust the fact that I was doing it to myself, and that he was a good man. I had to just trust in something bigger. Step back Alana, step back and see Stacey for who she is, does she really want this war with you?"

Alana calmed down as she listened and took in the words that Jane had spoken to her. Stacey had gone through her parent's break-up, watching her father suffer through her mother leaving him for another man. She had confessed to Alana on that last night before they entered Limbo that she was happy to finally have a mother figure who really cared about her and her dad. Alana could see that Stacey was being honest and telling the truth, she wanted to start fresh. But, Alana hated the fact that she would have to break down her barriers to Stacey after all that she had done. What if they all became a close family and her mother and Stacey's father split up? What if Stacey was just baiting her for yet another practical joke?

"If only I knew how Stacey really felt, if only I knew what to do. I wish I had all of the answers."

"Don't we all!" Jane said as she smiled. "Would it really change anything if you knew all the answers Alana? It could make things worse. Sometimes we just have to leave it to faith."

"I just want peace in my life Jane, I just want to know what to do to get that."

Great love poured from Jane's heart, she hoped that she had said the right things that would help Alana to feel confident in herself. To acknowledge the remarkable human being that she was.

"I wish that for you Alana. I wish with all of my heart that you can truly know how to let go. I want you to be set free from your suffering."

The two girls were looking eye to eye. Jane had her hands-on Alana's shoulders and as she finished those very words a long sharp vibrating noise started. It then became louder and louder echoing throughout the forest.

"What is that?" Alana was scared by the weird sound.

The trees began to sway as the wind picked up. Jane knew what this noise was, something was about to happen in Limbo. The girls looked around as they held onto each other's arms. It felt as though an earthquake was coming, the ground rumbled beneath them. The swaying trees began to move quicker and quicker.

"Jane what's going on!" Alana screamed.

"I don't know, just hang onto me."

The wind blew more viciously until it felt as though it was trying to tear them apart. Slowly they were being dragged from one another. They fought to keep their grip, but the pressure was too great and sure enough they could no longer continue the hold they had. Then the wind stopped around Jane, but it didn't stop around Alana. It was so strong that it began to pick her up and keep her in the air.

Boom, was the loud sound made from a huge glass pane that fell between the two girls splitting them apart. The wind stopped, and Alana fell to the ground. The annoying vibrating noise also stopped. Standing up Alana looked on as she stared at Jane through the glass. They moved closer to each other realising that they had been separated by this large glass barrier that went on for as far as the eye could see.

As Alana placed her hand upon the glass fixture she began to bang on it yelling out Jane's name. She could see the forest and Limbo in the background, but for Jane the vision was completely different.

Through the glass pane with Alana banging on it calling her name, the back ground was no longer Limbo but a high school. There were teenagers talking, muffled in the background. Lockers were clanging. Alana could see the shock on Jane's face. Turning she saw her fellow school mates back at her high school.

This was the moment, the last time she remembered her life before Limbo. As she walked through the hallway the other students that passed by never noticed her. Alana stood there for a moment taking in her surroundings trying to understand why she was there. Had she returned back to the real-world, but it didn't feel right.

"Wait, I remember this now," Alana said softly to herself as she looked around, she then started to become agitated. "Oh my God I remember what happened!"

Alana let out the biggest and most fearful scream as she turned back to Jane, running back to the glass.

"Get me out of here, please!" She begged Jane as she banged harder and harder on the glass panel with both of her hands.

Jane was in shock not knowing what was happening, she had no clue how she could possibly help her. She moved closer to the glass and placed both of her hands onto it so that Alana could see them there.

"Please Jane something bad is going to happen, please, he's coming!" Alana was hysterical.

"I'm here Alana, I'm here!"

Jane felt useless. She watched on as the front doors to the school opened. The light flew in from behind the person who opened the doors making it hard to see. But as the light dimmed there stood a boy with dark hair holding a rifle in his hands. He was angry.

Jane watched the commotion begin. The high school students started to scream and scurry away in all different directions trying to find a place to hide. Jane was paralysed. Fear for Alana's safety grew and all she could do to help her was to scream with all her might, "RUN!"

CHAPTER 21

The ability to make things right has no time limit.

It appeared that tricks were always being played in Limbo. Jane had to stand by and watch as Alana ran for her life. She ran away from a boy who had decided that today was the day that he would pay back all of his school mates that had tortured him throughout the years.

It was Thomas, the very boy that Alana had verbally abused that morning. He must have gone home and armed himself after their argument. Had Alana tipped him over the edge?

Thomas was looking to confide in someone, in Alana that morning, he thought she was feeling left out just as he was. When she also turned on him and treated him badly, he snapped.

Alana ran as the gun shots echoed inside of her head. Her heart rate soared as she could feel the blood pumping through her veins. Sweat filled her armpits as she ran into a classroom where other students were hiding. The popping of the gun and the screams were hard to bear. But now there was nowhere else to go, they were trapped.

Then she noticed it, the room that she was in was where Stacey was hiding and where she was hiding. Not this version of herself but the actual real-life version of herself that had already gone through this moment before. She could remember it all from the past vaguely, but it was if Limbo were re-enacting those very moments and allowing her to see what really happened.

Alana realised that no-one could see her, not this version of herself. All they could see was the Alana from the real-world and so instead of running and being afraid she realised that all she had to do was watch.

Jane watched on also through the glass, like a television screen playing out a movie, "Alana are you okay?" she yelled.

Alana relaxed analysing the scenario that was happening around her, easing into the experience as if it were a gift to her.

"Jane!" she yelled, "I don't think anyone can see me, I think I am safe, it's like Limbo is replaying this moment for me. I can feel it. I think it's trying to show me something."

Jane prayed that Alana was right. Alana watched herself run and hide inside of the storage cupboard. She closed the cupboard doors behind her as she wept putting her headphones into her ears and turning up the music so that she could not hear the screaming happening outside. Others in the classroom hid behind desks as the door suddenly flew open. Thomas stepped in and found Stacey hiding behind a desk.

"Where is Alana?" he yelled to her.

"I don't know," she cried with fear, "I don't know," she repeated.

"I saw her come in here, now where the fuck is she?"

He pointed the gun at her warning her that she was going to die if she did not answer his questions. He heard whimpering coming from the storage cupboard which took his attention. He moved towards it hoping that Alana was inside. Stacey rose to her feet quickly and without hesitation she jumped in between the storage cupboard and the gun.

"Leave her alone!" Stacey demanded.

As Alana watched on she was struck with guilt. Stacey had risked her life to protect the Alana in the real-world. She did not remember these moments and she did not realise that Stacey had tried to protect her. This meant only one thing, that she truly loved her as a sister.

Everything that she had ever said or did to her before this very moment meant nothing.

Thomas grabbed Stacey by her long beautiful locks and dragged her out of the classroom and into the hallway. He threw her down onto the ground as she cried. He was going to show everyone that he meant business.

"I don't remember this part!" Alana told herself.

"This is what happens to you all when you pieces of shit abuse and abuse people over and over. You fucking pieces of mother fucking shit are now going to pay for everything that you have done to me and to all the others you have crapped all over!"

Thomas aimed the gun at Stacey's head, looked at her eye to eye and he pulled the trigger.

"No, no this is not what happened!" Alana screamed. "I remember running into the forest away from the school before we came to Limbo. She can't be dead!" The piercing screams of students came from all around. Alana fell to her knees looking upon Stacey's limp and lifeless body. "No, what have I done?"

Thomas then walked back into the classroom again where several students were still hiding under the tables and in the cupboards. He reloaded his magazine and randomly began shooting, he sprayed bullets in all directions. Alana rose from Stacey's side as she followed Thomas back into the classroom trying to hit him, but her punches made no impact to him at all. It was as if she were a ghost.

Continuing to watch this cruel devastation she knew that these were her final moments alive. She had died in the real-world. Her life was taken away by a boy who knew no other way to release all the locked away feelings that had made him so very angry that day.

Thomas walked over to the cupboard and he opened the door. Alana was sitting hunched in a ball with her eyes closed with the music playing into her ears. She felt his presence and opened her eyes and looked up at him.

"Why, why were you just like all the others? I thought you were different," Thomas told her.

A tear slowly fell down her cheek unable to say a word. Alana watched on unable to help herself in the real-world within this situation, instead having to remember that this was exactly how this day unfolded. Thomas lifted his gun, as Alana closed her eyes awaiting her fate. Thomas pulled the trigger. The sound of the bullet sent a noise that pierced through Alana's body as she watched her own dead.

The glass between Jane and Alana began to crack, the scene in front of them paused. The loud annoying vibration was present again. Both the world of Limbo and Alana's alter universe began to wobble and shake. The worlds were shifting again.

Alana moved towards the glass and placed her two hands where Jane had her hands. Together they watched and waited. The fierce winds started again, and Alana just cried. This was all too much for her as she looked at Jane in desperation.

"I'm so sorry Jane," she said looking through the cracking glass.

"We are going to be fine!" Jane yelled back.

"I'm dead Jane, we are all dead!"

Alana's words send fear throughout Jane, what if they were all dead and stuck here in Limbo? Maybe they had all done horrible things that they couldn't remember, and this was their punishment. Both girls closed their eyes and waited for the impact of what Limbo had in store for them. The vibration grew louder and the earth shook heavier. Then there was silence.

The abrupt halt to all of the noise and commotion made the girls slowly open their eyes and look around. They were both in the forest in Limbo where they had started. Alana fell into Jane's arms and wept.

"What the hell was that?" Jane asked as the two embraced within the silence of the trees.

Alana pulled away and as she looked at Jane she just whispered, "Stacey."

Off Alana ran through the forest and back to her house, Jane watched as she grew smaller in the distance. Jane then ran behind her and stopped at Law street watching Alana run inside her home. Jane was struggling to comprehend what she had just seen. Both Alana and Stacey had been killed by a gunman, what did this mean for all of them here?

Alana burst through the front door running upstairs to Stacey's bedroom. She stormed in pouncing on top of Stacey, waking her from her sleep.

"What the hell Alana, piss off! You know I wanted a sleep in today!"

Stacey's words did not change Alana's actions as she just hugged and hugged her sister. "I'm so sorry!" Alana blubbered covering Stacey's face with wet salty tears.

Stacey quickly sat up in bed, "What the hell has happened, what's wrong?"

Alana was able to settle down compose herself, "I'm sorry for everything, it's my fault we are here. I need you to know that no matter what happens you are my sister and you will always be my sister no matter the past."

Stacey just smiled. The both of them had done so many unspeakable things, not only to each other but to others. Stacey was sorry for all that she had done, but she was proud of Alana for acknowledging her part. Stacey honestly believed that they could all start again and try and be a happy family, it's all she had ever wanted.

"I truly love you Alana, you are the closest thing that I have to a sister. Your mother is the warmest and most caring woman I know, and I would love for her to be a mother to me. My father needs her, he needs you."

"I love you too Stacey," Alana whimpered. "You know that your dad it's pretty cool too. I think we are all lucky to have each other, I'm sorry for not trusting you, for not believing you."

They hugged again and there was a love between them that was magical. The strange vibrational sound started to happen again, but this time Alana knew what was happening, she could feel it.

"It's time to go home Stacey, it's time to make things right. No matter where we go from here I promise that I will always have your back. I promise that I will always be love instead of hate."

The two girls nodded at each other as they embraced again. The walls of the bedroom began to move and wobble slowly. The world around them began to vanish and then it came back again. Alana quickly stood up knowing that it was time for her and Stacey to leave. She ran to the bedroom window and hung out of it waving at Jane who looked on from the street below.

Jane was scared again, she knew what was happening this time, it was just like Sam and Cindy. Jane held out her hands as she stood there in Law street feeling the specks of rain beginning to fall.

"Jane, it was you!" Alana yelled out to her from the window, "you're the answer!"

As the building began to move and wobble in unusual ways in front of Jane some of the remaining neighbours began to run out into the street. The pouring rain had abruptly started, the sign that someone was leaving.

Oliver ran to Jane's side, "What happened Jane?"

Jane could not answer him because she didn't know. Alana continued waving from the window.

"It's you Jane!" she yelled again.

Stacey then ran to the window and as the two girls put their arms around each other they smiled as their two-storey home vanished from Limbo.

The vibration had stopped. Alana peered out from underneath her hands and looked around her bedroom. She had now found herself sitting on her bed with her hands covering her face. This was the moment at night time after she had had that horrible argument with Stacey and the rest of the family. It was the night before the school massacre. She quickly stood up and raced into Stacey's room where she found her just looking around stunned.

"Where are we?" Stacey asked her.

"We are home," Alana said as they hugged each other excited to have returned to the real-world.

Limbo had offered them a second chance at life, but the memory of what was going to happen tomorrow at the school became fresh within Alana's mind.

"Let's make all of this right," Alana said. "We have both brought so much suffering to this world and done so much damage to so many people, it's time to start making up for it."

"You're right," Stacey agreed, "It's time to do the right thing instead of thinking about ourselves all of the time."

They both ran downstairs as quickly as they could and hugged their mother and father. Their parents were astounded by the gesture from the girls because only five minutes before they were all inside a war zone. Bewildered by the girl's affection they chose to embrace the change instead of questioning it. They talked all night long as a true family unit, it was the beginning of something wonderful.

The next day Thomas was outside Alana's window just as she knew he would be, but instead of shooing him away nastily she ran out to greet him. Thomas found it hard to recognise her without all of her dark make-up on her face. Alana had decided that today she was going to be herself and no-one else. No longer was she going to hide behind a mask to hide her feelings.

"You look different, in a good way," Thomas said shyly.

"Thanks," she smiled.

Thomas was always a quiet boy, but Alana liked him a lot. He was very sweet, but she knew that he had his limits just as she did. There she stood unable to blame him for the future choices that in this very moment he had not yet made. Stacey came outside ready for school, Thomas squirmed by her presence. Stacey and her group had hounded him for years and years just as they had done to Alana.

"It's okay Thomas, we have been talking and we have all chosen to stop all this fighting nonsense. No more bullying or being mean," Stacey told him.

Thomas knew the pain that Stacey could inflict and could not believe what she was telling him, how could he.

"Truce?" Stacey asked Thomas as she held out her hand to shake.

Thomas uneasily shook her hand and as he did a peace fell over his heart. Something had happened between them all, they had finally accepted each other for who they were. They chose to be friends instead of enemies.

From that moment on, the three of them were a group. Stacey no longer hung out with the cool kids and Alana changed her gothic ways and friends.

Thomas became the kind soul he always was. He turned himself around with the love and support he had with the new friendships from Alana and Stacey. He became confident and strong. No longer was he abused and ridiculed every single day of his life. He was finally free. Free from his own self judgements and the bullying of the peers at his school. If anyone ever tried to say a bad word about him the two girls would shut it down quickly.

School became a place they all loved to go instead of being the hell they had once created. Their lives had changed completely because they had all chosen to believe in the truth. They accepted each other and loved each other. Limbo had given them the time to stand back and realise each other's worth. It had granted them a wish that many did not receive, a second chance at life that they gratefully took, grabbing it with both hands and with every inch of their hearts.

CHAPTER 22

What you give to the world is what will be returned to you.

Otto looked on from afar at the two-storey house disappearing. He had been walking through the forest when he heard Alana yelling. She was crying out to Jane from the window that she was the reason, that she was the key to all of this. He came and stood on Law street watching on at Alana and Stacey waving goodbye. He was thinking to himself that he was tired of watching people leave, he wanted to go home, and he wanted to go now.

In the past Mandy had shared different ideas with Otto about Limbo, and now it appeared that Jane was involved with the leaving process somehow, without even knowing. He wanted answers from the both of them, they knew more than what they were telling him. There was so many things left unsaid when he left the real-world and it was killing him inside knowing that he had left his wife and baby behind.

He thought back to the time when he was on duty with his partner Neil, they had been partners for almost two years. Otto loved to serve the community as a police officer. The Law was his truth and he believed in it, but the pay packet for a couple of cops on the streets was poor. Slowly the amount that he was earning was not enough to cover the necessities, especially after Stephanie his daughter came along, and his wife Kate was not working.

He tried hard not to think about what could happen if things didn't change. He loved his job, but it was all about experience within the force and doing your time before you moved on or up. This is exactly what Otto wanted to do, it was his dream, but he felt like time was running out. He needed more money.

Life became very tough, it was hard to survive the ever-rising expenses; the weekly rent, groceries, baby formula, nappies and utilities. The stress took its toll and the fighting between Kate and himself escalated.

Kate found herself a job at the local grocery store for the night time work and was able to get five shifts a week. It helped, but the exhaustion which followed was difficult for her to cope with. Taking care of a baby during the day and working at night was too much.

Otto was going to make it up to her when he got out of Limbo, he was going to do his best to make things right again after all that he had done. It was that moment, he remembered it, when he sat in his car with his face in his hands. He was scared wondering if he was making the right choices for his family, it was the turning point in his life. As Otto remembered this moment he began to cry. Leaving the street and heading back into the forest, he did not want anyone here in Limbo to see his sadness. The choice he made back then that day was unfortunately the wrong one.

Otto and his partner Neil had just helped to bust a small drug deal that was going down with the help of another police vehicle. This second vehicle was driven by Matt and Graham, two cops that had always been a tough and over-powering pair. Otto saw it as a trait that just came with the job over time. He himself had learned to become more aggressive and immune to the horrific things that you would see while being a street cop.

Neil had become a bit chummier with Matt and Graham over the last six months. Neil had tried to involve Otto in some of their drinking nights out, but he always passed them up. His family needed him, and Kate had to work. There was no time left in his life for drinking and carrying on.

After this latest bust Otto was pleased with the four of the officer's efforts. Matt, Graham, Neil and himself had followed protocol to a tee and the result was two bad men being put behind bars. Otto was relieved and grateful that everything had gone to plan. It was going to be a routine check on some of their usual street nuisances, instead turning into a fifty-thousand-dollar cash find and a few kilos of grass.

Matt and Graham had pulled Neil aside and spoke to him privately. Their eyes occasionally looked over at Otto which made him feel uncomfortable. After their conversation Matt put most of the cash into Otto and Neil's car.

"We will take the offenders in and process them," Matt said.

Matt and Graham drove away heading for the station. Otto looked into the boot of their car and noticed that most of the drugs were gone but most of the cash was still there.

"Where is the rest of the evidence?" Otto queried. "There is at least 10k missing and most of the drugs are gone."

"Otto, I want to talk to you," Neil said as he put his sunglasses on and lit up a cigarette. He offered one to Otto which he accepted, after the bust he was still a little shaky.

"What's up?" Otto was apprehensive.

Neil looked around trying to pick the words he was going to say, "things have been tough for you and Kate, haven't they?"

Otto nodded in agreement unsure where the conversation was heading. Neil closed the boot of the car and looked at Otto.

"Things have been really hard for me too Otto, my wife and I have two kids that we have to feed and send to school, it's not cheap."

"I know," Otto agreed.

"Look I'm just going to come out with it the way the other guys told me. There is a few of us who believe in justice, and I mean justice in the fact that us good guys do not get paid anywhere near the amount we should. We risk our lives every day and get paid like the scum of the earth and we are sick of it. I can't support my family any longer and I was about to lose my house…"

"I'm sorry man," Otto cut in, "I had no idea."

Neil smiled from Otto's concern, "Otto, when we find evidence like what we found today we don't always hand over everything we find, especially if it is cash."

Otto flinched.

"Now hear me out Otto don't judge it yet! We don't really hold any of the drugs back, we hand most of that in! But the cash, what we choose to keep is split between us, the three of us. I was hoping that it would be four after today."

Otto was speechless as Neil awaited an answer, "Are you serious, you want me to steal and become a criminal?"

"No, no, think about it Otto…"

"Shut-up Neil! I don't have to think about it at all!"

Otto began to pace back and forward as he thought about the information that he had to process.

"What am I supposed to do now, with this bullshit?"

Neil looked at him shaking his head, "These guys know I'm asking you to join them. I told them that you would become a part of it. I got you into this because I know how much you need the extra cash, I'm doing this FOR you!"

"Don't fucking do me any more favours!" Knowing this could put Otto into some serious danger, he was unsure of what to do next.

"Otto just calm down and listen to me. In the last six months I have taken home around twenty thousand dollars in cash, we all have. I was able to take my family out to dinner one night for no reason. My wife and I don't fight anymore, everything is sweet right now. I pay bills with cash, I even buy the groceries with cash and my wife has absolutely no idea. I control it all. Nobody has to know, no one."

Otto watched Neil's face as he spoke to him about how wonderful his life was now. It made him think about the fights that he and Kate had been having. He hated the fact that Kate had to have another job especially at night time, he was putting her in danger and there was nothing that he could do to fix it. Was this his opportunity to make things better in their lives, to ease the pressure that society was putting on them.

"I can't...." Otto began as he turned away rubbing the back of his neck agitated.

"Look all I'm asking you for now is to just think about it. The other guys have taken most of the drugs and ten thousand in cash. They will log it into the system and no one will know any different. The bag of drugs that we kept is for Matt and Graham to keep their snitch happy. None of us do drugs or get into any of that full-on bullshit, it's just the cash. Now we have forty thousand dollars in the boot right now and split four ways is, well you can do the maths."

Otto just stood there looking at Neil, both of them in silence. It was not an equation that Otto had to work out. Ten thousand dollars was huge, absolutely huge. That kind of money would change his life for himself and his family instantly.

How good it would be to use cash whenever Kate asked him to pick something up from the shop on the way home. He could pay the bills with cash, or even putting petrol in their old Holden that Kate used to get to work and back. The pressure that all these little things caused in their lives would just disappear.

"All we have to do is go to a meeting place that we all know about and be there in three hours from now. We can split the cash there and then leave and go home to our normal boring little lives. Come on Otto!" Otto stood there thinking. Neil could sense that he had nearly gotten him reeled in. "Come on Otto I can see that you want to!"

That was it, Otto nodded, and the deal was done. Neil laughed and slapped Otto on the back.

"I knew it! I knew we could trust you buddy! This is going to be fantastic you and me. Life is going to be great from now on, you'll see."

"Yeah great," Otto sarcastically repeated unsure of the depth of madness he had just agreed to.

Otto phoned Kate and he told her that he would be home later that night, he had to do a whole bunch of paper work after the busy day.

"Do you think you could have a night off tonight," Otto asked Kate. "It would be nice to just be a family tonight and spend some time together."

"We need the money Otto; how can I give the shift up?"

"Please babe, just one night, call in sick...for me."

Kate heard in Otto's voice that something was wrong. She thought about his offer and agreed to call in sick for her shift that night. Times were tough, but she knew Otto too well, he needed her. The pressure from his job and the daily finances had caused Otto to be an angry and frustrated individual, but Kate could see beyond that. Their love for each other was deeper than these problems. Otto hung up the phone relieved that he was going to be able to spend time with his wife and his daughter. It had been a long time since they were all together, not just crossing paths.

Neil's plan was to grab a bite to eat, get changed into their casual clothes and then head down to the drop off point to split the cash. Neil called Matt to confirm as he lit up another cigarette. Otto got into the driver's seat of his vehicle, he sat in the car awaiting Neil to finish his conversation. This was the moment that Otto sat in the car with his head buried in his arms, wondering if the choice he had made was going to fix his life or ruin it. He had decided to go against everything that he had ever believed in, he was a traitor. The pressure inside was growing, and he could feel himself starting to panic. Breathing deeply, he tried hard to control his racing heart.

"What have I gotten myself into?" he whispered to himself.

Otto sat with his hands upon the steering wheel watching Neil on the phone. He knew that he was telling Matt that he had agreed to the cash. Otto lowered his head into his forearms again thinking about the horrible thing that he was about to do. He never believed that he would ever compromise his morals for money, not ever. Who had he become?

"Come on! Let's go!" Neal yelled as he hit the front of the car.

Otto shot his head upright quickly, adrenaline flooding through his body. Neil got in the car laughing after scaring Otto half to death.

"Well that's it then we will go and grab something to eat and hang out for a bit until the boys are ready. Then we will go and meet them, and then my friend…you will be ten thousand dollars richer!" Neil slapped Otto on the shoulder, "Come on, I'm hungry, it's been a big day!"

Otto started the car and drove off hesitantly. That night after they called it a day, got changed and ate something at the local cafe, Neil and Otto drove to where the meeting point was.

It was underneath a bridge where no one would see them do their deal. Neil appeared excited as Otto wondered how many times he had done this previously. Otto was uncomfortable, and the other men could see it. Matt had thought that Otto was too much of a goodie-two-shoes to agree to become a part of this operation. He was worried that he was going to tell a higher authority about their secret business. Otto could feel his negative presence towards him, this was intense.

Neil opened the trunk of the car and that is when everything went wrong. Someone had discovered them. In the distance they were watching. Everything turned ugly, guns were drawn, bullets were flying. It had all happened so quickly.

Otto was able to hide behind a bridge post where he sat glued unable to move. He watched on as Graham drew his gun from behind his vehicles front opened door. Otto gasped when Graham was hit in the chest, he fell to the ground motionless. Neil and Matt were desperately trying to hold off whoever it was attacking them.

Otto felt frozen, sweat pouring out of his body. In the distance he could see the cover of some trees and decided to make a run for it, it was his only escape. With a deep breath he ran, and he ran until he hit the camouflage of the trees. He stopped and looked back watching the deadly fight continue. Down went Matt, down went Neil. Otto moved on through the woods and that is where he found the welcoming sign for Limbo.

Otto never saw his wife and daughter that night, he never made it home to them. Instead he left them wondering where he was. How could he ever forgive himself for what he had done? He had to get the hell out of this place and find a way back to his family, he just had to.

Jane was the key to doing just that, it was time to find out exactly what she knew.

Otto felt broken now that he had revisited his final moments before coming to Limbo. He had not allowed it to enter his mind for too long before this day. It had caused emotions within himself that he hated experiencing. Storming back through the forest he noticed that many of them were still looking upon an empty plot that once housed Stacey and Alana. It was time to get answers.

CHAPTER 23

Share your gifts with the world, it's why everyone is so different.

Otto walked straight up Law street and passed those that were standing there fascinated by another empty lot. He headed for Jane. Mary was there, of course she was.

When was there a time that she wasn't poking her nose into everyone else's business, Otto thought.

Jason and Louisa were watching on. Otto walked straight up to Jane and grabbed her on the shoulder, "We need to talk!"

Oliver moved across Jane forcing Otto to release his grip on her, "Step back Otto it's not the time."

"Bullshit it's not the time, she is the connection to the other side somehow and we all want to go home!"

"Enough, both of you," Jane yelled.

Jason overheard the commotion, "So you have been keeping secrets from us! You better bloody tell us how to get out of here!" he pointed at Jane.

Everyone was becoming agitated. Oliver was scared for Jane, they were starting to gang up on her.

"How could she possibly have anything to do with this, we both arrived after you all. Why would we both still be here if Jane knew how to leave?" Oliver's reassurance made complete sense.

"Do you know something Jane?" Mary questioned her. Jane stood there unable to answer.

"See she does know something," Jason groaned.

"Quiet!" Jane yelled, there was no way that she was going to put up with another one of Jason's tantrums. "Look something happened today that I just can't explain. I don't know what happened, I just don't, but I do feel that I somehow was a part of it," she turned to Otto. "I'm sorry, I am, but I don't know how to help."

Mandy ran in between them, she could no longer put up with everyone blaming Jane.

"You need to get your ass home Mandy, this has nothing to do with you!" Jason bellowed.

"No! Jane hasn't got anything to do with it. You are all so stupid, if she knew she wouldn't be here."

Mandy looked at Otto trying to get his attention, Mandy trusted him. Others thought that Otto was hot headed, sometimes he acted that way, but she knew him differently. He had a heart of gold. Mandy knew his secrets, she knew all of their secrets.

"Maybe we should all just sit down and talk about this, someone has to know something. This is two houses in the same amount of days. Jane you were there for both of them, surely there is something you know," Mary reasoned.

"I'm sick of all this crap! Tell us or I will make you!" Jason moved towards Jane with his fist in the air. Both Otto and Oliver stepped in.

"Ease up big fella, I don't want to have to shoot you…. again," Otto flashed his gun and grinned.

Jason backed off, "Come on babe let's just go home, they don't know anything," Louisa and Jason began to leave. "I'm not done with you all," Jason said as he and Louisa headed home.

"Mandy come home with us," Louisa ordered.

"No, I'm staying!"

"Mandy…."

"Leave her!" Jason yelled, "you know she just makes things worse for us."

Mandy hung her head from Jason's words. Louisa looked back at her daughter one last time, but she did not stop to console her. Instead she went home with Jason.

"What a dickhead!" Otto said making Mandy laugh. "You all right kiddo?"

Mandy nodded.

"Jane, what about you?"

"I'm fine Otto, I think he's right though. Maybe it is me."

Jane paced the street, people were disappearing around her and she did not know why. The residents were all desperate to return to the lives they once had, and it was frustrating Jane to know that she may be holding the answers.

Father James came over and joined the group. He never said a word, but he looked hard at Mandy. He was a good man that only wanted the best for everyone, but he was always trying to make Mandy do things in Limbo that she didn't want to do. He had been the one that had revealed to her all of the residents in Limbo's secrets, in the hope that Mandy could save them. She hated that he pushed her all of the time to help people that she didn't want to help. The problem was that Father James knew that Mandy was the one, the one that possessed the power to return. The voice she heard every single night in her sleep had told her the answers to Limbo.

"Mandy…" Father James began.

"I think I know how to leave," Mandy said quickly as she hung her head down again.

"What do you mean?" Otto could not believe that Mandy knew this and had kept it from him.

"I'm sorry, I am, but I am afraid,"

"Of what?" Jane asked as she went over to comfort her.

"Leaving," Mandy answered.

"Well I think it will be best if we all just sat down together and heard what Mandy has to say over a nice cup of tea," Mary announced.

"I only want to talk to Jane and Oliver, no one else."

Otto and Mary were surprised. Otto was the one that had instigated this, he had helped Mandy through some really tough times. His heart fell, and his disappointment was obvious. Mary was no longer hanging around where she wasn't invited. Offended by Mandy after all that she had done for her since being in Limbo, she turned and headed home.

Father James smiled at Mandy's truthfulness, he was pleased that she had finally told someone about her secret. "I think my job here is done," he said as he tipped his hat and headed home. On his way he collected Frank who was starting to walk towards the commotion. Camilla had sent him out to see what was happening in the street. Father James decided to go inside and pay Camilla a visit. It would be best for him to talk to Frank and Camilla about Alana and Stacey leaving.

Otto stood devastated in the street, but Mandy had no intention of leaving him out. She didn't want Mary and Father James a part of what she had to say. It was best that Mary and the others didn't know that Otto was going to be involved.

"Go home Otto," Mandy told him. "In about an hour head to Jane's house. Make sure that no one sees you when you do. I don't want anyone else knowing that you are involved, especially Mary. She needs to work her own stuff out with Daniel before she learns anything else."

Otto was so relieved, "Are you positive that you want me there?"

"Yes, of course Otto, I trust you. I'm sorry I just had to get rid of everyone else. You have helped me many times here and I will never forget what you have done for me."

Otto finally felt for the first time here in Limbo that his true self had shone through and someone had noticed. That someone was Mandy. Otto knew he wasn't a bad guy he had just made some poor choices, that's why he came across angry all of the time. Mandy was a good kid and he wished that she could have a better life.

Mandy left with Jane and Oliver back to their house and they left Otto alone in the street. Otto looked down and watched as Mary entered her house, he strangely felt sorry for her.

When Mary arrived home, she found it hard to interact with Daniel. She was tired of being treated so rudely by all of them. Jane still had not apologised for their last confrontation. Mary was feeling so upset, everyone appeared to be against her. All she ever did was to try and help people feel more comfortable in Limbo. Why didn't she leave with Colin when she had the chance? Her life could have been so different.

Doubt was eating away at her. Daniel and herself had made a pact to stick together throughout this time in Limbo, it was Daniel who approached Mary with this idea. Now he was the one breaking it. Mary had a choice to leave with Colin and she didn't because Daniel had confronted her and begged her to stay. Their past was filled with an unbreakable bond, they loved each other deeply but they weren't in love. It was killing Mary not knowing the secrets that Mandy kept. If it were true and Daniel was betraying her then she was desperate to leave.

"Everything fine outside my love?" Daniel asked.

"Yes fine, nothing to worry about."

"That's good to hear."

Mary smiled.

CHAPTER 24

It takes time to learn new things, be kind to yourself and before you know it you will be the teacher of it.

O tto found his way to Jane and Oliver's house unnoticed by the other Limbo residents. He was nervous and excited because he felt like this was his opportunity to really understand what Mandy and Jane knew about Limbo. Thoughts of returning to his life and holding his wife and daughter again brought a smile to his face. When he arrived, he was surprised when he was happily welcomed through the back door. Otto shook Oliver's outstretched hand, it was the first time that Oliver had let down the walls between them.

Jane sat down next to Mandy on the couch. Otto sat at the dining table and Oliver stood while he leaned against the wall. It was time to finally analyse what had been happening here in Limbo. They all sat and wondered who was going to start this conversation.

Otto could wait no longer, "Please Mandy, I need to know. If there is anything that you can tell us, please."

Mandy took a very deep breath, "What if it is something that you really don't want to hear?"

Otto looked into her eyes and he lent back a little, "I need to get back to my family, to my baby girl, please. I've made some mistakes and they need fixing," he begged her.

Mandy nodded her head and she said bluntly, "Everyone here is dead."

Otto's body unnaturally twitched, "What?" he asked her vaguely.

Oliver moved uneasily, and a deep dark feeling hit him inside the pit of his stomach.

"What do you mean Mandy?" Jane softly asked her.

"Everyone here in Limbo died before they got here, they just don't remember their final moments, everyone is dead except myself and…. Jane." Mandy looked at Jane concerned of what she would think. Otto stood up and began to pace up and down the room.

"We are all dead?" Otto had to reconfirm. "Why not the both of you, I don't understand."

"I don't know why. All I know is if you can bend Limbo then you are not dead in the real-world, you are still alive in some form."

"In some form?" Jane was afraid of what that meant.

"How do you know this?" Oliver asked.

"Every night when I fall asleep a man visits me in my dreams and tries to explain things to me about Limbo. He does this so that I can leave and come back home to the real-world. But I can't, I don't want to leave."

"A man?" Otto was intrigued. "Who is this person?"

"I'm not sure who he is although he seems so familiar. I think that he tries to tell me, but I feel like I'm not allowed to know. Limbo stops him from being clear. Sometimes the things he says are vague and it's like he has to constantly tell me the same information over and over again every night so that I can remember it. He seems so kind and I want to listen to him and do as he says but…."

"But what?" Jane asked as she moved closer towards Mandy holding onto her arm.

"I'm scared, I don't want to leave. I don't know what it's going to be like if I go back. If my mother and Jason are both dead and I'm not, then what will happen to me?"

200

"So, this voice in your head while you sleep, tells you how to leave Limbo?" Otto stood there unmoved awaiting his question to be answered.

"Well he tries to explain to me how it works, how I need to feel."

"How does it work then?" Otto did not want Mandy to stop talking.

"It's about how we perceive this place, ourselves and others. Limbo is just a state of mind it isn't a place. We can change the surroundings in our life whether here or in the real-world at any time. But there are certain laws to it all, universal laws that cannot be changed."

"Like what?" Jane asked her.

"Like belief, there is a saying that you are what you believe. Although this seems like just words it really is the truth of it. If it is your belief that you are stuck here, then you are."

"That's all! But I believe that I can get back home to my family and I am still here, I don't understand this stuff," Otto was trying so hard not to become frustrated.

"It's really hard to explain and put into words, I'm sorry I'm not making any sense. I find it hard myself to understand what the voice is trying to tell me over and over again."

"You are doing amazingly Mandy," Jane told her. "Please just do the best you can, and we can try and understand it in our own way."

Mandy nodded again and continued while closing her eyes trying hard to recollect all that had been said to her within her dreams.

"Firstly, he reassures me that at the moment everyone is safe here in Limbo. Then he told me that it is definitely possible to leave if you understood why you were here and learnt how to adjust yourself correctly to match the universal idea of yourself."

"What the hell does that mean?" Otto was anxious.

"Hey!" Oliver made Otto look. "Let her go on."

Otto nodded, he was finding it hard to listen, but he knew that Oliver was right. He had to make sure not to upset Mandy.

Mandy opened her eyes and continued, "We have all decided at one point in our lives to believe in a perception of ourselves, of others and of the world that is incorrect. The lies in our lives have continued to grow. These lies have caused us suffering and to make choices which have ended in dying prematurely. Not everyone in the world that dies gets a second chance. The universe selects a handful of people, the ones that are needed to somehow change the real-world in a positive way or people that need to be connected somehow. Life is about free choice and following our purpose but sometimes we don't fulfil our purpose enough. That's why we have been chosen to experience Limbo."

"So, what you're saying is that everyone here in Limbo still has a second chance and that we can go back to our lives?" Jane reiterated.

Otto felt butterflies in his stomach. The thought that he was dead had scared him. Now he was one of the lucky ones, chosen to return if he could understand why he was here experiencing Limbo.

"Yes, we all do. The only difference between all of you and Jane and I is that we have the ability to bend Limbo," Mandy suddenly began to tear up. She covered her face embarrassed.

"What's wrong Mandy?" Jane put her arm around her while the two men came in closer concerned.

Otto bent down onto his knees, "You are doing great! I'm actually feeling excited now instead of being my grumpy old self."

Mandy had a small laugh. Otto's voice was so soothing, it always reminded her of her Papa Joe. Oliver sat on the coffee table near Mandy and Jane, they were all close together now.

"We are all here for you, you know that," Oliver added.

It had been a long time since Mandy had felt so supported and loved. She felt as though she had done them all a dis-service.

"I'm sorry I should have told you all sooner."

"You're telling us now," Otto comforted her.

"I feel like this Limbo is not the only one. There are many like this one just like there are many different universes that we don't know about. The voice told me that I was sent here to be the one that would release you all from Limbo. I was meant to teach you and make you understand how to return back to the real-world so that you could change your fate. I've let you down because I'm scared to go back. I don't want to ever go back, and I am scared about losing you here as well."

"Why wouldn't you want to go back? Look what happens to you here, the horrible way that you are treated. Surely you want to leave this place and go back to life as you knew it?" Oliver said.

"Life as I knew it was worse than here. At least I only have to deal with my asshole of a step father in Limbo and not all the bullies at school, the stupid teachers. I was losing my mother to Jason more and more each day, at least here we are a family and I know what to expect."

Jane thought there was a lot more to what Mandy was saying, why on earth would she not want to go back to her life.

"Mandy please, there is something you are not telling us."

Mandy paused.

"The night my family came to Limbo I watched Jason beat my mother to an inch of her life and I knew that she was going to die. He then came after me. I don't know why but I have survived, somehow, I am still alive, but my mother and Jason are dead. I heard a gunshot as I laid on the floor the day that he went too far. I had watched from the crack in my bedroom door as he tore into my mother like she was a rag doll, they had been fighting over me. He wanted me to be sent away. He even spoke about me being adopted out. I ran to my cupboard and I sat in there with my hands covering my face, crying. I remember being so scared. He then came for me, I could hear his heavy boots stomping towards my room. He found me, dragged me into the lounge room and he beat me so bad that I couldn't move, but I was still conscious. He left and a few moments later he was crying and then a gun went off. I prayed that he had killed himself. It was then the final moments just before we ended up in Limbo. My first memory was different though when I came to Limbo. I was able to run away from Jason and I found myself in a forest. But recently the voice was able to show me more about what really happened that day. Limbo makes us forget."

"That piece of shit!" Otto clenched his teeth as he stood up. "I feel like going over there right now and giving him a bit of his own medicine, how dare he?"

Oliver was stunned by Mandy, they all had a story to tell. He could not comprehend how much this young girl had gone through.

Jane began to cry, and she just held onto Mandy, "I'm so sorry sweetheart."

But Mandy did not cry instead she became angry.

"If I teach Jason how to change, how to return to the real-world then he will get a second chance. I will not give him another chance to do more damage to the world, to me and my mother. He deserves to die and if my mother chooses him over me then she deserves to die as well! I would rather lose her than to allow Jason a new beginning."

The way that Mandy spoke was full of hate, she was not going to give them their freedom back. Every day they stayed in Limbo was another day that she saved the real-world from Jason's evil nature.

Suddenly something different happened, it was not the vibration they heard or the movement of the walls. Instead there was a deep groaning. It was a sound that got underneath your skin, like death itself was preparing to come. Mandy breathed deeply and realigned herself so that the groaning would stop. She knew that it was the sound of Limbo reminding her that she was not allowing others to choose their own fate.

"What the hell was that?" Otto was not impressed by the indescribable vial noise that shook his nerves.

"I don't know but it can't be good," Oliver said as they all looked around at each other.

"I'm sorry it's me moving Limbo, it is because I was angry. It is Limbo reminding me that I am not here to be the one that chooses for everyone else. They are to choose their own fate for themselves."

With the cruel noise dissipating Otto wanted to confirm what Mandy had said, "So, it is up to us, we can still choose to go home if we understand how to?"

"Yes, that's right. Look, my parents at times can be wonderful people, I've seen it…" Mandy now started to cry, "but they don't know how to stop themselves. Their cigarettes, booze and drugs always come first, they come before me, they always have. I can't believe that they will ever change and even if they could, why should I allow them the option. They don't deserve it!"

There was silence, all were horrified by what Jason was capable of. Oliver took in a deep breath and ran his hand through his hair, this child had so much pressure on her shoulders.

"Wait," Oliver was curious, "so what you are saying is that you can bend Limbo and so can Jane. You feel like you were chosen to help everyone back, is that right?"

"Yes," Mandy softly answered.

"Then why is Jane and I here, why can she bend Limbo like you can?"

"The voice told me that she was sent here for her own reasons. But sadly, also because she would now be the one that would take over from me. I chose not to allow anyone their understanding of Limbo. I was not giving the people here a chance to learn and evolve and return."

"Why wouldn't you teach others, I understand not allowing your parents to leave but why not everyone else?" Otto asked.

"When Colin left I was broken up. He was the only one here that fought for me. Others helped but he was the only one who took me in. When I told him about Limbo, when I slowly told him what the voice was telling me he left. He left without a goodbye. I know that he wanted to take Mary and I with him, but I told him that it didn't work like that."

"Work like what?" Jane asked.

"We all come from a different time of the world. Colin thought that he and Mary could leave Limbo together, but you can't unless you want to leave. Even if Mary and Colin understood how to leave Limbo at the same time they would both separately leave back to the time that they were originally from. Time is not like how we know it, it happens all at once. It is not the past, present and future, there is only the now. Everything is happening at the same moment."

"We are all living at different time frames on earth, different years, is that what you are saying?" Oliver was absolutely intrigued.

"Yes, that is correct," Mandy turned to Jane. "Please Jane you don't understand, if you keep allowing these people to leave like you have been doing then there will be no one left. I will be alone with my mother and Jason and I don't want to be left alone, please."

"But I don't know what I am doing that is helping them all to leave, I honestly don't! Mandy you know how to go back so you can leave Limbo whenever you like, even if you leave your parents behind. It will be okay; the voice tells you that."

"No, it won't be! When you realise Jane how to leave, when you harness that power within yourself you start to bend Limbo. Others like Colin, Sam, Cindy, Stacey and Alana as soon as they clearly understood they had to leave, they had no choice about it, it was instant. Colin was drunk at the time and when he was sober he vanished. The others vanished instantly as soon as it became clear to them. The thing is that if you leave Jane, then you are choosing to leave us all behind and you seal our fate. None of us can leave after you go, we will be lost forever."

"Wait a minute!" Otto interrupted. "You're saying that if she leaves before us we are stuck here forever. Why can't you help us out of here? You just said that you could bend Limbo too."

"I no longer possess the power to help others to leave, Jane does. I can leave and all I can do is tell you what I know. I abused my right by not doing what I was meant to do. I am afraid that if you leave Jane we will all be doomed."

"Doomed is a bit harsh!" Otto corrected. "So, we all have to leave before Jane leaves?"

"Yes," Mandy sadly agreed.

"Holy shit!" Oliver sat up annoyed. "So, I'm dead and married to a woman that can send me back to my life giving me a second chance, but I can't go back to see my son because everyone here will be lost forever unable to return! This is just too much, screw this it I'm having a scotch!"

"Pour two mate, you're not the only one that needs it!" Otto begged as he watched Oliver storm off to the kitchen.

Jane just sat back in the chair trying to comprehend all of this information that Mandy was loading them with. Mandy had really grown up in Limbo, she was wise beyond her years. Jane wondered why she was the one that had been chosen to help the residents of Limbo back. It was hard enough to try and know what to do to get herself home.

"Jane, listen to me!" Mandy instructed. The boys had headed to the kitchen and Mandy whispered to her. "If you try and get people to understand and they don't listen to you then they will stay here. But if you decide to leave us behind then Limbo does not continue, we will all die. The second chance will be taken away from us all. Our fate will seal itself, everyone who is still in Limbo will die if you leave."

"But you told me that you and I weren't dead, that we were the only ones still alive! If I leave here, then won't you be safe?"

"I am alive, like I said in some form and you will send me back. I'm scared that my body will be messed up so much that I will never be the same. I don't want to go back to that! I won't! Everyone else will continue the fate that they were dealt. They will die, but I will be something that I can't guarantee. Jason messed me up so badly that day, there is no way that I could survive what he had done to me. I will be physically and mentally scarred beyond repair! Please Jane," Mandy was so afraid to return.

Jane was also scared to think how she herself would be in the real-world if she returned. Was she hurt as well? The last thing she remembered was that both her and Oliver had been involved in a small accident but was it more than what she was remembering. Then Jane thought about Alex. All that she cared about was getting back to him, no matter what she returned to.

"I can't stay here Mandy, I just can't. My son needs me," she watched Mandy's face drop. "I don't even know how I was able to help

Alana and Stacey. I didn't know what was happening at the time, it was just happening out of my control. It can't be me, it just can't be."

Mandy wiped the tears from her eyes, she felt like she had said too much. If she went on to tell Jane, the core true laws of Limbo and how it really worked then she was just going to leave them all anyway. She would be like all the others and leave her there to rot, not knowing what would become of her.

"What else does the voice say to you Mandy, is he ever repetitive in what he tries to tell you?"

"The voice tells me the same things over and over again until I remember, but the one thing he always tells me is to leave. He constantly assures me that I will be safe and that it is fine for me to leave, but I can't."

"Why don't you trust him?"

"Because every time I trust someone they hurt me, and I'm tired of being hurt all of the time. Limbo can send you crazy Jane, maybe I am just hearing voices in my head because I am crazy."

Mandy appeared exhausted. Jane could not imagine what her life had been like. This poor child having to grow up quicker than she was supposed to, she was incapable of trusting people anymore.

Jane pulled her in tight and hugged her with all of her might, "It's going to be okay, I promise you."

Mandy gently smiled within Jane's grasp, "I know you want to believe that everything will be fine Jane. I thank you for trying, but you can't promise me that. You just don't know, just like I don't."

It was true, Jane had no idea how all of this was going to turn out. In her hands she held the fate of everyone that was left here in Limbo, it was fearful not to understand the power that she possessed.

CHAPTER 25

Loving unconditionally is loving without judgement.

Camilla was a soulful woman, she was a child of God and everything she did was for her maker. In the real-world she had been blessed with five beautiful daughters who used to visit her often and two handsome sons, one of which still lived with her at home. She loved them all very much, but she always had a soft spot for Frank. He was the one that took care of her every day and lived with her in their original family home together. She knew his secrets and although many in their congregation also knew his secrets they seemed accepting and loving of him.

Living a long hard life, Camilla married her husband Stan when she was very young. Stan was a bit older and wiser than she was. For decades she obeyed his every command and allowed his constant beatings. Twenty years ago, when she was sixty-one years old she realised that her husband was a violent narcissist. Growing up as she did she never really knew much about anything. Her parents never told her about life or what people could be like, she was just taught to obey her husband and to do whatever he wished of her.

Camilla had learnt all by herself throughout her life how horrible people can be. Through all of the bullying and harsh ways that she and her family were treated because their skin was different, because she was a woman. Things had changed now that she was older. Camilla had watched over time the change towards black people, the change towards women and the change towards people that were different.

Stan was a very disciplined man who used the old ways on their children and on Camilla. Everything was always about him and when it wasn't he would explode until everyone conformed to his many demands. He was able to manipulate his family and he had this constant hold over them. Camilla lived daily with a man that made her feel not good enough. But times were changing, and Camilla was changing.

After the decades that Camilla had spent with Stan, she realised that her husband was not who she thought he was. It had taken her a long time to understand that Stan was a manipulator and a narcissist. She was expected to be the perfect mother, the perfect wife and whatever he wanted he got because that is just the way it was. Not anymore. Not now that Camilla was learning how people who loved each other behaved. Had Stan ever really loved her or was it just all for convenience? She was a very young girl when she met Stan, the infatuation towards him had blinded her from what love truly is meant to be.

There is only so much that one person can take. Although Camilla was a woman of God she was still human, and this beautiful, joyful soul had many secrets. All of her children loved their father, but they knew his ways. None of them were happy with the way that he continued to treat their mother, they knew it was manipulating and many of them begged her to leave.

But Camilla did not want to leave, this was her home, this was her community, and this was her life. Why should she leave? For the first time in her life she took control of her own destiny and that of her husbands. Even though the death of her husband came as a shock to the whole family, it was not a shock to her. There is only so much a person can take before they snap.

Camilla cried deeply at Stan's funeral and she mourned the loss of her soulmate, but his death was by her hands. Day by day she did exactly what he wanted. She cooked for him, cleaned for him and she kept everything in perfect order just as he liked it. In those very moments that she fed him wholesome and loving meals, she slowly poisoned him until the day came that his body could no longer deal with the over load of toxins. Believing that she had every right to take from him what he had taken from her; her freedom, her life. It was now time for her to start living.

Camilla was a very religious person and believed in all things that were good. She also knew that her son Frank was not right in his mind. Camilla took it upon herself to be the one that God had chosen to change the wrongs in his life and make them right, just as she had done with Stan.

God's law was the only law. In the Bible she knew that being gay was wrong. Stan, when he was alive wanted to throw Frank out of the house and disown him, but Camilla knew that her son just needed some guidance and divine intervention. After begging Stan to have some compassion for Frank he finally agreed that he could stay in the house.

Their community and congregation had lovingly accepted Frank just as he was, which was a gift. Due to this acceptance Stan eventually did not feel the need to repel Frank. Stan's name was no longer being tarnished. Camilla thanked God that the times were changing and that the world was becoming more accepting, especially now that it had allowed her son solace in their family home. It gave her time to find a way to cleanse him.

It had been nearly eighteen years since Stan had passed. Although Camilla believed that she could still save Frank from his evil thoughts and ways, deep down in her heart she had the knowing that he would never change. Instead of allowing him his life and his choices, instead of accepting him like so many others had done she could not. The bible clearly states that what he was doing was against God, it was sinful.

If you were against God, then you were against her and you were never going to see heaven. Camilla knew that Frank was having a relationship with a man, secretly sneaking around behind her back scared of receiving her judgement. Camilla was living in a world of torment. The heartache she was suffering brought so much pain to her daily life. As she slowly grew older, the more tired she became. She realised that maybe she had to take matters into her own hands once again.

Frank was always going to be the same way, he couldn't change. Camilla had tried her best over her life to save his soul, so he could return to his home in heaven when he eventually passed. It had been her life's duty to make sure that her son was safe when he passed and returned into the arms of his maker. Sadly, she had failed. This meant that he would in no way return to his home. It was one of the greatest sins to be gay and she knew that she no longer had the energy, or the power of prayer left inside of her to fix Frank. How sad it made her feel.

Camilla was now eighty-one years old and, in a wheelchair. She was limited to what she could and couldn't do, but in her mind, she was strong and vibrant. There were many different plans that she played over in her head of how she would save her son. The final plan.

She remembered the day that this one idea kept coming up over and over again. Camilla sat outside in the sun with a blanket over her legs wondering when Frank would return home. Crying she thought about her life and what she had endured, as she cried she placed her hands over her face for a few moments, welcoming the darkness. Slowly she lowered her hands, grabbed a tissue and wiped her eyes. There was only one choice left to make, she had to follow through with the plan that her thoughts were creating, it was the only way.

Camilla's plan was that she herself had already in her life committed one of the greatest sins, she had slowly and knowingly murdered her husband by poisoning him to death. By doing this she had agreed that her soul would already be doomed to hell after her own death. She had accepted this outcome; her life had given her such peace after Stan's passing. No more pain and no more beatings, her mind was set free of his demands and containment. It had been worth it. After making this deal with the devil eighteen years ago, Camilla would not allow both her and Frank's soul to be sacrificed. She would save him.

Camilla took her time with her plans, desperate for them to work. Although she was physically restricted in the things that she could do she knew that this time she would not just take Franks life, she would take her own also. Camilla wanted the two of them to go together. She would sacrifice herself and she would take her sons life knowing that he would be sent straight to heaven because he was

212

murdered. He was innocent and innocent souls are always saved. He would be set free.

Frank was a smoker, another trait that Camilla did not enjoy, but she was accepting and allowed this one obsession in his life. Compared to the other things that he was doing it was something that she looked passed and understood his addiction to it. It was his release for being the way that he was. Camilla picked up Frank's lighter that he had left on the counter and placed it into her cardigan pocket.

The day came, Camilla was sad hanging her head low for the entire day, but she was ready. Making sure that the day was a special one she pampered Frank with all of his favourite foods and never said a bad word or a smug remark when he lit up a cigarette. She allowed him to sneak off and see his boyfriend behind her back, unbeknown to Frank that it would be his last time. When he returned home for a hearty roast, Camilla asked him about his day. Still he did not allow her the truth. Camilla didn't mind that Frank did not trust her with his secrets, being a mother, it was her job to know everything about her children. That's just what mother's do.

That night when Frank finally fell asleep, Camilla pulled out the lighter of Frank's from her cardigan pocket. Lighting up a cigarette, she puffed on it slowly enjoying its deep rich flavours. Maybe she was the one who was hiding all of the secrets.

Slowly and quietly she went into Frank's bedroom and placed the burning cigarette near Franks hand on his bed. She sat there in her wheel chair as she watched the cigarette start to burn the bed covers.

Camilla then wheeled herself back quickly to her bedroom locking the door behind her, making her way towards her bed she lifted herself up onto her bed laying herself down peacefully. She closed her eyes allowing the sleeping pills to continue to slowly take effect as they had done with Frank.

Of course, she had given him a lot more than what was recommended. It would be horrifying for her to think that Frank would wake up during the fire. For Camilla she took the sleeping pills at a much lower dose not caring if the inferno that was about to rage through her room caused her physical pain. Deep down she felt like she deserved this end, the agonising pain and all.

How at peace she was at this moment as the smoke began to pour underneath her door. She began to cough from inhaling it. Slowly she could feel herself drifting away into a silent slumber which slowed her breathing down. Instead she began to take in the smoke like she was smoking a cigarette and welcomed it instead of rejecting it.

Her mind began to drift away, and she felt safe. Although she knew where her fate was heading, nothing was going to take this freedom away from her. She was saving her sons soul and she knew that she had won, her job was complete.

The next morning Camilla woke inside her home on her bed as if she had slept peacefully all night long. The smell of bacon and eggs wafted under her bedroom door instead of the smell of burning debris. Slightly confused Camilla managed to wake herself from her dazed state and lift herself into her wheelchair. Unlocking her bedroom door, she headed towards the kitchen. Frank was cooking her breakfast and he was singing joyfully. Camilla looked around the house and she stared inside Franks bedroom that was fine and intact with no signs of any fire damage.

Frank, after having the best sleep he had ever had in his entire life was exhilarated by the strong inviting smell of the forest. The morning breeze that filled his lungs brought joy to his heart without him even knowing it. He had not noticed the brand-new view that now displayed itself from their front lounge room window. The misty and airy site of a forest that once before never existed to them until now.

This was the moment that Camilla discovered that they were both living in Limbo. It was the moment that she felt God took justice upon her for all of the terrible things that she had done. Frank was stunned when Camilla showed him the forest view out the front of their lounge room window. Limbo was now their new residence.

Slowly they discovered what Limbo was. Camilla started to have her nightmares, this place was her hell. Limbo was a dungeon that she had sent both herself and her son Frank to. How could she ever forgive herself for what she had done? Her plans of saving him from a nightmare only created a different one. The only thing that eased her mind was that they still had each other.

CHAPTER 26

An ending is secretly just a new beginning.

F ather James had not noticed any changes to Limbo since he had last seen everyone in the street the day before. He was curious if Mandy had done as she said she was going to do and tell Jane and Oliver everything she knew about Limbo. He slowly limped down the street crossing over the road heading towards the forest. It was still very early in the morning. The forest was extra misty today and it made the forest cooler, but Father James liked its mysteriousness.

Watching he saw Mandy escape out of her bedroom window making her way to Jane and Oliver's house. Oliver let her inside. Father James made his way gradually to his favourite spot within the forest, which was where the old fallen hollow log was. He enjoyed sitting peacefully upon it as he listened to the various sounds of nature.

Limbo was definitely more intense than life. Father James was saddened that so many of Limbo's captives were reduced to numbing themselves or taking their own lives to try and leave Limbo. Why didn't they just look for the reason, the reason why they were there in the first place. Luckily Limbo is graceful and kind. It can see through any human dysfunctional thought allowing its laws to assist everyone to see the truth. Well he hoped that much for all of them anyway. Each person had a choice, what they chose was up to them.

Jane ran through the coverage of the forest making her way to the old fallen hollow log where she would usually stretch her body. Today she noticed Father James sitting there.

"Good morning Father James, how are you?"

"Oh Jane! You startled me. I am very well thank you very much."

"I'm sorry Father."

"No worries Jane, I was just listening to the birds that's all, they are so magical."

Jane went and sat down on the log with him.

I've never really spoken to Father James in depth before. It would be nice to have a conversation with him.

"You know, I was just thinking the same thing," Father James answered Jane's thoughts.

Jane was taken back by this priest. She was wondering if she had said what she thought she was thinking out loud or not. No, she definitely had said it inside of her head. Father James smiled at her.

"You seem very wise Father, like you know more than what you are saying. You knew about Mandy."

"Yes, I did," he answered her without any delay. "I came here today specially to talk with you Jane, it seems as though it is time."

"Time for what?"

"Well to be honest there really is no time here. I just used that word because it is what the human experience has become comfortable with. Time is actually linear, it is all happening at once moving along the same frequency but on different threads."

Jane's mind started to race, his words had confused her.

"Time happens all at once, how is that possible?"

"The human mind is not strong enough to understand what really is," Father James giggled. "If makes me laugh how people are so intent on trying to understand the universe and God when they are beings that cannot withstand that knowledge. Only in death and when you have been set free from your human shells, that you are able to comprehend and contain the knowledge of what truly is."

"But why is that, why can't we understand. Why do we live a life?" Jane wanted Father James to reveal all he knew to her.

"For the experience of course! We have been given life to be able to experience limitation, to experience choice, feelings, emotions, and to learn how to GROW the human experience into something that is greater than itself. Evolution my dear."

Jane paused for a moment, even though what Father James was saying was so intense it actually made sense to her. She would never question the presence of something greater ever again. A being, God, or a knowledge that was more than what she was in her humanness seemed definite now. Limbo proved it.

"Why are we here Father, why am I trapped inside this place away from my son unable to be with him?"

"Oh, Jane you are not trapped, and you never have been," Father James grinned.

"What?"

Father James took a deep breath and squirmed a little closer to Jane, "Dear Jane you have always been able to leave you just didn't want to."

Jane was certain that what he was saying was not true, of course she wanted to leave. She became upset that maybe she had subconsciously chosen to be away from her son for such a long time.

"Jane please don't be hard on yourself, you just don't understand that's all."

"What is it that I don't understand Father?"

"What you don't understand is that you are not away from Alex at all. Like I said before time is linear. Your consciousness at this very moment is on this thread in Limbo and not the thread that you are used too, which is what everyone here seems to call the real-world. All you have to do is to turn down the thread that you want to be travelling along," as Father James answered Jane he used both of his hands as a visual explanation by using them in a crossing motion.

"I don't have to be here, I can leave?" She asked.

"Of course, everyone can. Here's the thing, because you are using your human brain your understanding is that you are actually trapped, but you are not. You have given yourself this time here in Limbo because your true-self, your light or soul, if that is what you want to call it, can see your future. In this future you will not be completing the path that you have been destined to accomplish if you continue this way. You have signed a contract of what this lifetime has to teach you but on your current earthly journey you have been overtaken by the ego. There have been many times that your light has tried to encourage you to return to your purpose, but you have continued to ignore its cries."

Jane could think of many wonderful opportunities in her life that she had chosen to let go of or shut down. It was like Father James had this ability to inject his thoughts into her mind so that she could see all of the times she had chosen to give up on herself and her abilities.

"The world needs you Jane. It needs you to experience and be the person that you want to experience in this life time so that you may evolve as a soul. Evolution and growth is the most important facet to the human experience. If you deter from your vision and make the wrong choices, then death with take you. You will then be given another birth and another life to try and experience the things that you had originally wanted to experience. Limbo is a place that you have chosen instead of resetting your soul into another birth or life. Your soul is pleased with what it has achieved but the potential it can see excites it and it wants to remain as it is in this human form. Do you understand?"

"Strangely it makes sense to me, I don't understand how you know all of this?"

"I am the keeper of this Limbo realm, I am James the prophet. I have lived many human lives and I have done so to the point where my experiences have made me enlightened. I no longer have to live as a human to evolve. I have evolved enough that my vibration now matches that of our makers, which is the goal of all souls. I can be anywhere, do anything and enjoy being a guide to those who are learning. You are a higher levelled soul Jane just like Mandy. You both have the ability to stay or to go whenever you have decided that you have understood the reason for your momentary pause in your human life."

"What about Oliver and the rest of them here, who are they and why are they stuck?"

"None of them are truly stuck Jane, each of them has you to guide them. With you giving them clarity, it gives them an opportunity to step outside of their lives and to look over it, like a preview I guess. It is up to them to either forgive themselves and others or to accept the consequences if they choose their ego instead of their light."

Jane could not understand why she had been chosen, "what is so important about me, how can I give them this clarity?"

"Each person here has done something that has shaded their hearts and souls into a place where they have doomed themselves to death. It may be because they have refused to forgive another person who has done them wrong. But in most cases, they have refused to forgive themselves for the things that they have done in their own lives. Enlightenment comes only through forgiveness. You can't experience life to its fullest without forgiveness. Each person here has to understand the law of Limbo and that is to see themselves for who they truly are, and that is eternal."

"But how do you forgive others or yourself for things if they are terrible, terrible things?" Jane found it difficult to understand why people should forgive those who cause pain.

"A human body and mind is a creation of its surroundings and most importantly it's thoughts. The ego plays a big part here. You can either be controlled by your light or by your human ego. On earth balance is the key. A human ego is very important to the experience of life, but it many cases individuals give it the power of control which can do devastating things.

"Forgiveness is what brings the balance back. If you cannot bring the balance back through forgiveness, then you will have to suffer the consequences. You must live with the choices that you have made in that particular human life while the ego is allowed to be in charge. Usually ego dominance in a human experience will either lead to death or it will be traded as a long life that is of no worth to the expansion of a soul. A bit like a waste of time for a soul that wants to become enlightened. If you really looked at those people who do terrible things, do you think they want to be like that? They don't! They just don't know how to be different, that's why forgiveness and teaching others through love is so very important."

"What about those people who die young, and what about all the sadness in the world. How do you explain that?"

"Everyone has their own contract, those souls that have died young are mostly higher levelled souls. These souls do not need a full length of life to experience the knowledge they need to attain in that lifetime. Sometimes they agree to live short lives so that they can make sure that other souls can be encouraged to attain their knowledge in their current lifetime."

"Are you saying that if someone loses a person they love very young, like a child, it is because that child has agreed to a short life. That they have done so, so that the experience can help the people around them? That seems crazy, how can suffering help someone?"

"Jane everything that is, is perfect. There are no mistakes. Although the human experience sees things as good and bad, there is always a reason that in the end it is for the greater good. Everything happens so that each soul is constantly pointed in the right direction. This is so they can obtain the knowledge they have asked to obtain in that particular life, it's that simple really."

"So how do I tell everyone here how to go home?"

"You don't, they already know Jane," Father James stood up and stretched his sore leg. "All you do is help them understand their life at this moment from another point of view. Like Alana for instance. You see, we all get stuck in life because we blind ourselves from the answers that are so freely available to us. All they have to do is step outside of their normal thinking. They need to understand as they look at themselves deeply what is needed for them to be the person they were always created to be. So Jane, now you know the answers to Limbo.

Remember if you choose to leave, which you can do at any time, if you leave then this particular Limbo will vanish."

"I can't leave the others here, I can't!" Jane became upset.

"Jane if they choose in their final moments to stay and they allow their ego to rule their life over love, over forgiveness and over their true paths then death is what they need."

Jane stood up, "I can't just give up on them like that!"

"If you don't go soon Jane then you will be giving up on yourself, and the life that you need to experience! Sometimes it is better for souls who are caught in the ego to just start over."

There was a loud noise and great movement within the earth which shocked Jane. It was that vibration sound again and Jane was afraid that she had started the process for herself to leave without even knowing.

"Please Father…"

"Don't worry Jane it is not for you!"

Jane was surprised, if Limbo was not changing to send her back, then who.

"JANE!" A voice yelled from behind her.

As she turned she saw Otto. There he was standing behind a large glass wall just like the wall that Alana had been stuck behind when she had seen her reality in the real-world.

Otto began to smile at her, "I have seen it Jane, I understand now!"

Otto had heard the whole conversation between Father James and Jane, he had understood and chosen to return to his life. It was now time for him to leave.

"Thank you so much Jane," Otto yelled, he then turned to Father James, "thank you!"

Limbo then took Otto. He vanished leaving Jane and Father James to be covered in the pouring rain that came bucketing from the sky. Limbo had refreshed another soul back to where they belonged. Jane did not understand. This time she had not been a part of Otto's past review as she was with Alana, or was she?

"Otto has overheard us Jane and he no longer needs you or me. Everyone leaves differently from Limbo, they all understand in different ways. Be happy for him that he has understood enough to make the right choice!"

The earth stopped shaking and the vibrating noise settled to silence. The rain continued to pour. Jane stared at the empty forest where the leaves of the trees were draining water onto the very ground that Otto had once been standing. That's it, he was gone. She was happy for him, but she would miss his infectious and annoying personality.

CHAPTER 27

Learning from mistakes is what makes us stronger.

It was so very dark and Otto had no idea where he was. It took him a few seconds to realise that he had his hands covering his eyes, when he took them away he almost peed his pants. He was sitting in his police car leaning over the steering wheel. Outside the car he could hear Neil talking on the phone. He had returned to the moment after the bust, just after Neil had asked him to become a part of their dodgy, money stealing plan that he had agreed to. This was his second chance.

His thoughts went to Jane and Mandy, there was a guilt that he had left them behind. In Limbo Otto had re-experienced his last moments right before he left. It was like a movie playing around him, but this time he remembered how his fate really ended.

During the shoot-out under the bridge where Otto was able to escape into the woods, he had instead seen his true reality. All four of them; Neil, Graham, Matt and himself died that day. A local gang had followed the police officers after becoming suspicious. They had been watching them meet up to split their cash and drugs for the last three months. The gang intersected this deal killing the four officers and taking their cash, leaving their bodies to be found by a taxi driver.

The news had promoted all four off duty officers as heroes, describing the incident as a failed under cover take-down of an aggressive gang. The funeral was dramatic. Otto watched on as he saw his wife unable to cope with the fact that he had been murdered.

Knowing that he had been killed because he had agreed to do something unthinkable broke Otto's heart. He had made one stupid mistake, but he was adamant that he was going to change it. Limbo had offered him this second chance so that he could make things right.

As Otto sat in the police car he had thought over and over in his head how he was going to get out of this situation. Suddenly he no longer had to worry. It was strange, he felt as if Limbo was still talking to him, it had become a part of him. He now embraced and understood that no matter how bad things seemed to be there is always an answer to staying true to yourself.

Otto stayed with Neil as he had done previously, and his life seemed to play out exactly the same. The only thing that changed was right after they arrived at the pick-up point underneath the bridge, a swarm of police cars flooded the area. The huge amounts of unexpected police officers scared off most of the gang members that were preparing to jump. They arrested all of the unaware rogue officers, all except one.

Otto stood there with his hands free of cuffs as he watched the unbelievable scenario take place underneath that bridge. Gang members that were not quick enough to leave were arrested. Neil, Matt and Graham were escorted in handcuffs into fellow officer's police cars as they were taken to jail. Otto's Boss, Sargent William Smith had acted quickly from the phone call that Otto had made to him moments after he had returned from Limbo. It was the only real window he had to try and get William's attention without causing suspicion.

Luckily Sargent William already had eyes on Matt and Graham. He had been building a case against them for months hoping that Neil and Otto would not become a part of it. Otto breathed a big sigh of relief as Sargent William patted him on the shoulder.

"Good Job Otto!"

Otto looked over to see Neil staring at him and shaking his head from the back window of a police vehicle. Otto did not even flinch, for he knew that he had saved all of their lives, they would be dead if he had not intervened. He thought about his beautiful wife and his baby at home, he had not seen them for so long.

"Hey Sarge, can I go?"

"Mate, go home to your family. Come in late tomorrow and then do the paperwork. After that I want you to take a week off, you deserve it."

Otto nodded. There were no words that could describe how Otto felt when he got home that afternoon. He wrapped his arms around his wife and kissed his daughter. They ate a beautiful meal together and Otto could not stop staring at his girls. He was the luckiest man alive.

At the end of the night he excused himself to take a long hot shower. He wept uncontrollably on the showers tiled floor as he gently whispered under his breath, "Thank you," to Limbo. Life was a gift and he would never do anything to jeopardise it again.

CHAPTER 28

We are all limitless.

Otto was now gone, another had returned to the real-world. Jane was happy that Otto had finally found his way home and she closed her eyes praying that whatever it was that had brought him here was forgiven. When she turned to look back at Father James he was also gone.

The rain was saturating through her clothes and she decided that it was her time now. There was no reason for her to stay for she had gotten out of Limbo exactly what she needed. The insight that had grown in her soul was magical and instead of hating this place she respected it for what it was, time to heal. Her mind was clear and focused, no longer was it cluttered with lies like it once was in the real-world. Her body felt strong. It was the best she had felt in years and she thanked Limbo for it. She was at peace.

The sky began to change. Jane ran back to her house; this rain was very different, it was harder and stronger than usual. It was a warning sign. Jane had subconsciously set in motion the final exit to Limbo. The storm brewing in the distance was like a timer ticking away until the final siren. It was now up to Jane to make sure that she did as she was meant to do, offer everyone who was left the guidance to leave. The choice then was up to each person individually. They could return to their lives by choosing to love or destroy themselves with their ego.

Oliver opened the front door just before Jane reached it grabbing her in from the monstrous rain.

"Jane what's going on this doesn't feel right?"

"It is different," she said as she grabbed a towel from the laundry. She wiped her faced which made some of her make-up smudge.

"Oliver something is happening, and I think I started it."

"What is this Jane?"

"It's the end Oliver."

"What have you done!" Mandy cried out from the stairwell. Her eyes were so big and wide.

There was no time for fighting and Jane was tired of putting everyone else first before her son, "Mandy we are leaving!"

"No!" She returned.

"I am leaving and so is Oliver, he is a part of me and my healing and so he is leaving with me. You have to leave, you must!" Jane grabbed Mandy on both shoulders staring into her eyes, "it is time Mandy. You know what will happen if you don't let go."

"So, this is it then," Mandy said quietly, the storm outside was howling. "I'm afraid Jane, so afraid."

"You do not have to be afraid, I am here, and all will be well on the other side. I have to go, I must give everyone an opportunity to leave before the storm comes."

Mandy nodded and both Mandy and Oliver watched Jane leave. Jane ran to Camilla and Frank's house first. Frank opened the door.

"Frank…"

"I know Jane, we can feel it. Thank you for all that you have done for us."

"Done for us!" She heard Camilla screaming from inside. "You have doomed us all to hell you selfish girl!" She wheeled her wheel chair close to the front door pushing Frank out of the way. "What do you say about that Jane, you have allowed us no more time, nothing! What will happen to us?" Camilla growled at her.

"Well," Jane looked at Camilla, "that is completely up to you isn't it? I'm tired of having to baby sit you all while you decide. It's time you finally get on with it and face your own demons. Good luck Frank!" Jane turned, and she left.

As Jane headed back down the street she ran past Father James' house and watched him tip his hat to her from his front window. Branch debris started to toss around the street as Jane ran. The storms intensity was growing. Firstly, she would go to Mary and Daniel's house and then Jason and Louisa's.

As she ran past her own house Oliver and Mandy followed behind her. They decided that it would be safer staying with Jane. Mary and Daniel would not answer but she could hear them arguing inside. They had chosen to ignore her, and so Jane moved on.

Jason came out of the front of his house before Jane had reached it and so she stopped at the front fence.

"You have to leave!" Jane yelled through the rain.

"You have done this you fucking bitch!" Jason screamed at her pointing, "that brat of a kid has told you."

Jason charged through the rain and down his front path as his eyes burnt from the rains force. His anger was like fire, but Jane was not afraid, all she wanted to do was to go home.

"Aarrgghh!" Jason yelled grabbing Jane unexpectedly by the throat with his right hand. Jane's reaction was to grab his wrist with both of her hands. He began to lift her from the ground, the wet rain making her grip slip. She was struggling for air; her throat was being crushed and the force of the storm made her shut her eyes. Oliver was no match as he began to hit at him, Jason just pushed him away with ease. His strength was unbelievable, it was the drugs again. Mandy stood there screaming, begging for him to stop. Louisa was now outside doing the same.

Jane continued to struggle. She was doing what she thought she was supposed to do to survive and then she realised that she no longer had to. She stopped her human thinking. In that moment she understood that she was the storm, she was its power, she was Limbo and Jason was no match for her. Immediately she stopped struggling. Letting go of her grip on his wrist, she lifted both her palms to his chest and forced an energy pulse from her body onto his. It pushed Jason all the way back to the entrance of the house, smashing his body into its exterior wall. He slumped to the ground unsure of what had just happened.

The bricks of the house were broken and cracked, and Louisa could do nothing but cover her mouth in disbelief. Jane walked briskly down the front path, fearlessness on her face for she no longer had time for the same old crap.

"I am leaving!"

Jane turned towards Oliver and Mandy, Mandy helping Oliver up from the puddles on the ground. Jane looked back at Jason and Louisa, "WE are leaving!"

"What about us?" Louisa begged as she moved over to Jason and bent down to comfort him.

"Mum please," Mandy begged, "Come with me…Please!"

Louisa looked up at her daughter and she began to cry, she was afraid, and she didn't know what to do.

"Don't leave me babe, I need you," Jason muttered as he lay hunched by her side.

"Mum," Mandy said again. Mandy went over to her mother, passing Jane as she went and knelt by her side. "Please come back with me."

"I won't go back if you are with us, you are nothing but a trouble maker!" Jason's harsh words continued to hurt Mandy.

Louisa cried and cried as she shook her head holding onto Jason. Mandy could see that even in this moment she was choosing Jason over her. What was Mandy to do, her heart was broken. What kind of a life would she be returning to without her mother. Mandy thought that maybe it would be best if all three of them just allowed Limbo's storm to consume them. The world might be a better place without them all.

"Mandy," Jane called her name as she moved closer to her, "don't choose because of them, choose for yourself!"

Mandy stood and moved towards Jane but in that moment a giant glass wall split them apart. Oliver and Jane on one side and Mandy, Louisa and Jason on the other.

"Jane!" Mandy yelled. "Don't leave me!"

Jane yelled Mandy's name over and over as she repeatedly banged on the glass wall. Oliver came over to do the same, he had no idea what was happening, and he was afraid for Mandy's safety.

"Jane please, you can stop this I know you can, don't leave me!"

Jane did not know what to do. She stopped banging on the wall and instead stepped back and tried to concentrate while the wind and rain became fiercer and fiercer around her. Closing her eyes, she focused. She pushed the fingertips of her right hand into the glass wall pushing them further and further inside until her hand made it through to the other side.

Mandy grabbed hold of it as if it were her safety net. The two girls held hands just staring at each other, Mandy's tears flowing down her face as Jane watched the fear in her grow. The rain was beating down upon them, the wind was intense as they stood there looking at each other through the glass.

"Please," Mandy begged one last time sobbing.

"I will never leave you," Jane told her, but it was too late.

The storm grabbed Jane and Oliver ripping Mandy from her grip. All Jane could see was the world around her spinning as she tumbled and twirled. Oliver was screaming beside her. Jane was unsure if she was the one being taken by the storm or if Mandy had. Oliver and Jane could not make sense of what was happening until everything stopped and went black.

CHAPTER 29

Sometimes we don't know what we've got until it has gone and returned to us again.

BANG!

Jane jumped from fright and it took her a few moments to realise where she was. She was all dressed up again in that black number that had annoyed her every day she woke up in Limbo. But this time things were different. Looking around she understood that she was in the toilet cubicle at the awards night. She had returned to that very moment when she had covered her eyes trying to find a place of solace to hide inside of. That moment she remembered well, it was the lowest point of her life.

Adrenaline had pumped through her body from the shock of the toilet door slamming next to her, but that shock could not stop her joy knowing that she had finally made it home, back to the real-world.

Tearing up she busted through the toilet door, stepping out of that cubicle like she had released the world from her shoulders. The beautiful exotic woman that was standing at the sink jumped. That woman was Giselle. The last time Jane was here she was feeling like the world was crashing down on her, this time she felt more powerful than life itself. Jane was going to make sure that this woman knew that Oliver was her man.

"You're Oliver's wife, aren't you?" The woman spoke softly and seductively into the mirror.

"I sure am!" Jane happily answered, "And he is one hell of a guy. I'm so proud of him and his work!"

"Yes, yes he is good at what he does, very beautiful work, it's captivating."

"Captivating indeed, just like me!" Jane laughed.

Jane went to leave and then she stopped, turned around and said, "You know he is good at everything......everything!"

"Wait!" The woman made Jane stop, "Jane isn't it?"

"Yes," Jane's proud stance began to dip as she noticed that Giselle seemed different this time. How weird it was that she was now standing here more confident than ever, but Giselle was the one who appeared deflated.

"Jane, well this may seem strange but, well I noticed how wonderful both you and Oliver are together. The way he looks at you..." Giselle was uncomfortable but needing to tell Jane what she wanted to say. "What I mean is I love how much he loves you, how you love each other. I just wanted you to know that."

Jane was now saddened by the way Giselle was looking.

My goodness have I judged her all wrong.

The last time they were here she was certain that this woman was trying to steal her husband, but it was all in her head. Jane's body was flooded with this weird sensation like Limbo was still teaching her. It was telling her that the last time this moment happened she had turned it into something that it wasn't. The mind has this ability to create stories that were never real, and Jane had done that. Judged everyone and everything.

"Giselle, are you all right?"

"Oh, yes!" she answered, "I'm so sorry I have wanted to talk to you for so long, but I just haven't been able to."

"Talk to me, why?"

"Nothing, it's just silly," Giselle said as she moved uncomfortably.

Jane stepped closer to Giselle, "You can tell me, I won't bite."

"Well, Damien just told me that Oliver said no to going to Europe with him…"

"He did?"

"Well yes. It's hard for me Jane, I don't really know anyone here and Damien and I have only been married a year. When he goes away I just miss him so much. I just thought that maybe we could…. I don't know, get to know each other better." Giselle was afraid that she had said the wrong thing as Jane appeared surprised by her words.

Giselle looked away briefly as she fiddled with her handbag, "I know it sounds lame, but I'm not one for all these silly parties and going out. I just love how you and Oliver behave together, it reminds me of Damien and I. All the other friends we have are so fake and mean. Oh my, I think I'm making it worse!"

Jane just laughed, it was a good laugh and Giselle laughed too. Jane was blown away, this poor woman had been judged, hated, and used as a weapon against Oliver by her to make herself feel like she had the right to give up on her life. Jane was ashamed at how she had judged Giselle so completely without knowing her.

"I know what you mean about these functions," Jane agreed. "I'm really a pizza and tracksuit girl at heart, but I can't remember the last time I did that."

Giselle's shoulders dropped from her ears and the relief that swept over her was obvious. "Oh Jane, I have been so scared to talk to you for so long, I thought you were just out of my league."

"Out of your league?" Jane repeated. The two girls naturally moved closer towards each other.

"You're so refined," Giselle added.

Jane laughed, "Refined is definitely not how I would have described myself." Jane looked down to the ground as she shook her head.

"What is it Jane?" Giselle asked.

"I think that I misjudged you also."

"You did, how?"

Jane touched Giselle on the forearm, "I guess I thought you were just like all the other girls I knew. You're so beautiful, I think I just thought that you were...."

"A slut?"

"No!" Jane quickly rebutted.

"It's fine Jane I get that a lot. Look at me, most of the married men here tonight have been talking to my boobs instead of my face. All of them except Oliver of course!"

Jane and Giselle giggled together, and Jane just looked at Giselle smiling. "You know what Giselle, I would love to have you guys over for a pizza night, how does that sound?"

"I would absolutely love that Jane, there is only one rule though?"

"What's that?"

"No make-up! I hate it!"

"Done!"

The two girls felt so comfortable with each other that they embraced. The main bathroom door opened, and Sarah came in.

"There you are girl, I was wondering what was taking you so long. Here you are chit-chatting."

"Sarah, this is Giselle, Damien's wife."

"Oh yes Giselle, how are you?" They shook hands.

"I'm great thanks, Jane and I have been talking about our boys. Anyway, I really should get back, thanks for the talk Jane. Great to meet you Sarah," Giselle left the ladies room leaving Sarah and Jane alone.

Jane could not help but grab Sarah and squeeze her as tightly as she could, "I have missed you so damn much!" Jane squealed.

"What the hell is going on with you?" Sarah pulled her away. "Look I don't know what is happening, but Oliver just did the same thing at the table. It was like he had been gone for years and then came back. He was hugging and kissing us. I know these awards nights can get boring but for heaven's sakes, what is going on with you both?"

Jane started at Sarah as she spoke, "Oliver!" She yelled.

A group of women entered the ladies room giggling and talking loudly. Jane grabbed Sarah by the hand and pulled her quickly towards the exit, Jane even rudely pushed her way past the other women. She could not wait. Dragging Sarah back out to the main dining room where the awards night had been set up, she saw Oliver sitting at the table. Unable to contain her excitement she let go of Sarah's hand and ran towards him.

Oliver saw Jane coming in the distance and he stood quickly from the table with a smile on his face that was so big he could not contain his joy. Oliver started heading towards Jane. Jane moved even faster, maybe she was running. They embraced each other tightly. Oliver spun Jane around in his arms and after she landed they both stood there looking at each other with huge smiles on their faces.

"You know that she just went to the toilet, right?" Andy said to Oliver as he watched on at the two of them embracing.

Oliver and Jane just laughed at Andy's comment and Jane whispered gently, "We did it."

"No Jane, you did it."

"I want to go home," Jane tenderly said to Oliver.

"Let's go home my beautiful Jane and see our son!"

"What the hell is up with you two?" Sarah had finally caught up.

"I told Damien that I wasn't going to do the Europe job," Oliver wanted Jane to know that he had turned it down.

"It's okay, we will talk about it later," Jane said, and Oliver nodded. The two of them grabbed their coats from the backs of their chairs.

"Wait where are you going?" Andy asked. "It's not over yet."

"We have to go! I'm sorry Andy but something has come up and we have to get home," Oliver said ready to leave.

"Is everything well with Alex?" Sarah was worried.

"Oh, he's fine we just have to get home," Jane added.

They quickly said their goodbyes and Jane and Oliver went to leave. Jane waved to Giselle who returned a wave and a loving smile from her table across the room.

"What on earth was that?" Oliver couldn't help but grin "I thought she was the enemy."

"I don't know what you are talking about," Jane fluttered her eyelids as they both left arm in arm.

Andy and Sarah sat down exhausted by the carry on. Andy shrugged his shoulders, they had never seen the pair act like this before. "Maybe they are trying for another baby?" Andy said.

Sarah just gave him a death look and then whacked him on the chest, "Idiot!"

Andy thought it was a good explanation.

Jane and Oliver got into the car, the weather was just as bad as when they had first arrived.

"Another way home?" Oliver asked Jane.

"Definitely!"

The drive home was longer, but it did not worry the two of them. Instead the joy they both felt was so empowering and energetic. The thought that they would soon wrap their arms around Alex almost had Jane crying with excitement.

"I love you Jane," Oliver held her hand tight and looked quickly over to her.

"I love you too Oliver, now put your hands back on that wheel and stop perving on me. The weather is still horrible, and you need to concentrate."

Oliver smirked, it was the old Jane back. He could see the light pouring from her, it was life itself beaming from her skin. She was an amazing woman and he loved her with every inch of his being. They finally arrived home and for some reason it was bitter sweet. There was still that fear inside of them both that this was not real, and that Alex would not be in his bed fast asleep.

They jokingly fought their way through the garage door into the front lounge trying to squeeze through the door both at the same time. Grace was startled, it was too early for Oliver and Jane to be home, but as she came around the kitchen corner to her surprise it was them.

"What are you doing home so early?" Grace chirped.

"Mum!" Jane wrapped her arms around her mother and hugged her so very tight, "Is Alex asleep?"

"Yes, yes, he is, but..."

Jane started heading up the stairs. Oliver stood there happily looking at Grace which caused her concern, "Mum," he said as he grabbed her and planted a big kiss on her head.

"What the hell is wrong with you both? You're scaring me!"

Grace watched the two of them head up to see Alex. Jane in front of Oliver. Jane turned quickly around while halfway up the stairs and looked down at her mother, Oliver leaned out of the way.

"And don't think I don't know how many cookies you gave Alex tonight either mother!"

Jane pointed at her and smiled. Grace turned away with the guiltiest of looks upon her face. Oliver pushed Jane to hurry up the stairs and they both arrived at Alex's room. They were hesitant, but they slowly opened the door and peered in. There he was sound asleep in the darkness of his room. Jane covered her mouth, she couldn't believe that it was him. There was this feeling inside of Jane, one that she would never be able to explain, it was more than just relief. Oliver knelt by Alex's bed while Jane sat on the bed. Alex slowly opened his eyes.

"Mum, dad!" he sat up and Oliver and Jane hugged him. Jane began to kiss him all over his face. It was hard to stop the tears, she had missed him terribly.

"Mum what's wrong?" Alex asked.

"Nothing my sweet, nothing at all I just missed you."

"I missed you too," he said as the three just held each other for a few more minutes.

This was the very moment that Oliver and Jane had prayed for, for so very long. They were grateful to have this moment. Alex laid back down and although it was hard Oliver and Jane left him to sleep, closing the door behind them. They both stood outside of his doorway and hugged each other.

"I'm worried about Mandy," Jane whispered into Oliver's chest.

"So am I, but we will find her, somehow," Oliver reassured her.

Jane did not want to let him go, fear now took over from her joy. She had no idea what had happened to those left behind in Limbo, what had become of Mandy? The last thing Jane told her was that she would never leave her, but she did.

CHAPTER 30

*Never stop doing what you love. Be passionate with your
purpose and do what makes you happy, fearlessly!*

Life was different, it had changed. Jane had such a powerful
passionate feeling about her life now, but the dark shadow
of fear still continued to guilt her. Oliver and Jane both
found it hard to be normal, whatever that was. When they
first discovered that their electronics worked again it was like a couple
of children playing with toys. It didn't last long before the novelty wore
off.

Jane did not attend the soccer meeting that she was meant to
attend. Instead she quit all the PTA appointments and any future
commitments, going against the advice of Marianne. Jane was not
worried about what Marianne or what the other mothers thought of her,
let them talk. It was time for her to have purpose in her life and that
started with her trying to find Mandy.

Jane sat on the computer for most of her days trying to find some
evidence of the people they had known in Limbo. How silly that she
never knew any of their last names. Limbo withheld so much
information from them. There was always that thought that they were
all living in different times, maybe even in different worlds, who knew,
after what Jane had seen in Limbo anything was possible.

Then finally she found something, a small hope. A newspaper
article that was two years old. It was about a twelve-year-old girl who

had been beaten by her stepfather and left for dead. The stepfather had beaten the mother to death and then shot himself afterwards.

"Oliver, come look at this," Jane looked over at him.

Oliver came over from his side of the dining table and peered over Jane's shoulder. They had been looking for a couple of days and found nothing on Mandy. Oliver slowly read over the small newspaper article, it described how the girl had been in a coma for two years and was still to this day in a coma at a hospital in another state.

"What do you think, it could be her, couldn't it?"

"Maybe," Oliver said. "It sounds very much like the story she told us that day."

Jane looked up at him, "What should we do?"

"What was her last name, does it tell you?"

Jane looked through to the bottom and answered him, "Simpson, her name is Mandy Simpson."

"Look her up, for a photo or something."

Jane then put that name into the search engine and clicked on the images section.

"There!" Oliver pointed.

In front of them was a picture of Mandy. Jane clicked on the image and the picture took her to another website that had the news story about her family and their final moments. There was even a family photo of the three of them, Jane felt shivers go down her spine.

"Oh my God," she whispered.

Does this mean that Louisa and Jason are dead, did they not receive their second chance at life? Oh no, I left them for dead, how could I?

Jane had to turn away from the screen. Although Jason was a man who had done many horrible things, the thought that she had taken away his second chance made her feel sick in her stomach. What about Louisa, did she not deserve another chance also?

Oliver squeezed Jane's shoulder tightly, he came around and sat at the dining table. "You know that you did everything that you could. It was their choice to stay."

Jane was not convinced and instead just looked down towards the ground, "I killed them."

"No!" Oliver stopped her. "Jane, Mandy is still alive, and it is up to us now to find her and do something about it. You can't sit here and worry about what you could or couldn't have done. You gave them a choice and they took it. We couldn't have stayed there any longer. You did what had to be done and you should not feel guilty for that."

It was hard because Jane knew that he was right, she had given them the chance to change and they did not take it. After knowing how to leave Limbo there was no way that Jane could agree to stay there. They had to return to Alex.

"I know you're right Oliver, I do, but it doesn't stop the pain of it."

"Jane," Oliver moved closer, "Mandy is alive let's go get her."

"But how?"

"I don't know, but if she has no one left in her life then we need to be the ones that are her family."

"She's in a coma Oliver, it's been two whole years. She might never come out of it now that I have left her in Limbo all alone."

"Maybe she is just waiting for you to come and get her Jane."

Jane was amazed by Oliver, he truly was such a loving human being and he was exactly what she needed just at the right time, like always. How could she leave Mandy to rot in a hospital bed? She couldn't.

"But there would have to be someone paying for her care, surely."

"I don't know," Oliver said, "let's go and find out."

Jane smiled, "What about Alex?"

"No one gets left behind, not now Jane. Call your mother and tell her that she is coming interstate with us. She will love the spontaneity of it all!" He was right Grace loved to be whisked off at a moment's notice and by the next morning they were booked and ready to board a plane to take them to Mandy.

Jane was afraid. What if Mandy looked just as Mandy had feared she would look. Jane had felt responsible for allowing her own wants before the others. Her selfishness had caused Jason and Louisa's death and maybe even compromised Mandy's way of life, if she ever did wake up from her coma. Jane thought of Mandy brain damaged and needing care, why couldn't she get these horrible thoughts out of her head?

Oliver and Jane left Alex and Grace to enjoy the day and investigate together. Although Grace did not know why they were there or what Oliver and Jane were up to, she knew to trust her daughter. Her job was to create a wonderful day for her grandson in a new place that they had never explored before. Oliver and Jane headed for the local hospital, Jane's anxiety grew. They both approached the nurses desk and inquired about Mandy.

The nurse frowned, "Are you relatives of the patient?"

"Not relatives," Jane paused, "we are more like old friends."

"Just wait a minute please," the nurse went over to an older nurse and they spoke for a little while. The older nurse headed their way smiling as she lowered her glasses.

"You're here to see Mandy Simpson, is that correct?"

"Yes, we are," Oliver confirmed.

"Well, it's actually nice to see some new faces in here to visit her, you are…?"

"Oh, I'm Oliver and this is my wife Jane, we knew Mandy when she was younger, and we did not know about what had happened until yesterday. As soon as we heard we came right here."

The nurse smiled again, appearing to be happy with their answers. "Come and follow me," she said as she walked on in front of them. "Joe never told me about anyone else, it's been a long time. It's a shame that no one except Joe has come in to visit such a precious girl."

"Do you mean Papa Joe?" Jane asked.

"Yes, that's actually what most of the staff call him around here. He comes in everyday and sits with Mandy talking to her, hoping that she will wake up."

The nurse stopped by a room door and nodded to Jane and Oliver, they had reached their destination.

"Thank you," Oliver said as the nurse left.

"I'm scared," Jane was finding it hard to enter the room, but Oliver desperately needed to see Mandy, so he went straight in.

Mandy lay in the bed perfectly still with all of the medical apparatuses attached to her beeping as they do. To the both of them she looked fine, just asleep. Jane went over to her and inspected her, she had some scars on her right cheekbone but that was all of the injuries that Jane could see left behind from Mandy's ordeal over two years ago. Jane slowly and softly ran her finger along the scar.

"She actually looks really good," Oliver said.

"She does," Jane gently answered.

Mandy looked older but that was because she was older, two years older. Jane wondered how long the hospital would keep her here in this condition. The older nurse entered the room and began to check Mandy's machines and charts.

"Is she okay?" Oliver asked thinking that maybe it was a silly question.

"Oh, yes," the nurse happily said, "she is one of the healthiest patients I have!"

"What about her injuries from when she was brought into the hospital?" Jane asked.

"Well, she had multiple injuries from the incident but after the two years of being in a coma she has made a full recovery. The only thing we don't know is if she has sustained any lasting brain injuries."

"Are you saying she could be brain damaged in some way?" Jane was upset to think that it was a possibility.

"Well we just don't know. She had substantial swelling, the only time we can know that answer is when she wakes up, then we can see what she can and can't do for her."

"But if she is so physically well then why is she still in a coma?" Oliver did not understand. The nurse stopped what she was doing.

"The human body is a strange thing, Mandy is one hundred percent fine on our charts. But for some reason she has not chosen to wake up from her coma yet. We have tried many things over the past two years but sadly to no avail. It could be that she has sustained too much brain injury. It could be something that we can't see on our tests."

Jane and Oliver were unsure of the fate of Mandy, would it even be a positive life for her if she did choose to wake up. Jane was broken.

"Who maintains her care?" Jane asked.

"Mandy's grandfather is now her sole carer and like I said he comes in here every day to sit with her." The nurse stopped and smiled, she was pricking one ear up listening to something from the hallway. "Here he is now, I can hear him whistling through the hallways."

There was the sound of old nursery rhymes being whistled which echoed against the hallway walls in the hospital. It grew closer and closer and Jane rose to her feet in anticipation to meet Papa Joe.

The door gently opened with such a joyful push and there stood an old man with a cane. This man stopped in his tracks as he looked upon Jane and Oliver. He was a little man, must have been in his late eighties but still quite vibrant, even though he was using a cane to help him walk. It must be Mandy's Papa Joe that she had told them all about, her father's father. There was something so warm and familiar about him. Oliver's face lit up and the old man did too.

"Oliver! Jane!" The old man yelled.

Oliver moved in quickly hugging him first, shaking the hand of the older gentleman, both of them laughing. Jane stood back until Papa Joe's eyes met hers.

"Otto?" Jane's voice cracked as she asked.

"Jane, I cannot believe that I am looking at you with my weary old eyes!" They both embraced each other, and tears filled up Jane's eyes, she wiped them as they parted, and joy blessed her heart.

"I don't understand," Jane said.

"I think I will leave you all to it," the nurse said exiting the room with a huge loving smile on her face. It was a moment that she had been a part of that would stay with her forever.

Oliver whacked Otto on the back in awe of how old he was, "Look at you! My goodness!"

"Oliver it has been so long since I have seen the both of you, I just can't believe it, I can't."

Jane allowed Otto to sit down in the chair next to Mandy's bed and he held onto Mandy's hand. "I knew that we had a connection, but I didn't know how. All the time that she talked about her father and her Papa Joe I never realised that it was me she was talking about!"

"Why does she call you Papa Joe?"

"My name is Joe," Otto said. "Otto was given to me in university after a party I went to and it stuck. I liked it, so the nickname was what I used most of the time."

"This is incredible," Jane threw her hands into the air.

"I have sat here every day talking to my beautiful granddaughter trying to tell her how to escape Limbo, I know that is where she is. She is lost. Every day I try and tell her how to leave that horrible place we were trapped in."

"Oh my God, you're the voice, the voice that would talk to her in her sleep every night," Jane told Otto.

Otto looked up at Jane and smiled, "I hope that is true!"

"What's happened since you have come back Otto, obviously you lived in a different time to us. You are so much older than when we last saw you about a week ago," Oliver was intrigued to find out.

Otto smirked at the fact that to them he was a young man and the time frame was only a week since they had last seen each other.

"When I left Limbo everything changed, I made things right again and I worked my way up in the police force. I had a wonderful career and I supported my family by working hard and getting promoted. I had two sons after my daughter and I have been the happiest man ever. How can you not be happy when you know that you have been given a second chance at life? Thank you, Jane. It has been sixty years since I have returned, and I have lived every single one of them."

"Wow," Jane's mouth opened wide, sixty years, it had been only a week to them.

"Tell us more Otto, about your life with Mandy," Oliver happily pushed.

"Well, my older son of the two boys, Patrick brought home this girl one day, her name was Louisa. I tell you something I was blown away when I saw her because I remembered her from Limbo. But she did not know me, not yet anyway. It was too early in her life to have known me in Limbo. I chose to say nothing to my son about her, they were so good together. It breaks my heart now to know what happened to them after Patrick's death. They disappeared without a trace. I never spoke to Mandy in detail about her life or her father when we were in Limbo. All she told me was that I reminded her of her Papa Joe. While I was in Limbo I never asked anyone about themselves which makes me so mad now, I was such a selfish idiot back then. Maybe I could have stopped my son's death, I could have stopped all of this from happening!"

"Come on Otto don't be so hard on yourself," Oliver told him, "you weren't that bad… most of the time!"

The boys had a laugh together, their bellowing voices infecting the quiet hallways of the hospital. This friendship had not started out well, but now they were closer than ever.

"I'm sorry Oliver for being such an ass to you!"

"All is forgiven old man!"

Jane smiled at the two boys teasing each other. She looked at Mandy soundly laying in the hospital bed, "Why doesn't she wake up?"

"You know what she was like in limbo Jane, she was so very scared to return. Every day I try and tell her that she will be all right if she returns to the real-world. You know, I felt something today. I knew that today something was going to be different, Limbo was telling me."

"What do you mean?" Jane asked Otto.

Otto shook his head, "I can't explain it to you Jane, Limbo has stayed with me throughout my life guiding me. I thought that today something was going to be different and here you both are. Wait, if you are both here and Mandy is still in her coma... Oh no! Does that mean she is lost, she did not choose to leave before you?"

Jane did not know how to answer him, "When I left Otto, I was scared that she would not leave. I couldn't stay any longer, I had to come home. I don't know what Mandy chose to do in the end that's why we are here to tell her to wake up."

Otto feared for his granddaughter. He began to remember what Mandy herself had told them in Limbo, that if Jane left then they would all have to make a choice or accept their own fate. For most of them it would mean a final death, but for Mandy he did not know what her outcome would be. Otto prayed that it would not mean that she would be lost inside a coma forever. He stood up and held Mandy's hand.

"Please baby wake up," he whispered into her ear.

Suddenly there was a loud beep that screeched from the machine that was attached to Mandy. Then a whole bunch of scary noises that sounded bad. Nurses began to run into the room pushing them out of the way to get to Mandy.

"What is it, what's wrong!" Otto yelled backing away from the bedside.

"We are losing her!" the older nurse screamed.

"No," Otto muttered under his breath.

CHAPTER 31

Karama is a bitch.

The storm in Limbo continued to whirl around, a tornado was slowly and fearfully being created. Mandy watched as Limbo began to destroy itself. It started with Camilla and Frank's house piece by piece.

Mandy had been sucked up into the tornado after Jane had been separated from her. She was now floating inside the storm somehow, Limbo was personally showing Mandy everyone's fate. Maybe it was a gift to her or maybe it was her punishment for not doing what she was meant to do here. Now that Jane had chosen to leave the rest of them behind, those that were left were doomed to their own individual outcome. Mandy watched on as each resident made their final choice.

Frank was screaming at his mother Camilla as their home bit by bit began to tear away and disintegrate. It didn't seem like the time to fight with each other, but Mandy did understand that the both of them lived different lives.

Camilla was angry after finding out that Frank was having an affair with Mary's husband Daniel in Limbo. She thought that by bringing them here he would learn that being gay would send him straight to hell, this was his last chance at salvation. She had given up everything in her life for her children, especially for Frank. She had given her own life so that he would be saved, and this is how he repaid her by continuing his unruly behaviour.

"How dare you!" she screamed at him. "Look what you have done!"

"Mother please, we must leave, you must forgive me. You have to forgive yourself!"

"Forgive myself, I have done nothing wrong, you my son have broken my heart!"

Frank bent down in the chaos and knelt on one knee in front of his mother in her wheel chair. "Mother you don't understand, I love Daniel. Don't you see that, this is who I am, this is how God made me."

"No! That is not love, it is not what God intended for you or for any of us!"

Camilla was like ice, she was unbreakable, stubborn and angry. Frank rose to his feet in front of her and backed away with a few steps.

"I forgive you Mother for all that you have done."

Camilla's face changed, she did not understand why her son was forgiving her for she had done nothing wrong, not in her eyes.

Frank continued, "I forgive you for telling me my whole life that I was not normal, that there was something wrong with me. I forgive you for murdering my father and I thank you for protecting me from him. I forgive you for murdering me in my sleep and sending us here because you thought that you were saving me. But mother the thing you need to know is this, I am perfect just the way I am. You may think differently but it took me a long time to finally understand that the God that I love is love itself. I believe that God made me, and I do not believe that he could possibly make any mistakes, for then he would not be God. I have forgiven you for this. I have forgiven myself for treating myself badly and thinking terrible things about who I was, the things that I had been taught. I am letting you go mother. I thank you for doing all that you could for me even though what you believe in is not what I believe. I have never pushed my ways onto you, instead I have lived my life in the darkness to avoid your judgements, but not anymore. I love you, but I need to let you go. You are choosing to die, and I want to choose to live. I beg you to do the same!"

Camilla was shocked by Frank's words, he had never spoken to her like that before. His words hit her hard and even though she sat there thinking briefly that what he said may just be true her ego mind could not allow him to be right. She had lived by her religious rules her whole life and she knew nothing else. How could she forgive her son when she believed so deeply that what he was doing was wrong?

Maybe that judgement was not hers to give. Her thoughts seemed to whirl as intensely as the storm that swarmed around them, but she could not agree with her son. She loved him, but she could not forgive him.

"You are doomed to hell!" Camilla screamed at him.

"No mother," Frank calmly said. "You are!"

Mandy could feel and hear everything that they were both going through inside this intense moment. She could feel the emotions from both of their lifetimes making the choices that would finalise their decision in this precious time. It saddened her that Camilla could not forgive her son, that she didn't understand that it wasn't her job to forgive him. Instead it was her job to accept him and love him unconditionally no matter what the circumstances.

Deep down in her heart Camilla could not forgive herself either. Frank had surprised her by knowing all of her dark secrets, the secrets that she believed did not earn her the right to forgiveness. She believed that she did not deserve a second chance. This whole time in Limbo Mandy had not given much time to get to know Camilla and Frank, and she was sad that this was going to be how it ended.

Frank continued to step back, away from his mother until he got to the front door, he walked through it leaving his mother inside. She was heartbroken that he had gone. They had been together throughout their whole lives, she hoped that it wasn't her fault that he had chosen his sinful ways.

Camilla looked around her as her house broke away, it's pieces spinning in the air like a perfect symphony of music. The walls began to hiss, and the smell of smoke suddenly filled her lungs. She blinked and realised that she had returned to her bedroom, she was lying in her bed. Camilla had been returned to that fateful night that she had chosen to take both her life and Frank's by starting a fire in the house.

Although that night she had taken sedatives, she awoke suddenly seeing that her bed and her clothes were engulfed in fire. Screaming she felt the pain of the flames melting her clothes into her skin. The pain turned to a numbness as she watched her body burn, the smell of her own skin singeing was terrifying to her, what had she done?

Frank was running down Law street trying to make it to Daniel and Mary's house. He stopped when he heard the dreaded screams coming from his home, smoke began to pour out of the windows and instead of the storm taking it, the house now began to burn. Flames swallowed it whole and his body felt ill hearing the deafening screams that he knew was coming from his mother's mouth. He began to cry, falling to the ground full of guilt. Limbo was taking her to her death, the death that she had planned and agreed to when she followed through with it on that original night.

Mandy had to close her eyes as she watched Camilla scream and slowly burn until she passed out from the pain. The house began to vibrate and move like it did when Limbo was taking someone, it did so until it eventually vanished. The storm headed towards Father James' house, but this sight was more comforting to Mandy. She watched Father James inside his home waving to her like he could see her in the storm, it was strange because Camilla and Frank could not.

He placed his hand over his heart and then he tipped his hat. Father James was pleased with her, it was strange the feeling Mandy received from him, it made her think that he was somehow a part of Limbo. He was not choosing, he was not getting a second chance and he was not dying either. He was a soul that was everlasting and when he vanished she felt that he had returned home, to his real home. Mandy was given a small ounce of peace from Father James. It made her think that everything would be as it is meant to be, no matter the outcome.

Mandy then watched Frank as he lifted himself to his feet trying to out run the storm that was heading down the street towards Mary and Daniel's house. He had to try and make it there so that he could somehow save them both from making the wrong choices. The storm continued to disintegrate everything in its path, turning it all into a black abyss of emptiness. The empty lots that used to hold the houses of those that had escaped were slowly being chewed up.

Frank barged through the front door of Mary and Daniel's house and found the two of them embracing, the noise was piercing through their ears and it was hard to hear. Frank fought his way towards the couple and as he did Daniel let go of Mary and embraced him instead. Frank was apprehensive, he did not want to hurt Mary. Mary smiled at Frank gently.

Mandy was overjoyed as she watched on from the heart of the storm, because she could sense Mary's forgiveness. Mary had been so cold at times, but Mandy knew it was only because of her loneliness. Mary had always wanted to be a mother and she had felt that Daniel had lied to her their whole time together. Mary loved Daniel and Daniel loved Mary, but they were never in love.

Mary had originally wanted to trap Daniel within Limbo so that he too would not be able to find happiness with another, it was her reason for not leaving Limbo. She feared being all alone, and this fear stood in her way of allowing Daniel forgiveness, or even forgiveness for herself.

It was finally time. The three of them stood there while the storm began to close in, they all hugged each other unsure of their fate. They embraced in a circle as the storm started to hit the house. Their hearts were full of love, they were all happy to accept themselves and each other and whatever future was being given to them. They had even accepted death.

Limbo opened up its dark and endless mouth, swallowing the three of them whole. They were gone. Miraculously it was like the storm stopped for just a moment. During this pause, Mandy was blessed with three separate visions, each vision showing the fate of Frank, Mary and Daniel.

Then the storm ignited again, and Mandy was thrown up inside of its core. The howling became louder as the storm drew closer to her home, it was the last house left in Law street. The time had finally come to seal Mandy and her parents fate. When Mandy reached her front door the whirling storm somehow spat her out of its rhythmic flow pushing her inside into her room, she covered her eyes and braced herself for the fall.

There was silence. Her hands were covering her eyes and as she took them away she noticed that she was hiding inside of her closet. She could hear the screaming coming from the lounge room as Jason abused her mother. That was when Mandy realised that she had returned to that fateful moment that Jason had killed her mother and beaten her to an inch of her life.

Quickly without thinking she left her cupboard and went to climb out of the window, but she stopped, maybe she could save her mother. Over the time spent in Limbo she had become stronger, it was time for her to stand up for her life, for what was right. Instead Mandy ran out to the lounge room grabbing the vase near her bedroom door. Jason was hitting her mother. Mandy jumped on the couch to give her height as she slammed the vase as hard as she could over Jason's head.

Jason fell to the ground in agony, but it did not stop him. Mandy's decision was now making her feel sick, had she made the wrong choice? She watched as her mother squirmed slowly along the lounge room floor, the blood pouring from her face, she was still alive. Jason turned his anger towards Mandy. He raised himself up and he punched Mandy so hard that she flew across the room. She slammed into the wall near the hallway table and she sat slumped in the corner after hitting her head viciously against the wall. There were cuts on her face from the blow that Jason had ploughed her with, her skin torn open from its force.

He was such a big man, but Mandy was no longer afraid of him, she had endured this so many times before. If this was going to be the last time he would beat her, then she would embrace its finality. Mandy sat in the corner winded as Jason began to kick into Louisa once again, Mandy cried unable to help her. The memories of what really occurred on this very night began to play out inside of Mandy's mind.

Mandy did not run like she originally remembered when she entered into Limbo, instead she was beaten and left for dead. What Mandy also recalled was hearing Jason open the draw of the hallway table, pull out a gun and shoot himself. He had done this after he had thought that he had killed them both, his guilt had taken him over.

This time Mandy would not give Jason the chance to hurt her like he had originally done this night previously. She did not want to be beaten to the point where she would not be able to recover. Slowly Mandy dragged her pain riddled body over to the hallway table and glided the draw open. Desperately she tried to reach higher, feeling around inside the draw. Maybe it wasn't in there. Finally, her finger touched its metallic skin and she pulled the gun out of the drawer.

Mandy knew a lot more than she used to. After being in Limbo for so long and having friends like Otto she now knew how to use a gun. She was such a young girl, but she had lived through a lifetime of hell. Otto had shown her how to release the safety and how to shoot. Otto was initially taken back by Mandy's request to show her how to use a gun, but he was impressed by how well she handled it. *What harm could it do in Limbo anyway,* Otto had thought at the time.

Without even thinking, as Mandy sat slumped in the corner of the lounge room watching Jason slowly killing her mother she changed her fate. The noise of the gun going off was deafening. It was like the bullet had shot itself, moving in slow motion. Jason looked up at Mandy and with surprise he was hit with a bullet from his very own revolver straight in the throat.

For Mandy the look that was carved onto Jason's face was priceless as he fell to his knees, both hands wrapped around his bleeding neck. This time he knew he was not coming back, he was not getting a second chance, he had chosen his fate.

"Eat that, you piece of shit!" Mandy wept for what she had done, lowering the weapon to the ground. But it will never be anything that she would have to forgive herself for. She had been preparing for this moment for a very long time. She had saved herself. Jason's body fell face first into the carpet, his blood staining it. He gurgled for a few moments and then he was still.

Sirens wailed in the background and Mandy desperately tried to make it over to her mother, she was not moving. Scared and fighting to stay awake Mandy dragged herself closer and closer to her mother but it was just too hard for her little body and she eventually passed out.

Voices echoed inside of her darkness. It was the sound of doctors and nurses fussing over her, they were in desperate need of Mandy's attention, but she was content where she was. There was no anger, no negative feelings at all and so she chose to stay inside the comforting darkness. She felt safe, for the first time in a long time she felt safe.

A light began to shine in the distance and she took in a deep breath which felt like pure love. She began to hear a familiar voice, it sounded like her father.

"I will always be with you," he told her.

"I love you daddy!" Mandy yelled to him.

The light began to fade and then she heard Jane's voice, oh how much she missed Jane and Oliver. Then she heard Papa Joe gently singing to her. Finally, she believed that is was fine to let go.

CHAPTER 32

Having the courage to love yourself will truly save your life.

So, what actually did happen to Frank, Mary and Daniel? Mandy had witnessed their individual fate. She was pleased at how much they had evolved since being inside Limbo, especially Mary. Limbo was not just about learning, although it taught every single person there something quite unique. For Mary Limbo was about her ability to forgive, it was about her being able to forgive not only Daniel but herself.

Mary had learned how to trust herself once again and to let go of the wrongs that had been done against her, because holding onto such things just traps you in the same place. That is not living. Life is about moving forward, which is something that you definitely can't do when you are choosing to be stuck. The universe wants more for you than that. So, if you are privileged enough to have Limbo intervene then you should really count yourself lucky, not everyone gets a second chance.

What would you do if you had been told to marry a man that was convenient for your parents? Mary was such a people pleaser even from an early age. She did what she was good at and so she agreed to please her parents and marry Daniel. It really wasn't a bad deal for she already loved Daniel. Growing up together was fun, but she was never in love with him. In her heart she had always hoped that Daniel would ask her to marry him one day, because she had been hurt by someone already.

It was easier for her to be around Daniel, he never expected anything of her. Not like the other boys.

It was when she went to Daniel one night after her boyfriend Jimmy had tried to have his way with her. Luckily, she managed to escape, and she headed straight to Daniel's house. Daniel had promised her that he would always protect her if she needed him, for he loved her like a sister.

Daniel was always a confused boy. Even though he was strong and independent his parents knew that he had no interest whatsoever in finding himself a girlfriend. They were afraid that he would be left alone his whole life. Ashamed of how he felt inside, Daniel knew that the right thing to do at the time was to marry Mary. He loved her so much and he wanted to keep her safe. He never told her he was gay.

In the whole time they were married Daniel was never interested in having a sexual relationship with Mary, although he knew that it was his duty to give her children. After trying and failing many times, he could no longer keep doing something that made him feel so uncomfortable inside.

How could he ever tell Mary how he truly felt about being with her; that it made him feel physically sick. It didn't take too long before Mary decided to stop hounding him about having children. When she told her family and friends she blamed herself for not being able to bear children. This was a time in her life that haunted her, she had lied to them. Mary had given up so much in her life to make sure that Daniel's secret was hidden. What would people think of him? Decades flew past and eventually their relationship became a deeper friendship. They became each other's companions and although they seemed to have their separate secret lives they continued the facade that they were in love.

Mary never really understood why she didn't just leave and have a life of her own, find someone else to have children with. In her heart she thought it was her responsibility to protect Daniel just as he would protect her. As time moved on the thoughts about leaving became less and less, with both of them just accepting their fate with each other.

Why was it such a hard moment for Mary to see those male magazines that day, hidden in the locked drawer? This was the day she found herself in Limbo. Hadn't she already known that Daniel was gay? Had she pretended that there was something wrong with herself and that was why Daniel did not want to be affectionate towards her this whole time.

It was because in that moment she realised how much she had lost. If everyone truly only ever gets one life, then her realisation had become that she had wasted hers on a person that had never actually revealed the truth to her. She felt betrayed, and although it seemed that the betrayal was felt for the first time, in that moment it was a feeling that had always haunted her soul. Daniel had never actually explained his motives to her. He used her as a façade, so he wouldn't be judged.

All of those negative feelings flooded her body. Daniel's constant betrayal, knowing that he was having affairs with other men behind her back, thinking that she had no clue. Living a life that was false and wasteful. She had given up being a mother, she had given up her career to wait on him, she had given up her life. Maybe the anger was actually being felt towards herself that day. She had been stupid enough to give up so much for a man that continued to happily do as he pleased, but she would not allow the blame to be cast solely upon herself.

Daniel was easier to blame and the anger that consumed her whole life aimed its vengeance towards her husband. This anger continued from that day she first came to Limbo and it did not stop. Not until today. Today it was time for her to choose her fate and Daniel's fate inside Limbo. The storm was coming.

There they stood together, Daniel and Mary in front of each other. They did love each other, but they had both been each other's crutch to maintain a life that did not serve them.

"My darling Mary I am so sorry, what you have been through with me is just unforgivable. I have been selfish and uncaring towards your own well-being. I wish I could take it all back, I really do and there is nothing in this world that could ever take away the guilt that I hold in my heart. So many times, I have tried to tell you about who I am, about what I have done. I have deceived you my beautiful Mary my whole life. I deserve to be banished to darkness for the things that I have done."

Mary looked deep into Daniel's eyes as the storm that Limbo created began to hit near their home. They both knew that their time in Limbo was coming to an end. Inside Mary's heart she realised that Daniel had been a wonderful companion, she had allowed hatred to consume her for so long. Daniel had done the very best he could to make sure that she had the best life possible, what more could she have asked from him. But it was herself that she had to forgive. For allowing her life to be as it was, for not choosing herself, for not loving herself enough to have the life that she had always dreamed about.

"Promise me that if we get a second chance that you will love me enough to let me go," Mary told Daniel.

"Mary, I love you more than life itself. I have tried my best to be the man that you needed me to be, but I just couldn't be that man. I am sorry for that. I promise you that if we make it back I will let you go. I will not be afraid of losing you, or what people will think of me for who I am without you. You deserve better."

"No," Mary said as she ran her fingers through his hair, "I honestly have loved our time together. You are a remarkable man and it is my own fault that we have been allowed to live a life that wasn't real. We are best friends and we always will be. I will have to let you go also. I want you to be free to be yourself as I me. I don't want to lose you, I just want us to be honest with ourselves and each other."

Daniel nodded as both of them began to cry, they tenderly embraced each other as Daniel whispered, "You are the most magnificent woman ever to have lived."

If only they could return home and back to that moment Mary felt lost, when she had found those magazines. Mary knew that she could make things right again. Sadly, she began to remember her last days in the real-world. Her and Daniel were having dinner at a friend's house, she remembered feeling so angry because of Daniel's betrayal and she could not take anymore. On the drive home she confronted Daniel about being gay and also about the magazines. They fought, and Mary begged that he pull over and let her out of the car. Daniel refused, it was too dark and unsafe to leave her on the side of the road. He could not put her in danger, he loved her.

Mary was so tired, physically and mentally and she yelled and yelled trying to make him understand what he had done to her, but he already knew. Mary grabbed the steering wheel pulling it so that Daniel would pull over onto the side of the road. Instead it just caused a chain reaction that lead them to their death.

What had they done to themselves and to each other? They stood there together as they both remembered their final moments in each other's arms. They were devastated.

"I am so sorry for blaming you for the choices I made. I knew, I always knew about who you were Daniel, but you were my rock and I was afraid of what people would think not just of you, but of me. That is being selfish my dear. I love you and I am truly sorry," Mary confessed.

"I love you too my cherub, with all of my heart and I am sorry for the things that I have done. I need to tell you…."

"I know," Mary began. "I know about Frank, I always have. I understand."

Daniel just looked into Mary's eyes stunned that Mary was so understanding towards his ways. She had forgiven him, and he felt free. He embraced her again and that was when Frank came barging through the front door. He staggered up close to them fighting the storm. Mary smiled, Daniel went and embraced Frank. Mary then embraced Frank also.

The three of them hugged tightly in a circle as the storm that Limbo had sent to destroy them was welcomed by the forgiveness that each of them offered. They had a bond that nothing could break. They shut their eyes and prepared for whatever fate was given to them.

It was only a second before Mary heard silence, not a sound. Her hands were covering her eyes and she remembered this moment, she was sure it was the moment she had found Daniel's magazines. As she slowly opened her eyes she felt different in her body, it felt lighter and freer. She had not felt this way for such a very long time. Something was not quite right.

"Mary! Mary!" she could hear Daniel calling to her, "I can't believe it, we did it!"

Daniel was laughing, and Mary was in disbelief. She was wrong. She had not returned to the moment she had found Daniel's magazines, instead she was sitting on Daniel's bed when they were much younger. She had been crying, it was the night she had come to him after her boyfriend had tried to rape her.

"Mary would you look at us, we're young again!"

Daniel was pacing the room looking at his hands, then looking into the mirror at his young perfect complexion.

"How can this be?" Mary asked.

Limbo had given them a gift, it had not returned them to the time they had left from like it had all the others. Instead it had given them a whole new chance at life from this particular moment.

"It's our second chance Mary, can you believe it!"

Mary just screamed and began jumping up and down with joy, they hugged each other as they jumped and eventually fell onto the bed rolling onto the floor. Daniel's father came into the room finding them both on the floor wrapped around each other. Instead of getting angry he was happy that he had caught his eighteen-year-old son rolling around on the floor with a girl.

"Oh, I will leave you," he said with a smoke jiggling up and down upon his lips.

As he went to close the door, Daniel called to him. He stood up, hugged his father tight, ripped the cigarette from his mouth and put it across the hallway into the bathroom sink.

"I love you dad and I want you around a long time. I don't want you to smoke anymore, deal?"

His father grinned at the compassion he saw within his son's eyes. Desperately from that day on he tried his hardest to please his son and his wishes, but his addiction was too fierce. He would still die of lung cancer at the age of fifty-nine.

Daniel and Mary did not get married, but they moved in together and started a life as friends instead of husband and wife. Eventually Mary became a teacher and married a nice gentleman called Max from the same town who had his own garage. Over time they had four children. Mary started young and wanted to have as many as she could. Her husband Max died when she was fifty, it was an accident in the garage. The car he was working on fell onto his chest collapsing his lungs. Daniel was by her side every step of the way supporting her, they had always continued to be in each other's lives.

Mary and Daniel decided to travel the world for a few years. Her kids were all grown up now and although Daniel had been in a few relationships it was hard for him to maintain them. The times were still not accepting of how he decided to live his life.

Daniel felt safe with Mary, but he had learned to let her go. She had been so happy in her life and Daniel was pleased to have watched her live it. Daniel and Mary decided to move and settle into a city that was full of hustle and bustle. Strangely it was not like them at all, but there was a connection here and Mary wanted a new start. One of her daughters was living here, the one that was married and had three children. Daniel had become uncle Dan to all of them.

Mary accepted a job in a college teaching teenagers English. She had always wanted to get back into her teaching, it was something she was very passionate about. On the first day she was able to meet many of the teachers, that was the day she met Colin the sports teacher.

Well, when they met they just laughed and laughed. Colin could not believe that Mary was standing right in front of him. They were both the same age they had met while in Limbo and Mary realised that she had now lived two full lifetimes. Colin had only just returned from Limbo, it had been a few weeks. He had stopped drinking and he had begun his life again after his wife had left him for another man.

Colin and Mary eventually married, and their families merged together wonderfully. It was an enormous family event when celebrating at Christmas time and she loved it. Daniel loved it also as he was always a huge part of her family. But Daniel felt a loneliness deep inside that Mary could not fill. He had watched on as Mary had enjoyed her life and found what she had always been looking for. Sadly, he had not.

Daniel decided that it was time for him to leave Mary to her own life, he would tell her today at their Christmas luncheon that he had decided to move back to their hometown. Strangely this Christmas day he decided to walk to her house. On the way to Mary's house was a quaint little store that he had always wanted to go inside of but never did.

Daniel entertained his inquisitiveness and he went inside wondering why the shop was even open on such a special day. It was an old book shop that appeared to have been there for decades. As he entered, the small bell on the door dinged to tell the owner that there was a customer. A tall slender man had his back to Daniel, but he turned to see who this customer was on Christmas day. To Daniel's surprise the owner of the shop was Frank. Isn't it strange how the universe can put you in the right place at the right time when you allow it to happen.

Daniel never ended up telling Mary that he was going to leave, instead he made Frank close up his small little book shop and join him for Christmas lunch. It was a miraculous Christmas, and life as they knew it was more than any of them could have ever wished for.

CHAPTER 33

The fear of the unknown is the power that helps sculpt us into becoming…fearless.

O tto could not lose Mandy, she had been taken away from him once before when Jason had taken her. He could not bear it again. Jane felt guilty, she believed that Mandy's fate was in her hands and that she had doomed her when leaving Limbo without her. They both yelled hard at Mandy's lifeless body. Otto begging her not to leave him and Jane yelling at her to wake up. As the doctors and nurses were desperately trying to revive her, it seemed useless. Time was ticking by slowly, it felt like forever since her heart had beaten.

Then there was this sudden gasping of air. Mandy's chest elevating itself dramatically towards the heavens and then back down as her lungs filled with the oxygen they were starving for.

Mandy gasped again, and the monitors beeped a happy beep, showing everyone that her heart had decided to start working again. It's rhythmic beat singing gracefully as if nothing had ever been wrong. The doctors and nurses looked at each other in awe, her heart had settled so quickly, they had never ever seen this happen before.

"Welcome back," the older nurse told her as she smiled.

"Where…." Mandy tried to speak.

"You are in the hospital Mandy," the nurse told her.

After checking Mandy over, the doctors were pleased that her vitals had returned to normal. They left leaving Mandy with her family.

"Mandy!" Otto moved as quickly as he could to her side and grabbed her hand.

"Papa Joe," her voice was meek and crackly, it was hard for her to talk. Jane and Oliver went around to her other side. "Jane, Oliver…. But how?"

Jane grabbed her other hand. "Try not to talk Mandy," Jane found it difficult not to cry. "You have been through so much, we are here for you and we are never going to leave you again. I'm so sorry, I…."

"No," Mandy said, "you saved me."

Jane and Mandy looked at each other. Mandy smiled at her and then she closed her eyes, "Thank you."

"Mandy are you all right baby," Otto said.

Mandy opened her eyes again and she looked at her Papa Joe, "I missed you Papa Joe, thank you."

"For what?" he asked her.

"For finding me, for talking to me every night in my dreams in Limbo and for looking out for me in Limbo also, you protected me from Jason."

Otto smiled but put his head down, "I'm sorry I was so stubborn, if I had known in Limbo that I was your Papa Joe I would have been a better person to you, to everyone. I would never have left you like I did, I was such a selfish man there."

"No Papa Joe, you had to leave. Don't you understand, it was all for a purpose."

Otto did not understand, but what she had said was comforting. Mandy closed her eyes again, tired from the internal energy that she had used. She fell asleep. Otto was nervous while Mandy was asleep, but he could tell that it was different than the coma she had been in for years. It was a normal sleep as she moved and turned over to get more comfortable.

The three of them took it in turns to stay by Mandy's side sleeping on the horrible chairs. Otto did most of the day shifts as he was older and unable to rest his weary body overnight on such hard and uncomfortable beds. Jane wanted to be with Mandy and she was happy to do the night shift. The ward was so quiet at night, it gave her time to think easily. She wondered what would happen when Mandy was released from the hospital.

After two nights and three days Mandy was released in one hundred percent health. It was weird the first time when Mandy looked at herself in the mirror she looked different, more grown up. Her legs were like jelly and it would take time for her body to get used to being mobile again. But Mandy was not one to just sit around waiting, she wanted to be up and about as soon as possible. Jane pulled Otto aside and asked him what his future plans were.

"Well, I am her guardian now as she has lost both parents, until she is eighteen. I have money but there is nothing really keeping me here, no family at all. I was thinking that I might go visit my daughter and her family although she always seems to be quite busy all of the time."

Jane moved closer towards him. She did not want him to move somewhere where she could not be a part of their lives.

"We have a huge home, you could both stay with us."

Otto was not sure what she was asking, did she mean forever, or did she mean to just come for a holiday.

"Jane, I am an old man and I know nothing about bringing up a teenage girl. All I know is that I cannot leave her or be without her again."

"I feel the same, I don't want to be without her either. Please if it is an option at all for you come and live with us we would love that."

Jane thought about the stairs and how difficult it would be for Otto to manage them. She was willing to sell up and move if she had to get them both to stay in their lives. The guest room was downstairs, and it had its own bathroom, she hoped that it would be enough for Otto to at least give it a thought.

Oliver moved into the conversation and without even thinking he tried hard to make Otto agree to Jane's request. He was apprehensive to think what life would be like with so many people in the house, but his heart jumped thinking of all the happy times they could have together. He too wanted them in his life. They had all changed so much, Limbo had been good for them.

"Let's just have a holiday for now and then we will see how it all goes shall we?" Otto told them both.

Jane hugged Otto tight. He let out a small chuckle, he was unsure how well they would all live together. But he knew that Oliver had some good quality scotch in his cabinet that he could help polish off.

CHAPTER 34

The Universe has always got your back.

Months then passed and Jane could constantly hear Limbo inside of her head, it was like an old friend. She listens to that voice and embraces it now instead of drowning it out with her ego that tells her lies. Limbo is with her to guide her, it's her heart talking to her.

Maybe it isn't Limbo at all, Jane thought. *Maybe it's Father James telling me what to do!* Jane giggled to herself as she stacked the dishwasher. It was a funny thought.

Today was going to be a great day, Oliver had suggested a sea change and Jane agreed. They bought a beautiful house in the western suburbs and Jane pulled Alex from his school, enrolling him into a new one. She wanted a new life and she wanted to find new friends. No more gossip queens that judged everything that she did. Today was moving day.

Otto and Mandy had been living with them for about two months now. They had decided to sell most of their belongings and bite the bullet and move in with Jane and the family. So far so good. Although it was only early on Jane was excited to have them both so close to her. Mandy was like a daughter to Oliver and Jane and Alex loved having an older sister.

Otto was staying in the downstairs guest bedroom as he was having trouble with the stairs. It was only for two months and everything he needed was on the lower floor of the house anyway, he had never lived in such a big place before. The house they had purchased by the beach was slightly smaller but that still meant that it was big enough for all of them.

Otto headed into the kitchen, "Good morning sunshine," he said to Jane.

"Good morning ratbag!" she answered.

You could hear Oliver snorting out the back after over-hearing Jane's comment.

"Well that is hospitality isn't it?" Otto scalded.

Jane handed Otto a freshly brewed coffee, as he sat up onto a stood by the kitchen bench. "Jane there is something I want to talk to you and Oliver about, but firstly I want to know if you are absolutely sure that you want me here pestering you every day…forever?"

Jane immediately stopped what she was doing and focused on Otto, "Of course I do! We love having you here."

"I can be a grumpy old man sometimes Jane!"

"A grumpy old man sometimes?" Jane teased. "You were grumpy when you were young as well you know!"

"Ha!" was Oliver's input into the conversation. Jane and Otto could not see him, but they could hear him. Oliver entered in through the backdoor, "She got you, old man!"

Otto smiled, he loved being here, "I want to be serious for a moment. I have been thinking about Mandy and, well, I'm am old, and I have decided that I really want you both to adopt Mandy."

Oliver and Jane just looked at each other, they were surprised by Otto's request.

"But what about you?" Oliver asked him.

"Is there something wrong?" Jane jumped in hoping that he was healthy.

"Oh, I'm fine, just fine. The thing is I am an old man and Mandy needs a mother and a father. She needs a father to walk her down the aisle one day and she needs a mother for all that girl stuff that happens. I want you to do this for me," he insisted.

Oliver was lost for words and so he just went over to Otto and shook his hand.

"Otto there is nothing more in this world that I would want to do than to have Mandy become my daughter, but I can't stop thinking about you, what about your other family?" Jane asked.

"Mandy is my granddaughter and I love her, but you both are my family now. We have been through so much together and I know that she is where she is meant to be with the both of you and with Alex. I want you to be her parents, please do this for me."

Jane and Oliver both nodded and were overwhelmed with the offer that Otto had given them. Jane began to cry and as she did Mandy and Alex came into the kitchen.

"You all right Mum!" Mandy asked grinning.

Jane's mouth dropped, "Are you serious!"

"Don't worry Jane, Papa Joe and I had this planned for at least a month," Mandy teased.

Jane picked up the tea towel and threw it at her, she then raced around the kitchen bench and grabbed Mandy as hard as she could. Oliver got in on the hug. Then Alex, and then they all moved around so that Otto could reach his arm out and be a part of it also. They were all in such a good place right now.

The doorbell rang.

Jane left the kitchen to see who it was. As she opened the front door there stood Father James with an enormous smile upon his face.

Oh shit! Why is he here?

"Hello Jane."

"Father James, what on earth…."

Oliver and Mandy came over and were also surprised to see him. They were not sure if it was a good visit or if Father James was going to whisk them all off to another version of Limbo. Fear briefly entered their bodies as they waited for an answer as to why he was there.

"It looks like you are all getting along so well but there is someone who really needs to meet you all."

"Who?" Jane said ever so slowly.

Jason? Louisa? Who? Was Mandy going to be taken from her again? Oh God, what now?

Father James motioned to a young girl in her twenties who was standing next to him. She was holding an old book and appeared nervous to meet Jane. Oliver and Mandy were curious and by now Otto and Alex had joined the view from the front door.

"This is Alexia," Father James began, "she is the great-granddaughter of Samuel Patterson and Cindy Patterson."

Jane smiled from ear to ear, "You're Sam and Cindy's great-granddaughter?"

"Yes," she answered as she nodded.

"Can we come in?" Father James asked.

"Of course!" Jane was so curious.

As Jane went to turn around and let them inside she almost fell over everyone else that was standing in the doorway.

"Shall we sit in the lounge?" Jane pushed them all.

Everyone was fascinated with Alexia, she was feeling a little uncomfortable as they all stared and smiled at her. She looked so much like Cindy, such a beautiful thing. Alexia sat opposite Jane, Oliver and Otto while Mandy and Alex sat on the floor. Father James nodded to Alexia as she began to show the book that was in her hands.

"This is my great-grandmother Cindy's diary. It has been passed down since she died and the stories inside of it has been told to all of us children over generations since we were born. I have always wondered if what was inside of this book was true. I can remember my mother telling me about her mother's time in Limbo and that we were all lucky to be here, together. It gave us a sense of gratitude for being alive."

Jane looked at Otto and then at Oliver.

Alexia continued, "When I met Father James at church last week I told him about my great-grandmothers book and he wanted me to come and meet you."

"Alexia," Father James pointed at Jane, "this is Jane, that is her husband Oliver, and this is Otto. The lovely girl sitting on the floor is Mandy. Next to her is Alex, Jane and Oliver's son, the one that you are named after."

"Really?" Alexia questioned. "Well that is just amazing. You are all named after the people that my great-grandmother wrote about in this book. She called it, Law of Limbo. She told me that I was named after an Alex, a little boy who Jane and Oliver were trying desperately to get home to."

Alex was young, and he did not understand, "How is she named after me?" he looked upon his mother for an answer.

"It's a long story," Jane told him.

"Come on kid," Mandy pushed Alex, "let's go upstairs and play."

"Thank you," Oliver told Mandy.

"How much do you know about Limbo Alexia? What does it say in her diary?" Otto was fascinated.

"Well it's like a story, but it is in diary form. Everything that happened to her in Limbo is inside it. She would tell the story over and over to her kids and that story was passed on. She believed that if everyone knew the Law of Limbo they would have a long and prosperous life."

"May I?" Jane asked as she gestured to the book.

Alexia nodded, and Jane took the book from her. It was old and fragile and as Jane opened it and began reading its contents she became emotional. She missed talking to Cindy but reading the entries made her feel like she was with her.

"Is it you Jane that my great-grandmother talks about in the book?" Alexia asked. "Not many of the people in my family believed in the stories that my great-grandmother told, but I did. She told me that you were all from different times and that you might not even be born yet. I loved how real she made it seem. I believed every word."

"What if I told you that the people in the book are us?" Oliver said. "Would you believe me?"

"Believe you! I already know that it is you. I have read this book over and over and I know it's you, all of you, it just has to be!"

Jane went to hand the book back, "What do you want us to do about it?" Jane asked her.

Alexia smiled, "I know that you are a writer Jane, my great-grandmother handed me this book before she died and told me if I ever found you to give it to you. She wanted you to have it, she wants you to write it into a book so that others can use its wisdom."

Jane looked at Father James and he just nodded at her, he had used his influence to bring Alexia and the book to her. A great feeling of peace fell over Jane. It was time for her to start doing what she had longed to do, and that was to write. Writing was her purpose and so Jane kept the book honouring Alexia's request.

Over time Jane discovered its magical contents. After eight months she turned Cindy's diary into a full-length book that came not only from the diaries contents, but also from the experiences that they all had endured through Limbo. Although it was released as a fiction she knew that it was real, it was their truth.

The book 'Law of Limbo' was released and it was the first of many that Jane wrote. Everything that she published was filled with stories that would encourage others to choose to live their greatest life possible, just as she did. Just as they all did.

About the Author

Tarina Marcinkowski

(also writes children's books under Jackie Lukes),

Is a mother of two, her eldest son Jack is an angel in heaven, and her youngest son Luke is her inspiration that encourages her to write and create every day. Together with her husband and youngest son they all live happily in Adelaide, Australia.

The authors first book 'Just Believe' is the story about her eldest son Jack who passed away from brain cancer. This book is Jack's journey told through the authors eyes as his mother. From this painful experience grew the authors strength to follow her passion of writing and illustrating.

Delving into many different genres including fiction, the author also creates children's books under the pseudonym of Jackie Lukes.

This author is a true Australian inspiration.

Webpage: http://tarinamarcinkowski.wixsite.com/author

Facebook: https://www.facebook.com/tarinamarcinkowski/

Just Believe

Jack's Inspirational True Story Told

Through His Mothers Eyes

There is nothing a mother wouldn't do to save her child's life!

Challenged by the heartbreaking diagnosis of a brain tumour in her two-year-old son, Tarina writes her story about Jack from the heart.

Tarina's complete honesty will allow you to experience Jack's incredible journey through her eyes as a mother. Endure with her and her family the harrowing decisions they were faced with, and the devastating mistakes made by the experts they were supposed to trust. Tarina spares no details about the intense treatments that her son bravely endures within this battle to save his life.

Believing that Jack's story had to be told, Tarina's intention is to inspire all who read it. This little boy's spirit and courage will not only inspire you, it will change your life forever. A compelling true story of resilience by a family dealing with the greatest of adversities.

ISBN: **E-Book** – 978-0-6486855-0-0

ISBN: **Paperback** – 978-0-6486855-1-7

Broken Angel

Sometimes the only way to destroy the darkness is to be the darkness.

Azra does not know she is broken, not yet anyway. A confused soul torn in two trying to exist in two different worlds. In love with two separate beings. When she discovers her true identity, that she is half human and half angel, she is forced to see the truth: that if she can reunite her soul on earth she will become a weapon of darkness created by God himself. Her purpose, to protect the chosen one – A boy named Jackson.
This boy, the key to earth's salvation will be hells ultimate damnation. But hell has a powerful keeper- Cain. And until hell itself freezes over he will not be intimidated by a child and some foolish broken angel.
Cain can sense Azra's vulnerabilities- her manic human emotions. These emotions will betray Azra's heavenly connection, causing her to separate from the very powers she needs to eliminate Cain.

Who will win this supernatural battle?

Let the war begin.

ISBN: **E-Book** - 978-0-6482955-9-4

ISBN: **Paperback** - 978-0-6482955-4-9

Children's Books

by Jackie Lukes

One Awesome Alien

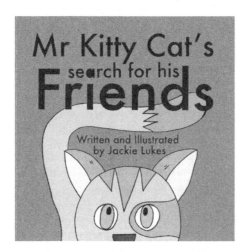

Mr Kitty Cat's search for his Friends

Webpage: http://tarinamarcinkowski.wixsite.com/author

Facebook: https://www.facebook.com/tarinamarcinkowski/

Printed in Great Britain
by Amazon

83724198R00163